I0694505

PROJECT
OBEDIENCE

PROJECT OBEDIENCE

Project Series 1

A. R. Stein

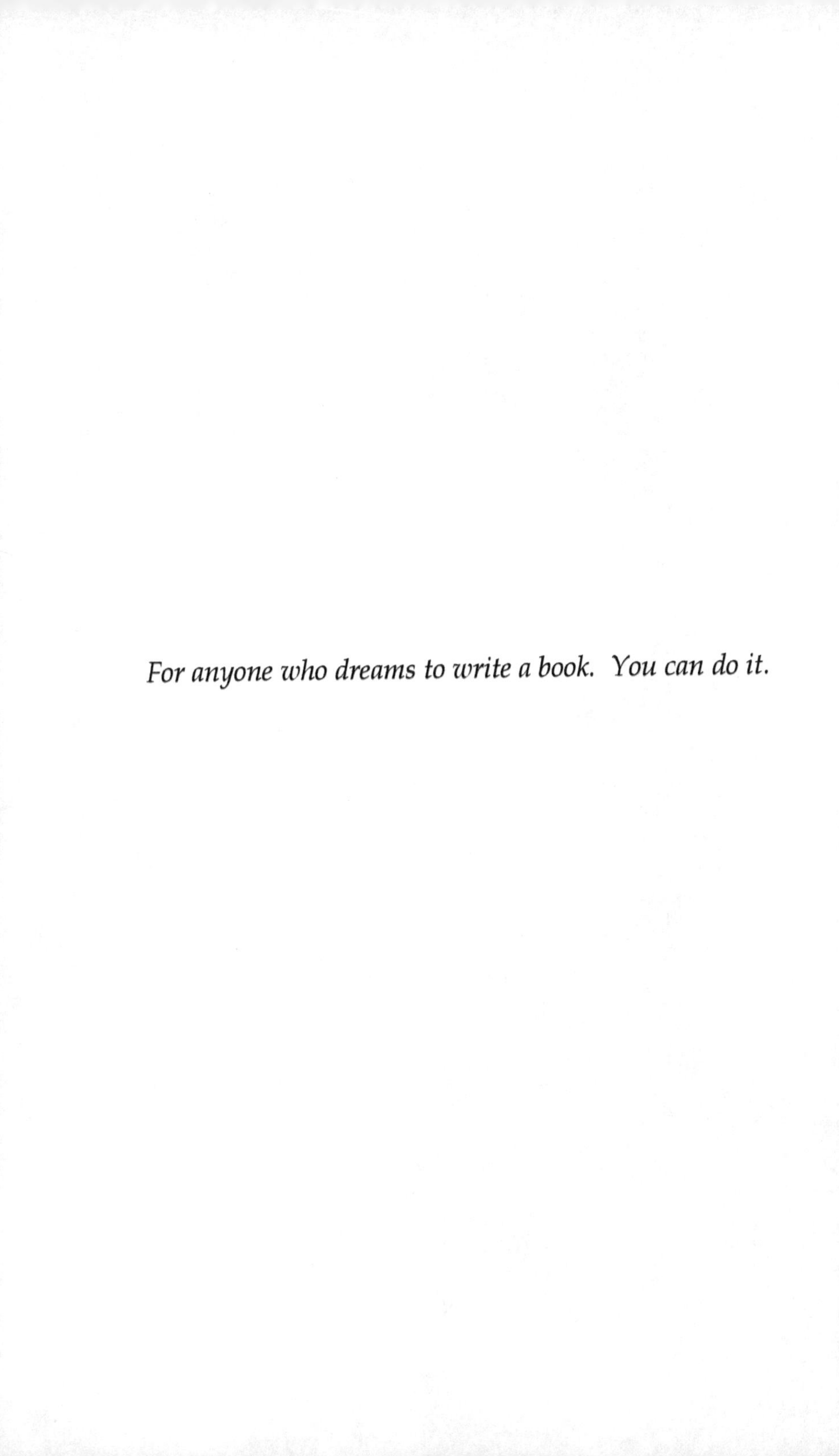

For anyone who dreams to write a book. You can do it.

PROLOGUE

The moment I met him, I knew he was destined for greatness. He was only a few minutes old, but I knew he would be extraordinary. My son. My beautiful boy. He looked like me, blond hair, blue eyes, dimples, and the same lopsided smile.

As I held him in my arms, he slept peacefully. His mother slept in the hospital bed across the room, exhausted from bringing him into the world. He stirred in my arms and I knew it was only a matter of time before he would wake up, asking for his mother to feed him.

I knew someone was watching me from the door. I could feel their presence. "Well, this is unexpected," his deep voice told me. Abaddon. My half-brother, who is now my enemy due to his betrayal on our kingdom.

Without turning around, I asked, "What are you doing here, Abaddon?"

"I've come to see where you disappeared to," he answered. "Looks like our laws don't abide to our King."

I turned around to face him. "You know I've wanted to get rid of that law for a while now."

"And yet, you still punish those who break it."

My face heated in anger. "I never want to. But until I can get the Council on my side, I have to punish the ones who break it." The baby stirred in my arms, sensing the tension in the air around me. I looked down at him and knew what I had to do. I didn't want to do it, but knew I would have to in order to keep Abaddon quiet. And more importantly, to keep my son alive long enough for him to at least have a chance to live his life. "If I never see him again, will you keep this whole ordeal quiet?"

He chuffed. "Why shouldn't I punish you? Allow the Council to punish our King?"

"Because losing him will be hard enough," I told him as I gestured to the baby, who was now looking up at me, in my arms. "That is a punishment in itself."

He sighed, "Fine. But if you come to visit him once, I will inform the Council of their King's affair with a human. And how you brought a Nephilim into the world."

I nodded. "Deal. Just give me one minute?" I asked.

He walked out of the room and I had no doubt that he was waiting outside.

I looked down at the baby in my arms. He was so content as he looked up at me with his beautiful blue eyes. I kissed him on the head and whispered, "I love you, Christian. Always will." I placed him in the crib the hospital provided and went over to his mother. I kissed her head. "Take care of our son."

I knew she would blame our son for my disappearance, but hoped she would get over it and take care of him. I walked out of the room and closed the door behind me. My heart ached at the thought of never seeing him again. At the thought of him being fatherless. The agony was harsh and real, but I knew what I was doing would keep him safe. And that's what any parent would do for their child, sacrifice anything to keep them out of harm's way.

Abaddon was waiting outside the room and I walked past him, knowing if I stopped, I would never have been able to leave.

CHAPTER ONE

"**G**et the hell out of our house now!" my foster dad screamed at me. "We don't want you here! You're now 18 and can fend for yourself!"

"Where would I go?!" I yelled back. "I don't have a job or anywhere to go!"

"Figure it out! I don't want a kid who is living here for free when he's not even mine. More importantly, a worthless one like yourself," he hissed. He threw my clothes and few belongings into my bag and pushed me out the bedroom door.

My foster mom just stood there with a scowl on her face. I never liked her; she never did anything as her husband beat me up.

He took the bag and threw it out the front door of the small one-story house I had stayed in for the past year and a half.

"Chris?" their son, Alex, questioned as he came into the hallway. Alex was eight years old and had autism. He adored me and I always looked after the poor kid when his parents forgot he was there.

I went over to him and bent down in front of him to look him in the eyes. "Christian has to leave now, buddy."

He looked at me with hopeful eyes. "But he will be back later, right? For dinner?"

The tears started building up in my eyes. "No. I'm sorry, but I'm not going to be back anytime soon. You be good for me, okay?"

"But who will make me mac-and-cheese?" he asked as his own tears started building up.

"I'm sure someone else will make it for you if you ask them to," I told him with a smirk. He started to cry. I opened my arms, and he walked into them to give me a hug.

My foster dad pulled me away from him by my hair, so hard that I fell to the floor. He kicked my chest and went for my face, but I protected it with my hands. He punched and kicked me until I was sure I wouldn't be going to school for at least a week, due to the bruises I would have. "Don't you ever touch my son again!" he yelled.

He pulled me up by my upper arms and shook me. Alex was crying as he hit his father's leg and told him to let me go. He released me and literally kicked me out the front door before slamming it shut.

I laid there for a moment before pushing myself up and picking my bag off the ground next to me. I winced with every movement; the beating took its toll. I walked down the short driveway to the street. I had a friend who lived a few minutes away, I just hoped his family would allow me to stay with them.

Once I made it to his house, which looked like a mansion compared to any of the houses I've ever stayed in, I walked up the driveway and took a shaky breath before knocking on the front door. Their dog barked and a moment later, my friend, Connor, answered. "Christian, what happened?" he asked when he took in my appearance.

"They kicked me out, but not before he beat me first," I told him. He was the only one who knew the truth about what really happened in my foster home and the only one who really cared enough to ask why I had bruises all over my body. "Can I stay with you for a few days?"

He gestured for me to come inside and closed the door once I was through it. "On your birthday too? That sucks, man."

I sighed. "Yeah, it does." Dakota, their Siberian husky, came over to say hello and I rubbed her behind her ears in greeting.

"Connor, who's here?" his mother, Linda, asked from the kitchen.

Connor told me to take my shoes off and to leave my bag by the front door before walking into the kitchen. I followed him and saw Linda was making dinner on the stove. It smelled delicious! The scent of garlic and spices filled the room and made me feel at home, something I hadn't felt in a long while. "Hi, Mrs. Peters," I said as I walked in.

"Christian!" she exclaimed with a smile as she turned to face me. Her smile dropped and she put her hands over her mouth. "Oh, honey. What happened?"

"I got kicked out of my foster home. He beat me before I left…"

"Well, you can stay here for as long as you want. You're practically family to us. Why don't we go get you cleaned up?" she said as she took my hand. "Connor, can you please keep an eye on the stove for me?"

He nodded, and she led me up the stairs into the guest room. The room had light gray walls with all white furniture. A dresser was along the left wall and a full-sized bed with a gray to white ombre comforter was along the back wall. A door to a connected bathroom was on the right wall; every bedroom in the Peters' house has a connected bathroom.

"Are you sure it's okay if I stay here?" I asked her as we walked inside. "You don't have to-"

"It's fine, Christian," she interrupted. "I don't mind taking care of a close friend. Why don't you go get a shower and then I'll get some ice to put on your bruises?"

I nodded. "Thank you. I really appreciate it."

She smiled. "I'll go get your things while you are in the shower. They'll be here when you get out," she declared as she walked out of the room. She turned to look over her shoulder and said, "You're a good kid, Christian. Never listen to what others think. I believe that one day you will do extraordinary things." She left without waiting for my response and closed the door behind her.

I went into the bathroom and closed the door. I turned to the right to look in the mirror above the marbled vanity sink. As I studied my bruised body, I realized that I had a black eye forming and a split lip that, thankfully, stopped bleeding. My bright blue eyes stared back at me and my blond bangs hung slightly in them. I've been told that I'm a mirror image of my father, although I've never met him. According to my mom, he dropped off the face of the earth the day I was born. Nobody knew where he went. My mom blames me for his disappearance, which is why I was a foster kid. She went off the deep end when she concluded that he'd never come back, and as a result, she neglected being my mother. She took very little care of me and beat me all the time as a kid until that one day…

I blinked back the horrible memories of that horrific day. It was the best and worst day of my life and changed everything.

I pushed my bangs back to reveal a nasty looking bruise forming on my forehead. I shrugged off my shirt, knowing my chest and stomach took the brunt of the beating. Sure enough, there were two boot shaped bruises on my stomach and another on my chest. I ran my fingers over them, making sure nothing was broken. I have had a few broken ribs in this past year and a half. I usually had to go to the hospital myself and say I either fell or got hurt at football practice. I knew I could have said something and gotten out of there, but didn't want to leave Alex or see him put into the system. That poor kid looked up to me and I couldn't leave him alone.

Once I was sure nothing was broken, I turned the shower on and took my remaining clothing off before stepping underneath the warm water. I sighed as it cascaded down my body, relaxing my tight muscles. I shampooed and rinsed my hair, and after I washed my body, I turned the water off and climbed out. I grabbed a towel out of the gray basket next to the shower door and dried off.

I thought about what Linda told me, that someday I would be extraordinary. I didn't know what to think of that. She knew I allowed all those hateful words get to me. That I was worthless, that I would never make it in life, and that I'm just a horrible foster kid. Before I let them get to me, I had such grand outlooks for my future, but now all I wanted to do was get out of Lincoln, Nevada. Get away from all the people who kept reminding me of my worthlessness.

"Is he okay?" I heard Connor's sister, Ginny, ask. Ginny is two years younger than us and looks up to me like her older brother. She is like my little sister and I have never seen her as anything else.

"I'm not sure how anyone would be okay after going through what he's been through," Linda answered. "I mean, he's been through hell. Not only these past few years, but his whole life. His own mother beat him until he had to be hospitalized for two weeks when he was only eight years old. He's been in and out of foster homes, and this last one was a lot like his younger life."

I wrapped the towel around my waist before opening the door. I plastered a smile on my face, but was surprised when I found the room empty. My bag was sitting on the bed and I went to open it. I was surprised because I thought they were for sure in the room. I could hear their conversation perfectly.

"Can you pass me the sauce, Connor?" Linda asked. "Thank you."

I widened my eyes in shock. They were in the kitchen, which was downstairs and on the other end of the house, but I could hear them as if they were speaking to me. What the hell was going on?!

CHAPTER TWO

Once I got dressed, I walked downstairs, through the dining room, and into the large white kitchen. "You okay?" Linda asked with her brows scrunched up in worry.

I nodded and shrugged, but grimaced at the pain that the movement brought. "I will be."

"I hope you're hungry," she declared. "We're having spaghetti tonight."

I smiled. "I'm starving. And it smells delicious."

I went over to the rectangular kitchen table near the French double doors leading to their back patio and pool. Ginny and Connor were sitting at their seats and I sat next to Connor. "Hey, Christian," Ginny said from across the table. Ginny looks like their father, Dan, while Connor looks more like Linda. Ginny has brown curly hair and brown eyes, while Connor has thick blond hair with mesmerizing green eyes. We always picked on Ginny because she is only four foot nine inches, way shorter than her family members, but she never seemed to mind as she simply claimed she was 'fun-sized'.

"Hey, Ginny," I told her. "How are you?"

"Pretty good," she answered as she popped a grape into her mouth. "Happy birthday, by the way."

I smiled. "Thanks."

Linda tapped me on the shoulder, and I turned to find her handing me an ice pack. "Put this on that eye of yours."

"Thanks," I told her with a grateful smile. I put the cool ice up to my eye and sighed in relief at the cool sensation.

"How bad is it underneath that shirt?" she questioned me with a hand on her hip. "I know you're hurting; let me see it."

I shrugged my shirt off, and they all gasped when they saw how bruised I was. "Oh, honey," Linda breathed. "That looks really painful. How are you even walking?"

I shrugged, but winced at the movement. "I'm used to it, I guess."

She tsked her tongue. "No one should have to get used to that." She walked over and opened their cabinet. After finding what she was looking for, she came back and placed two pills in my hand as she said, "Here are some pain meds. Hopefully, they will help ease the pain."

Connor handed me a glass of water and I swallowed the pills before saying, "Thanks."

"Dan should be here any minute, and then we will eat," she told us. I shrugged my shirt back on as she went to get plates and silverware.

A few minutes later, Dan walked in through the garage door connected to the kitchen. "I'm home!" He went over to Linda and kissed her before looking over at us sitting at the table. "Christian! Hey, man! Haven't seen you in a while." He took in my appearance and cringed. "Ouch. What happened?"

"I got kicked out of the house. Let's just say it wasn't a good farewell," I explained. "Linda said I could stay here for a while. Is that okay?"

He glanced over at Linda before smiling. "That's fine with me. *Mi casa es tu casa.*"

I smiled back and replied, "*Gracias.*"

He announced he was going to get changed, but before walking out, he turned to me and said, "Oh! And happy birthday."

"Thanks," I called after him as he walked out of the room.

Linda started serving us spaghetti, meatballs, and garlic bread. By the time she finished, Dan came back into the room wearing a white t-shirt and gray sweatpants. "Looks amazing, honey," he said as he sat next to her.

We all agreed, and she smiled as she said, "Thank you, guys."

We all prayed. They are a religious family and helped me become religious when Connor and I became friends in middle school. We then ate with small talk about everyone's day and the homework some of us still had to do. They all agreed to not send me to school tomorrow, and possibly longer, until I healed enough. I love their whole family like they are my own and know they feel the same.

After we all finished eating, we cleared the table and sat on the couches in the living room attached to the kitchen to watch some TV. "What do we want to watch?" Dan asked as he picked up the remote.

"I think Christian should pick," Ginny piped in, "since it's his birthday and he is our guest."

They all looked at me and I shrugged. "I don't watch a lot of TV. You guys pick." My foster family had a TV, but if they caught me using it, they would have beaten me. I always obeyed their orders the best I could to ensure I wouldn't be beaten later that night. They never wanted to see me, so I would have to go right to my room when I got back from school, would make dinner for everyone but me, and sometimes even locked me out of the house for the night, forcing me to seek shelter elsewhere. That was why I looked forward to turning 18; I wouldn't have to listen and obey any more foster parents and could finally make my own decisions.

"How about Game Show Network?" Dan suggested, snapping me out of the horrific memories.

We all agreed and watched a few episodes of *Family Feud* before I announced I was going to go to bed. "Okay, goodnight," Connor called. They all told me goodnight and I walked up the stairs and into the guest room.

I closed the door behind me and turned to climb into the comfy bed when I noticed something.

A pillow was floating over the bed. I walked over to it and ran my hands through the surrounding air, making sure it wasn't a prank. I looked back to make sure the door was closed before pushing it down. It floated back up as soon as I lifted my hand. "The hell?" I whispered to myself.

I backed up to the wall and it seemed to follow me. I flung my hands in front of me, not wanting whatever it was to get any closer. As soon as I did, it seemed to follow my movement and flung to the other side of the room. I walked over to it and lifted my hand, curious if it had something to do with me. It raised with my hand and moved wherever I wanted it to go. Whatever was happening, it had something to do with me. I heard a conversation from another room as if they were speaking to me! That's not normal. And now this? No, something was indeed happening to me. And I knew it would bring danger my way. I just knew.

CHAPTER THREE

I woke up the next day to the sun shining through the sheer-white curtains covering the windows on either side of the bed. I rolled over and looked at the clock on the nightstand and saw it was 10 o'clock. I quickly sat up, shocked by how late I slept. I froze, expecting pain to shoot through my body with the movement, but felt nothing. Instead, I felt… energized.

I pulled my shirt up to examine my bruises, but found nothing, Not even a scratch on my body. I took a few deep breaths to calm my rapid heartbeat. I got up and hurried to the bathroom to examine myself in the mirror. Nothing. Not even the slightest of evidence of what happened yesterday.

What was happening to me? Did I have some sort of…abilities? Would I be able to control them, or do they just happen whenever? Would I have to hide my entire life? What if I became some sort of lab experiment?

I gripped the vanity's corners tightly, feeling dizzy as a bunch of questions swirled around in my head. I forced myself to take deep breaths and looked at my reflection. My face was slightly pale, and my eyes were wide in panic.

Splashing some water on my face snapped me out of my panicked haze. I dabbed my face with a towel before going to get dressed. I changed into a pair of sweatpants and t-shirt I found in my bag. I then brushed my teeth and ran my fingers through my hair to tame it.

Nobody should be home. Connor and Ginny were at school, Dan was a professor at a local college, and Linda was a writer who liked to write at our local coffee shop. I walked downstairs and into the kitchen to get something to eat. I found some strawberry yogurt in the fridge and opened it. I got a spoon out of the drawer the silverware was kept. I then leaned against the granite countertop and looked out the window. I put the spoon in my mouth and took a few bites.

"How are you feeling?" Linda asked from behind me.

I jumped and turned to face her. I put my hand over my frantic heart and said, "You scared me! I didn't think anyone was home."

She laughed. "I stayed home today. Are you okay?"

"I'm good," I told her with a smile and bat of my hand.

She studied me closely. "How are your bruises gone? You look perfectly normal."

"Maybe my body is used to getting beatings and is healing faster now?" I suggested with a shrug.

I gave her the best smile I could muster, but was silently hoping she wouldn't become curious and start asking a bunch of questions.

Sure enough, she asked questions. "How are they all gone? There is not even a blemish or scar. I've never seen anyone heal this fast before."

I forced my face to remain expressionless. "I don't know. Maybe they weren't as bad as we thought they were."

She pursed her lips. "Maybe …" she said as if she didn't believe me, but dropped the subject. "I am going to the grocery store. You want to come or stay here?"

"I think I will stay here, if you don't mind. I think Connor will send me some notes and assignments over lunch, so I might just work on homework for a little while."

She nodded. "It sure helps that you two have all your classes together. I'll see you later. There are some leftovers in the fridge if I'm not home by lunchtime," she told me as she picked up her purse and walked out the door leading to the garage.

Once she was gone, I finished my yogurt and hurried back upstairs. I closed the door behind me and made sure I locked it before focusing on the pillow on the bed. I lifted my hand up, and it followed suit. I widened my eyes in surprise. *I don't think I will ever get used to this.*

I wanted to try something other than a pillow and decided on my bag. Sure enough, it worked. I wondered what else I could do and pulled a hoodie over my head before heading downstairs. I walked out the French doors in the kitchen and to the back-yard. I went around the covered pool and opened the gate surrounding their backyard to go to the woods behind their house.

I didn't know what to do. I just knew that I wanted to see if there was more to my abilities.

I walked around aimlessly until I noticed a few wilted flowers perk up as I walked past them. I stopped and turned around, bending down next to a few pink and white flowers. When I touched them, they seemed to open up and get brighter.

I pulled my hand back and they closed once again. *Interesting.* I ran my hand over them, and they opened once more.

I stood up and continued walking deeper into the woods. I wondered if I could do anything that I thought of and raised my hands over my head as I willed the wind to listen to me. The trees swayed and the leaves on the ground picked up and swirled around me, creating a tornado of orange and red.

I spun around and laughed to myself as I al-lowed them to swirl around me until I slammed my hands down by my sides. They dropped to the ground without a second delay.

This is so cool! I thought to myself. I froze when I heard a twig snap nearby and crouched low to the ground. A moment later, leaves rustled in a bush near me and I turned to look at it. I jumped when Da-kota came barreling into me, knocking me over.

She jumped on top of me and licked my face. "Hey, girl," I said as I rubbed her fluffy head. "You scared me."

If she was out, Linda must be home. I stood up and brushed the leaves off me. "Your mama is probably worried sick," I told her. "Why did you follow me?"

She just looked at me and ran towards the house, only to stop and look back at me as if to say, you coming?

I laughed and followed her out of the woods and back to the house. Linda came around the corner with a worried expression on her face. She looked at Dakota and bent to look her in the eyes. "I was so worried about you." She looked up at me and said, "Right when I came home, she ran out of the garage and into the woods. I called for you, but couldn't find you. I thought you were kidnapped or something by the way she was acting, but I guess she was just following you."

I nodded. "Sorry about that. I should have at least left a note for you."

She shook her head and pulled me into a hug. "I'm just glad you are okay. That's all that matters."

"Thanks," I told her as I hugged her back.

She let me go and I told her I should probably work on some homework now. I went upstairs and used the laptop Connor provided for me. He emailed me assignments and I started working on them.

An hour and two essays later, I decided to go get something to eat for lunch. Once I ate, I went back upstairs to finish my math homework. I tried something new and used my newly found abilities to move my pencil with my mind.

Once I found it worked, I smiled to myself and didn't use my hands at all. I found it easy to control them and was quite surprised because I expected it to be more difficult.

I was in the middle of writing when I noticed all the pillows floating around the room. *Maybe they aren't as easy to control as I thought.*

The door then swung open, and Ginny and Connor walked into the room without warning while everything was still floating around me.

CHAPTER FOUR

I slammed my hands down on the bed, making everything fall to the ground as they walked inside. *Why didn't my super-hearing work when I needed it?* I thought as they came over. They didn't seem to notice anything as they climbed in the bed next to me.

"Hey, Christian," Ginny told me. "How are you feeling?"

"Pretty good," I answered casually. "How was school?" I asked Connor as I looked up from my notes.

"Boring. Not much happened today and everyone missed you. Coach hopes you get over the flu," he gave me a wink, "before the game on Friday."

"I'm sure I'll be there tomorrow," I told him with a smirk. I was the football quarterback, while Connor was our running-back. I hoped and planned to play for college next fall. I still haven't decided which college I wanted to go to, due to foster family drama, and hoped to soon. I've already got so many schools asking me to choose them, and so far, Penn State University was the top runner.

"Good," he said with a slight smile. "You look better."

"Thanks. Although, I feel like I'm drowning in homework," I told him with a chuckle.

He laughed too. "I should work on mine."

They agreed to do their homework, so we could do something together later. Once they closed the door behind them, I laid back and sighed in relief. Thank God they didn't see anything or notice anything was off when they barged in.

I went to get up to lock the door, but stopped short when I got an idea. I concentrated on turning the lock with my mind. It locked. I smiled to myself, surprised by how well I was doing.

I just had to focus on not allowing anything to float without my consent, and then I would be in good shape. I just hoped I could control myself when I was at school. I practiced unlocking and locking the door while lying in bed for a little while longer before lying back and closing my eyes for a few minutes.

* * * * *

I MUST HAVE DRIFTED TO SLEEP because the next thing I knew, I was being gently shaken awake by Linda. "Hey, honey," she whispered when I opened my eyes and looked over my shoulder to find her sitting on the edge of the bed. "I just wanted you to know that dinner has passed. I didn't want to wake you, but I didn't want you to go hungry either."

I nodded and stretched my arms as I sat up. I looked at the clock and it read a little past 7 o'clock.

"Sorry. I didn't mean to fall asleep," I told her with a yawn.

"It's okay," she told me with a smile. "Why don't you come downstairs, and we can get you something to eat, okay?" She got up from the edge of the bed and walked out the door.

I slowly got up and followed her down the stairs and into the kitchen. Connor was sitting at the table with his laptop in front of him, while Dan and Ginny were playing a video game in the living room.

Linda handed me a plate with pizza on it and a glass of water. "Thanks," I told her with a grateful smile. I went to sit next to Connor and saw he was working on his essay for English class. "How's it going?"

He groaned. "I hate writing! I don't know how mom does it for a living. I mean, it's awful!"

I laughed at his struggling and gave him some pointers as I ate. Once he finished writing it, he closed his laptop and sighed in relief. "Thanks for the help," he told me.

I smiled. "No problem. Sorry we didn't get to do something tonight. I fell asleep after closing my eyes for a few minutes," I told him with an apologetic look.

He shook his head and said, "It's all good. I think Ginny is having fun with dad anyway."

We both looked into the living room and saw Dan and Ginny playing a competitive game. They were both yelling, cursing, and cheering as they played. Connor and I both laughed and got up to join them.

An hour later, we decided to go to bed because it was a school night. Connor, Ginny, and I all walked upstairs together and said our goodnights before walking into our rooms. I closed the door behind me and don't even think my head hit the pillow before I fell asleep.

CHAPTER FIVE

I closed my locker before heading to my last class of the day. I felt like I was suffocating, drowning. I knew it had to have something to do with my new abilities. *Maybe I have to use them a few times a day to be comfortable*, I thought as I walked into class.

I sat in my usual seat next to Connor in the back of the room and tried to listen, but the tightness in my chest was almost unbearable.

I asked to go to the bathroom and walked out of the classroom. I started walking down the hallway, but stopped when I heard a soft voice. "Please, just let me go."

"Oh, come on, beautiful," a male voice said. "Just one kiss, please?"

I followed the sound of their voices and found them in a corner behind a pillar, hidden from view. I saw the boy's broad shoulders and dark hair and knew who it was. Victor Rodriguez. A beefy junior football player.

He was pinning a girl to the wall with his hands on her hips. She had long wavy brown hair and a flawless complexion. She looked over his shoulder and her bright blue eyes met mine.

I stopped in my tracks, mesmerized. Her eyes were stunning; she was stunning. A shock went through my body and I felt an immediate connection with her. I didn't understand how, but I felt like I knew her, even though I never met her. However, the moment was short lived when Victor leaned down to kiss her.

It happened so fast. I pulled him away from her with my mind and pinned him to the pillar behind him as I walked over. I took hold of his shirt collar. "Don't you ever touch her or anyone else ever again," I told him with a clenched jaw.

His brown caramel skin paled and he nodded. "Okay. Okay. I'm sorry. It won't happen again."

I let him go and he ran away. I turned back to the girl, who was watching me with wide eyes. Not with fear, but with curiosity.

"I don't believe we've met. I'm Christian. Christian Hoyt." I stuck my hand out.

She hesitated before shaking my hand. "Eliana. Eliana White."

Her voice was melodic, like an angel. I released her hand. "Are you new or have I just never met you before?"

She blushed. "I'm new. Yesterday was my first day and I obviously got on his bad side for some reason," she rambled before chewing on her lip nervously.

"Yeah. My advice, stay away from him and his friends."

"Thanks for stepping in. How did you do that anyway?"

I rubbed the back of my neck. "I should explain, but I don't know where to start. Are you free after school?"

She nodded before stepping past me and started to walk away. She looked over her shoulder and smirked as she said, "I'll meet you here."

* * * * *

AN HOUR LATER, class was almost over, and I planned what I would say to Eliana in my head. We had 15 minutes left of class before school finally let out.

A knock sounded on the door and two men wearing military uniforms stepped inside. "Sorry to disturb you, but we are looking for someone named Christian Hoyt. Is he here by chance?"

My teacher looked over at me and pointed. "That's him right there. May I ask what this is about?"

"We have reason to believe he is someone we have been looking for," he responded. He gestured for me to go over to them.

I nervously got out of my seat and glanced over at Connor. He looked confused as I walked over to them.

"Give me your hand," the one closest to me ordered with an outstretched hand.

I did as he said while giving him a weary look. He grabbed my wrist and pricked my finger with a device without warning. I immediately pulled my hand back and cursed.

"Language," our teacher warned in a stern voice.

I ignored her as the device's screen lit up green a second later. He looked at the other man and nodded before looking back at me. "You will have to come with us."

I knew the device somehow told them about my abilities, but tried to keep my cool. "Why? I didn't do anything."

"I think you know why," he told me with a stern look.

I saw the man next to the one speaking take something out of his pocket. I caught a glimpse of the needle of the syringe before he made his move and quickly moved away.

They tried to tackle me, but I ducked, dodging them, and ran out the door. I ran down the hallway and went around the corner when five uniformed men stepped in front of me, blocking my path.

I stopped short and looked around. The other two were running after me, blocking me in. I saw my class rush out of the classroom to see what was happening. I looked over at Connor, who was standing in front and looking at me with confusion written all over his face.

I knew what he was thinking when I locked eyes with him. *Don't fight them. I don't know what you did, but I will help you get out soon.*

I figured I should give him a glimpse of why they wanted me before I surrendered. So, I lifted my arm and pointed at the man who tried to inject something into me earlier. His eyes widened in fear, as if he knew what I was going to do. I pushed him with my mind and sent him flying down the hall, landing in front of my class.

They all looked down at him and back up at me with wide eyes. The other men shouted, and one wrapped his arm around my neck from behind me. I fought his tight grasp, but he pressed a needle into the side of my neck, making me hiss in pain.

I immediately felt like a deflated balloon; my energy left me, and I knew that if he released his hold on me, I wouldn't be able to stand. He loosened his grip on my neck once I stopped fighting. He didn't let go of me until another put my left arm over his shoulders and the other one holding my neck did the same with my right.

They started carrying me towards the main doors and I saw Victor leaning against the wall with a smirk on his face. He must have been the one to call the military because he was one of two people who knew about my abilities. And I knew Eliana wouldn't betray me after I helped her, not before I explained myself.

He flexed his fingers up and down in a wave as he said, "Bye, Christian. See you soon."

I did not understand what he meant by that, nor did I care at the moment. I only glared at him as they dragged me out to a black SUV with tinted windows. One man opened the back door and the men carrying me put me in the right seat. The one who drugged me went to the other side and climbed in next to me after closing my door. The two others got in the front of the car.

The man next to me reached over and fastened my seatbelt. I couldn't do anything, could barely keep my eyes open. I rested my head against the window and looked at my classmates who gathered outside. I saw Connor arguing with one of the uniformed men. The principal, Mr. Lopez, was holding him back as he tried to fight the man he was yelling at.

"I'll effing kill you for this!" Connor yelled as tears ran down his cheeks. He looked at me, even though he couldn't see me through the tinted glass. "Christian!" he yelled. "Snap out of it! They drugged you! Fight back!"

I wished I could have told him that I knew they drugged me. That I was trying to fight the haze forming around my mind, but couldn't.

"Connor!" Mr. Lopez yelled. "Yelling at him won't help. He can't help it."

Connor broke down into sobs and stopped fighting Mr. Lopez's grip as he turned to cry into his chest. Mr. Lopez rubbed his back, trying to comfort him. The men outside must have brought their own vehicle because one waved us on and our car left the school.

I could have sworn I heard the men laughing as the movement of the car lulled me into a deep sleep.

CHAPTER SIX

I woke up when one of the car doors opened and then slammed shut. I couldn't open my eyes, so I just listened. Someone unbuckled my seatbelt, and I felt them pull me, so I was leaning against them as someone opened my door.

"How's he doing?" a deep voice asked. It sounded as if he was in charge, there was an authoritative tone to his voice.

"He's heavily sedated, if that's what you're asking," the man holding me said. "He's different than the others, he knows how to control his abilities very well."

"How much did you give him?" he asked.

"Two doses. One at the school and the other a few minutes ago when he started to stir."

"Let's get him inside. Everyone, clear a path."

Someone picked me up and carried me as if I weighed nothing. "You got any background for me?" the man in charge asked as they walked.

"Yes, we do, Sir," the man answered. It sounded like they were walking in front of us. "His name is Christian Hoyt, and he just turned 18 two days ago, on October 17th. He is a foster kid and has

been for 10 years. His mom beat him, and the last
foster family kicked him out on his birthday. He has
many friends and the teachers absolutely adore him.
His one friend gave us minor trouble, but we promised he could come to see him someday and he
calmed down."

"Well, thank God for Victor. We needed a
powerful male."

I heard a series of beeps and they soon placed
me on what felt like a bed, "You two, don't touch or
talk to him, or there will be consequences," the man
in charge said.

"Yes, Sir," I heard two girls softly reply from
somewhere in the room.

"Let me know when he wakes up," he ordered
one guard. "I will be in my office. If they touch or
talk to him before I get to, come and get me immediately."

"Sir, yes, Sir!" he replied.

"And remove his shoes," the man demanded
before leaving the room.

I felt someone lift one foot at a time and take
off my shoes. He then walked out of the room as
well, and I heard the series of beeps again.

I tried to open my eyes, but failed. It felt as if
someone super-glued them shut, so I eventually gave
up and gave in to sleep once more.

* * * * *

WHEN I WOKE THE NEXT TIME, I could finally
open my eyes. I stared up at the gray and white tiled
ceiling that had fluorescent lights scattered around it.

I turned my head to the right to come face to face with a gray brick wall. I turned to look the other way and saw the semi-sizable room I was in. A dark window was on the other side of the room and I could make out the silhouette of a man inside. A door was to the right of the window that connected the rooms together. Another window was on the wall in front of me, by my feet. It wasn't a tinted window like the other one, and I could see that it looked out into a bright hallway.

I looked over my shoulder and saw two other single beds in the opposite corner of mine. They both were occupied by two girls, who were watching me. They appeared to be around my age. One had black hair that was cut short, like a pixie cut, and the other had long black hair.

I sat up and swung my legs to the left, so they were hanging over the edge. My head spun, and I felt like I would be sick. They discreetly pointed to a door to the left of their beds, and I knew it had to be the bathroom.

I stood up on my shaky legs and hurried to the bathroom. I closed the door and threw up in the toilet to the right. I sat on the floor and rested my back against the dark gray wall. I didn't want to go out there, knowing that they would force me to accept this new life. But I knew that to get my answers to my never-ending questions, I would have to face them.

I pushed myself up from the floor and went over to the single sink across from the toilet. I splashed some cool water on my face and rinsed my mouth to get rid of the acid taste. Once finished, I opened the door and looked over at the girls, but they wouldn't look at me, it was almost as if they were scared to.

I looked ahead of me and saw that a man was standing in the middle of the room. He looked to be in his mid-forties, with black hair and bright green eyes. He wore a navy-blue suit and a black tie. He looked like a man who meant business.

"Hello, Christian," he said. I recognized his voice as the one from earlier, the one who was in charge. "I am Dr. Rodriguez, or Sergeant Rodriguez depending on who you ask, but to you I am Dr. Rodriguez. I am head researcher and commander at this base and expect you to respect me. Do you know why you are here?"

I shook my head, but responded, "I have a good idea why."

"You're here because you're special, Christian. You can do things others can't. We are researching people like you to figure out why you are different. So far, across the country, we have found 21, including yourself, who are like you. These two," he started as he gestured to the girls, "are like you. Girls, introduce yourselves to our newest angel."

Before they had time to introduce themselves, I interrupted, "Angel?"

"I'll have them explain," he told me. "I have to go pick up my son from football practice because his car is in the shop. I'll be back in a few hours," he said as he walked out. He used a keypad and punched in a code after the door shut behind him.

I turned back to face the girls, who were still sitting on their beds. "Hi, I'm Alis," the one with the pixie cut said. "And this is my sister, Angelica." She gestured to the girl next to her, who still wouldn't look up at me.

"Hi, I'm Christian."

"The reason they call us angels is that a week after we come into our abilities, after we turn 18, we come into wings. Black feathery wings. They aren't one hundred percent sure what we are, but we resemble angels, so that's what they call us."

"What do they do here?" I asked.

"We each have our own researchers. They have different techniques on what they do. Mine likes to focus on my flying and takes more samples, while Angelica's likes to practice with her abilities."

"So, you have wings?" I asked in shock.

She nodded. "Would you like to see?"

I nodded and she closed her eyes in concentration. A second later, black feathery wings emerged from her back, slipping through slits in her shirt that I didn't notice until now. I widened my eyes as they kept getting bigger and bigger. Her left wing hit Angelica in the face and she swatted it away. She looked up at me as she did so and I sucked in a breath. Her eyes, I've seen them before. They were forest green and I knew I'd seen eyes like hers before, but couldn't place where or when. She had a slight smile on her lips and blushed when she saw me staring at her.

I looked back over at Alis, and realized she had the same green eyes when she opened them again. We all jumped when a female walked into the room and said, "Alis, it's time to train." She looked to be in her mid-twenties, with blonde hair and enormous glasses.

Alis nodded and stood from her bed as she made her wings slide back into her back. She looked over her shoulder and smirked at me. "See ya later," she said before walking out with the girl. The door was locked with the keypad a moment later.

I turned back to Angelica and sat in her previous spot on her bed. She looked over at me and blushed again. "So, does this room block our abilities or something?" I asked her because I couldn't feel the power I have felt for the past few days.

She nodded. "They control our abilities, so we only use them when they want us to," she explained in a soft voice. "We only have access to our enhanced senses and rapid healing in here."

"That sucks," I said. "How long have you been here?"

"My sister and I have been here for about 8 months now. We turned 18 in February and were brought here a few days later."

"Oh. Have you ever considered escaping?"

"We did at first, but never found a way out."

"Have you ever gone outside in the time you've been here?"

She shook her head. "No, we haven't seen the sun since the day they brought us here. Nor have we seen anyone outside of this place."

"But they promised my friend he could come see me," I told her, remembering the conversation I overheard earlier.

"I'm sorry, but they were most likely lying to get him to stop fighting them," she told me with a sour face. "You most likely won't see him ever again."

CHAPTER SEVEN

A few minutes, or hours, later, I learned a lot about what goes on around here. I learned that most of their experiments were painless, but depended on what the researcher they assigned us to was like. I asked her who my researcher might be, but she just shrugged in response.

We both turned when the door opened, and Dr. Rodriguez walked inside. "Alright, my son should be here in just a moment. Angelica, it's time for you to go train."

She got up and brushed past me on the way out. After she was out of sight, Dr. Rodriguez's son walked in. I widened my eyes when I saw him. Victor Rodriguez stood behind his dad with a malicious grin on his face as he stared at me. *Could this day get any worse?* I thought to myself. However, I wondered how I didn't see it before; it was obvious from the start. He called the military, he told me he would see me soon, and he had the same last name as Dr. Rodriguez.

"Well, since you two know each other, I figured Victor could be your assigned researcher," Dr. Rodriguez said.

"What?!" I yelled. "He hasn't even graduated high school yet! How could he do research when he doesn't know how?"

"Victor is a very intelligent young man. He has been shadowing me for two years now. I figured that since he found you, I'd give him the privilege of assigning you to him."

Victor only grinned wider when he saw my outrage. He slapped his dad on the back. "Thanks, dad. It means a lot to me."

"Anything for my favorite son," Dr. Rodriguez replied with a smile. "You can start tomorrow after school. I'll go over things with you tonight and he will be ready for you tomorrow afternoon."

"Sweet," he said as he glared at me when his dad wasn't watching.

They walked out and locked the door behind them. I watched them through the window as they made their way down the hall and rounded the corner. I cursed and kicked the glass separating me from the outside world. Why did it have to be me? Why did Victor Rodriguez have to be my assigned researcher?

* * * * *

THAT NIGHT, I cried myself to sleep. They gave me sweatpants and a t-shirt to change into. The girls came in when I was in the bathroom and got changed before climbing into their beds seconds before the lights turned off. I faced the wall so nobody could see my tears.

I cried for my old life back, prayed to whatever God was out there to help me out of this mess. I couldn't believe that I went from having a hellish life to it becoming impossibly worse in a matter of a few hours.

For the first time in ten years, I actually missed my mom. I wished I had my mom here with me to hug me and tell me everything would be okay; that I would get through this obstacle in my life. She probably got the news and didn't even care: didn't care that her only son had become a lab experiment and might be for the rest of his life.

The tears eventually dried up, and I fell asleep soon after I couldn't keep my eyes open any longer.

CHAPTER EIGHT

The next day, the girls came and went throughout the day. While I sat there and waited for Victor. I took a shower in the morning and changed into the black t-shirt and shorts they gave me. I brushed my teeth and ate the breakfast and lunch they gave us.

I was bored beyond bored. I had nothing to do in the compact room they locked me inside. They gave me a tennis ball, and I bounced it off the wall and caught it from where I was sitting on the floor with my back against my bed. *They couldn't at least give me a book? I would at least be more entertained than I was now.*

I looked over at the door as it opened again, thinking it was one of the girls, but stood up when I saw Victor walk in. "You ready?" he asked with an amused expression on his face.

I sighed. "I guess if it means I will get out of this room of boredom. Even if it means I have to be with you."

He laughed. "It can't be that bad in here. You're sharing a room with two very attractive girls. What guy in their right mind wouldn't want that?"

"First of all, I am not sharing a room, I am locked in the room with them. And second, they haven't been here most of the day."

He just rolled his eyes. "Whatever. Let's go," he said as he walked through the door.

I followed him and saw the room behind the tinted glass had a chair behind a panel of buttons. I wondered what the buttons were for, but didn't have the opportunity to ask because Victor was already walking out the door to the right.

I followed him down the long bright hallway that had white subway tiled walls, white marbled floors, and bright LED lights along the ceiling. We passed many doors, all of which were closed, and I found myself asking, "What are all these rooms for?"

He shrugged. "Mostly to hold our research or where we perform certain experiments. You will be in some of them, but will be unconscious most of the times."

"Unconscious?" I asked in a worried tone. "Why?"

"Because some experiments we perform require you to be unconscious. Don't worry, I'm not allowed to take the samples, I only study them."

I got goosebumps just thinking about what they could do to me when I was unconscious. They could do anything, and I wouldn't be able to defend myself. "Where are we going now?" I asked him.

"We are going to see how powerful you really are. We have come to find that others all have a range of how powerful they are. Some can do things that others can't. But first, we will take a blood sample," he said as he opened a door on the left.

I followed him and saw the room resembled a doctor's office. It had a few chairs and a medical exam bed. Victor told me to sit on the bed and walked out of the room. I looked around the room and spotted a hidden camera above me, right next to the light.

Victor then walked back in with a woman in her late fifties. She ordered him to sit in the chair across from me and he did, I smirked, at least someone ordered him around here. "Hello, honey," she said as she washed her hands in the sink to my right. "I'm Lisa and I am in charge of taking your blood samples. Are you okay with needles?"

I nodded. "I'm fine with them. Although, I don't think anyone is truly okay with them."

Victor rolled his eyes, but Lisa laughed. "That's very true, honey." She looked over at me and smiled as she said, "My, you are a handsome one. My granddaughter would be all over you."

I laughed. "Thanks…I think."

"Which arm would you prefer?" she asked me.

I shrugged. "Doesn't matter."

"I'll do the left then."

I turned my arm over, and she gently took it. "How much are you taking?" I asked.

"About a pint, right?" She turned to Victor.

He nodded. "Correct."

She started cleaning my inner arm with an alcohol pad and tied a rubber band around my upper arm. She then told me to relax as she felt for my vein and prepared the needle. I felt the prick, and she connected the tube as she filled a pint-sized bag with my blood.

She finished a few minutes later and handed me some juice and an apple after sealing the bag. She handed it to Victor, and he got up to take it to another room where they would look at it later.

I ate the apple as she asked, "Are you feeling lightheaded or dizzy?"

I shook my head and smiled. "No. Not yet."

She cackled. "I like you, Christian. I wish I could help you get out of here." She glanced up at the camera nervously. I could tell she truly wanted to help, but didn't want to risk it. I grabbed her hand and squeezed, letting her know that I understood.

"Alright," Victor said as he came into the room. I quickly dropped Lisa's hand, so he wouldn't notice. "Let's go see what you are capable of," he told me with an excited grin.

"Woah, woah, woah," Lisa told him. "Not so fast. I just took a whole pint of blood. We don't need anyone passing out on my watch."

Victor sighed dramatically. "Fine," he mumbled as he sat in the chair he was sitting in earlier and crossed his arms.

"I want you to finish your juice and eat your apple before doing anything," she told me in a motherly tone. "I'll be back in a few minutes to make sure you're good to go."

I nodded. "Okay."

She walked out, and Victor and I had a stare down. He glared at me and I glared back as I sipped the juice Lisa gave me. "Just explain one thing to me," I started. "Did you set me up yesterday? Did you somehow know before you saw?"

He thought about how he wanted to answer before saying, "I knew someone in the school came into abilities. I have this device," he held up a device that resembled a phone, "to tell me when one is near me. I was going to the restroom when it went off. I saw the new girl, Eliana, and grabbed her to see if you would try to help her. And sure enough, you did."

"So, you set up the entire thing?" I asked.

He pursed his lips and nodded. "Yeah…pretty much."

"How could you?" I asked, angry that he would set me up like that.

"I did it because my dad told me that if I could find an angel, I could do my own experimenting and research."

"How's the football team doing without me?" I asked after a moment of awkward silence.

He chuffed and shook his head. "We're a mess right now. Connor wasn't at school today. Coach doesn't know what to do without his quarterback, especially with our big game in two days. And now that it seems that Connor won't be back anytime soon, we also lost our running-back."

"Well, that sucks," I said as I leaned back on my arms.

"Alright, honey," Lisa said as she walked back into the room. "Did you finish your juice and apple?"

I nodded. "Yep."

"Alright, you are free to go," she told me with a smile.

"Thank you, Lisa," I told her as I hopped off the bed and followed Victor out. "So, the girls told me we come into wings a week after our 18th birthday. So, that means I'll get mine-"

"In three days," he interrupted. "Four if you count today."

"What can I expect on that day?" I asked as we continued walking down the hall.

"You'll have the day off because you will be asleep almost the entire day. I'm not going to lie, it will hurt."

"Great," I replied sarcastically as I rolled my eyes.

"Since it will be a Sunday, I'll be here and will sedate you. So, don't worry too much."

"What should I expect my days to be like while I'm here?"

His features quickly filled with anger. "Do you ever stop asking questions? I mean, why not just wait and find out?"

I threw my hands up and murmured, "Well, sorry."

We stopped at the door at the end of the hall-way. "This room is the only room where you will have full access to your powers. I can control it with this device," he held up a device that had a big red button. "I will go in with you, but will press the but-ton if I feel threatened by you at any point."

He opened the door and let me walk in first. I took in the large football field sized room. Like the hallway, everything was white. It was oval shaped, no corners, and I took notice of the six cameras around the room almost immediately. I knew people had to be watching in case I did anything to Victor or tried to escape.

The power in my veins begged to be un-leashed the moment I stepped inside. "Welcome to the training room," Victor announced as he leaned against the door frame with an amused smile. "Go ahead," he told me with a wave of his hand. "I know you want to."

I turned to look back at the room. I didn't know what to do. It was different now that I was be-ing watched; being monitored.

I concentrated on my hands, focusing on forming a ball of energy in them. It did what I wanted it to do, glowing a bright neon blue, and I threw it across the room like a baseball. It hit the wall and sparked and cracked before dying out. The wall wasn't affected in the slightest.

I looked over my shoulder at Victor and saw his mouth was agape in shock. "How did you do that?" he asked. "You control your abilities so well."

I shrugged. "I just think what I want, and it happens."

"I've never seen any angel who could do that. And I've met 10 in my lifetime. None of them have been able to do whatever they want."

Dr. Rodriguez came inside and stood next to Victor. "I think he's perfect for it. Don't you think so?"

Victor grinned. "Definitely."

"Perfect for what?" I asked them.

"For an experiment we've wanted to do for a while," Dr. Rodriguez answered. "We've been waiting for the right angel to do it with. One that has lots of potential."

"What do you mean?"

"We want to make you a weapon for the military. We are calling it Project Obedience."

I shook my head. "No. No way in hell are you going to make me into some kind of weapon. I will never hurt people. I refuse."

He just shrugged. "Too bad. You don't have a choice. You see, this experiment will make you obey our every command."

"How?" I asked, growing angrier with every passing moment.

He ignored my question and looked at Victor. "We start tomorrow. I am giving you permission not to go to school tomorrow."

Victor only nodded and Dr. Rodriguez walked out. I was so mad that flames could have shot from my ears and Victor pressed the button as he followed

him. My powers immediately vanished; not a trace of
them.

CHAPTER NINE

I was in the middle of a battlefield. Guns and bombs were going off everywhere around me. I couldn't do anything, though; I couldn't move. It was almost as if something was holding me back. Then, Dr. Rodriguez was standing in front of me, looking into my eyes. "Kill all of them," he ordered as he gestured to the battle in front of us.

I had no choice but to obey. I took to the sky and created a deadly force of wind, making everyone below fall to the ground. I flew down and saw all the people, from both sides, dead. Dead because of me.

My hands shook as I took in the damage. So many people. Dead. I looked down at the person by my feet and cried out when I saw Connor's lifeless face, covered in blood.

A hand rested on my shoulder, and I looked up to come face to face with Dr. Rodriguez. "You did well. Very well."

I screamed in anger and lunged at him, but he disappeared. I turned to look for him, but instead of finding him, I found Linda stumbling over the bodies to get to her son.

She bent down to her knees next to him. She screamed in agony. In heartbreak for her dead son. She looked up at me and pointed as she yelled, "Monster!"

I backed away as she kept repeating it. My heart shredded into tiny pieces more and more until I realized I couldn't live with myself anymore; couldn't live with what I've done.

I looked over to my right and grabbed Dr. Rodriguez's gun out of his holster before he could even react. I held it up to my head, put my finger on the trigger, and pulled.

* * * * *

I WOKE UP TO ANGELICA shaking me awake. My breathing was quick, and my body was covered in sweat. "Shh," she whispered as she pulled me to her and rubbed my back. "It's okay. It was just a nightmare."

I sobbed into her shoulder, and she held me until my tears dried up and I pulled back. I wiped my tears away from my cheeks and looked into her eyes. They were so full of understanding. "Sorry, I didn't mean to wake you," I whispered, not wanting to wake Alis too.

"I was awake anyway. I couldn't sleep." She brought her thumbs up to wipe my remaining tears away from my cheeks. She quickly pulled away when she realized what she was doing. "Do you want to talk about it?"

I shook my head. "No." I just wanted to forget about it.

"Move over," she told me. I gave her a confused look and she said, "I don't want to be alone, and know you don't want to either."

I slowly nodded and moved so I was pressed against the wall. She climbed in next to me and curled into my side. I wrapped my arm around her and pulled her closer. She fell asleep within seconds, while I laid there and thought about the dream for hours until I finally fell asleep.

* * * * *

WHEN I WOKE UP the next morning, Angelica was gone. She and Alis were already out of the room. I got up and got dressed in the clothes I found lying at the bottom of the bed and brushed my teeth in the bathroom.

When I walked out of the bathroom, I stopped short when I saw Dr. Rodriguez and Victor standing in the middle of the room. "Time to start Project Obedience," Dr. Rodriguez said with a grin. Victor looked uneasy, like he wasn't exactly confident in their plans. "Let's go," he ordered as he turned and walked out the door with Victor following.

I didn't follow. I figured they would have to drag me out of that room before they did whatever they were going to do to make me 'obedient'. They turned when they realized I hadn't moved and Dr. Rodriguez tsked his tongue. "I will force you to come out," he told me in a stern voice.

"I guess you'll have to," I challenged.

He made his way over to me in three long strides and slapped me across the face so hard that I saw stars. He then gripped my arm tightly and dragged me out of the room. I tried to fight his grasp, but it was too tight.

54

He dragged me down the hall and into a room on the right. A chair you would see at the dentist was in the center of the room.

I fought harder when he tried to make me sit in it. Victor tried to help him by taking hold of my other arm. I kept fighting them until they got me in the chair and Victor straddled my body while holding my hands down on either side of my head. Dr. Rodriguez snapped cuffs over my wrists, locking them to the chair. He did the same with my ankles before Victor got off me.

Dr. Rodriguez came up to my face as I glared at him, and he put a gag in my mouth, securing it by tying it at the back of my head.

"Go get a sedative to calm him down," Dr. Rodriguez told his son. "Not too much, we don't want him going unconscious."

He nodded and walked out of the room. I glared at the man in front of me while he fixed his rustled suit and tie. He went to the corner of the room, where I noticed a video camera. He set up the camera, so it was facing me, as Victor walked back inside.

He prepped the needle and inserted it into my neck as I glared at him. He either didn't notice or didn't care as I started feeling out of it. He stood by my right side as Dr. Rodriguez pressed record on the camera and walked over to my left.

"This is Project Obedience, test one, subject: Christian. We hope to have full control of him by test seven." He nodded to Victor, and they hooked me up to IVs and let some liquid drip from the bags and into my veins. "The meds should start working within a half an hour," he told the camera.

They walked out of the room, leaving me alone. I looked up and noticed cameras in each corner of the ceiling. I had no doubt they were watching the footage.

I started feeling…. weird. That's the only way to explain what I felt. My muscles became more strained, and my brain became foggy. I blinked, trying to focus on fighting the effects of whatever they were putting in me. It didn't work; it settled over me like a blanket. I could barely focus on what I was thinking.

I don't know how long they were gone for, but when they came in, I barely noticed. "Let's see if this worked," Dr Rodriguez said as Victor unhooked the IVs.

"Should I uncuff him?" Victor asked.

"One second," he answered. He shined a light in my eyes as he checked my pupils. "Pupils have a delay, but it's expected." He stood up straight in front of me. "Alright, Christian. Focus on me."

My mind was torn between obeying or not, but I got an instant migraine when I fought obedience and had to look at him. He grinned, "Good."

He then nodded to Victor and told him to remove the cuffs around my wrists and gag from my mouth. Once the cuffs were off, my hands fell limp by my sides. I looked straight ahead because my mind wouldn't let me do anything without permission.

"Take this," he said as he handed me a pencil and paper. I did and waited for what I was supposed to do next. "Write down your name," he ordered.

Christian Hoyt.

"Your age."

18

"Your two biggest fears."

While my mind screamed at me not to, my hand wrote:

#1: I am worthless. My whole life has been a waste.

#2: Being alone for long periods of time.

"Well, Christian," he said, making me look up at him. "You're not worthless. Not anymore. You are a powerful weapon." He looked over at Victor. "Take the cuffs off his ankles." He did and stepped back. "Stand up."

It was almost as if my body wasn't mine anymore. I had no control over what I did as I moved to stand in front of him. My back was straight, and eyes were focused in front of me, on him.

"Take off your shirt," he ordered. I did, and he grinned wider. He looked over at Victor, who was standing by the door, most likely to block me if the medication wore off. He turned back to me and looked my body up and down in a creepy way that would have made me squirm, had I not been drugged. "He is in very good shape, don't you think?" he asked Victor without looking at him.

"Sure, dad," he answered while keeping his face expressionless.

I knew I was fit. Years of football and working out gave me abs and biceps girls went crazy over. However, it made me feel self-conscious and naked when Dr. Rodriguez was talking about me as if I was nothing more than an animal or object.

He walked over so his face was mere inches from mine. Without warning, he punched me in the stomach, hard. I couldn't do anything, though; couldn't even wince or grunt in pain due to the drugs in my system.

"This will be such a magnificent thing for our troops and research," he told Victor as he stepped back a step. "If he got slightly injured, it would barely affect him."

I finally started feeling the effects of the drug wear off and could think a bit clearer. "All right, Christian. Put your shirt back on."

Even though I wanted to, I didn't. I was still in a daze, but had control over my body again. He stepped up and examined me. "I think it's wearing off," he told Victor. "Sedate him before he snaps out of it. We'll have to figure out how to make it last longer."

Victor pressed a needle into my neck, but I barely felt it with the haze still over my mind. I hardly flinched as I fell into Victor's arms. He held my limp body to him, and Dr. Rodriguez helped him carry me back to the room and lay me on my bed.

The girls waited until they left before coming over to me. "What are they doing to him?" Angelica asked Alis.

Alis looked down at me with helplessness all over her face. "I don't know, but whatever it is, it's not good."

"Agreed," Angelica said.

I closed my eyes, no longer able to keep them open, and fell into a deep sleep.

CHAPTER TEN

I woke up and ate dinner before falling back to sleep. I could tell the girls were watching me with worried faces. They didn't ask the questions I knew they were thinking, and I was thankful for that.

I woke from a nightmare in the middle of the night and Angelica was by my side in an instant. She climbed into bed with me, and we talked about our lives outside of the lab. I found out she wanted to be an artist and maybe even an art teacher. She told me she had a boyfriend before they brought her here, and that he acted the same way Connor acted. I found out that her and Alis were foster kids too, and for the same reason. Their mother beat them after their father abandoned them.

We soon fell asleep curled in each other's arms, content to have someone who understood how hard it is to go on without our moms, no matter how horrible. And now, our freedom.

* * * * *

THE NEXT TWO DAYS were the same. They did their experiment, I would eat dinner, and wake up from a nightmare. Victor went to school on Friday, leaving his dad with day two of experimenting, but was here all day on Saturday. Dr. Rodriguez enjoyed hurting me. He would slap, punch, and kick me while the drugs had their effect. I couldn't even defend myself because I was told not to move.

When Victor was there, he would remain silent as his dad did his thing. Then, he would do whatever his dad asked without any hesitation.

I had Sunday off, but knew it still wouldn't be 'a day off' because I would be coming into my wings. That morning, I woke up with a horrible pain in my upper back. "Christian," a voice said from beside me when I groaned and rolled onto my stomach.

I opened my eyes and saw Alis sitting on the edge of my bed. The pain doubled as soon as I opened my eyes. I moaned and whispered, "It hurts."

She nodded in understanding. "I know it does. You have to keep breathing through it," she told me as she took deep breaths with me. "Good," she said with a slight smile.

I winced when it doubled again. She took my hand, and I squeezed it firmly. I closed my eyes tightly, praying it would go away soon. "Christian!" Victor yelled in panic as he rushed into the room. Alis moved out of the way and he kneeled by my side. He took my hand in his and I squeezed it, not caring if I hurt him or not. "Sorry I'm late," he told me. "I got stuck in construction traffic on the way here."

I only grunted in response. I was sure my entire body was covered in sweat, but didn't care as another wave of pain hit. He took out a needle and showed it to me. "Want me to?"

I nodded as I cried in pain, and he pressed the needle into my neck. It must have been a very high dose because I passed out almost instantly.

* * * * *

PEOPLE WERE WHISPERING somewhere near me. Their voices were laced with confusion and shock. "Why is he different?" Victor asked.

"I don't know," Dr. Rodriguez growled.

I heard his footsteps retreating from the room and felt someone run a hand over my back. It felt… good. Like a massage. I sighed at the feeling and Victor let out a breathy laugh. "Christian," he whispered in my ear, "you awake?"

I moaned and said, "Five more minutes?"

He chuckled, and I felt him touch my back again, only this time, it tickled. I opened my eyes and blinked a few times to clear my blurry vision. I looked at Victor, who was grinning down at me and then glanced back at something on my back.

I looked back and shot up, fully alert, when I saw wings sticking out of my back. However, they weren't black like I was told they would be. No, they were white. Pure white and huge. Each wing had to be at least my height in length, if not longer.

I looked over at Victor, who grinned from ear to ear. I moved so my legs dangled off the edge of the bed and went to stand on my shaky legs. I wobbled, not used to the weight on my back, and Victor grabbed my arm to steady me.

I couldn't stop looking back at them with wide eyes. Victor chuckled and said, "They're beautiful, aren't they?"

I only nodded and tried to flap them. They flapped, scaring me and making me jump back. Victor laughed, but said nothing as he held onto my arm. I flapped them again, and again, and again until I barely had to think about it, and it was almost like moving another body part.

"I think you've got the hang of it," Victor told me. "Alis is waiting for you in the training room if you want to learn how to fly."

I nodded. "But first, I want to go to the bathroom," I told him.

"Okay. You may want to make your wings go away before you do, though."

"How?" I asked as I tilted my head.

"From what I've gathered. You must picture yourself without wings and they should retreat."

I did as he said and closed my eyes as I pictured myself without wings. I felt a tingling sensation on my back and looked to see my wings sliding into my back. They disappeared and left no evidence that they were even there. "Wow," I breathed.

"Yeah, wow," Victor agreed.

I walked into the bathroom and walked back out a moment later. "Ready?" he asked.

I took a shaky breath and nodded. We walked out and went to the training room, where we found Alis waiting. She had her wings out already and smiled when she saw us.

Victor stayed by the door frame while I walked over to her. "I haven't seen your wings yet. How are they?"

I hesitated before saying, "They're good."

"Well, let's see them," she said.

I closed my eyes and willed my wings to come out. They did, and I heard Alis gasp. "It's you," she breathed with her hand over her mouth.

"What do you mean?" I asked.

"I've been having visions of a white-winged angel," she explained. "You're meant for extraordinary things."

I gave her a confused look, but she didn't go on. I decided not to push it and to ask her later, when we were alone in the room. "Okay. Let's get started. I want you to flap your wings once, just enough to lift yourself up in the air."

She demonstrated and lifted herself into the air with one powerful flap of her wings. She then slowly came down and gracefully landed on her feet. I tried and wobbled in the air. She came up and took my hands to stabilize me. She helped me by guiding me to the ground and helping me to my feet.

"This is a lot harder than I thought it would be," I admitted.

She laughed. "It doesn't come easily. It's like riding a bike. It takes a while to learn, but once you learn, your body always knows what to do."

I nodded. "I see that now."

She told me to try again, and a few tries later, I could do it on my own. "Excellent job," she praised. "Now, let's try to go a little higher."

She took my hands, and we flew higher, to the ceiling, which was about three stories above the ground. She smiled and I smiled back as we kept flapping our wings to stay up. She let go of my hands, but stayed close as I adjusted to flying myself. "You're doing it!" she exclaimed with a smile.

I was still slightly wobbly, but after a few hours, I was flying around the room on my own. We raced a few times, laughing the entire time. Victor came and went while Alis and I stayed in the room and enjoyed hanging out together.

"I could get used to this," I said as we hovered in the air. "Wish we could do it outside, though."

She nodded and pursed her lips before replying, "Me too."

We slowly lowered ourselves to the ground and made our wings retreat into our backs. I looked over my shoulder and saw Victor and Alis's researcher watching us with amused expressions on their faces. "You having fun?" Victor asked with a smirk.

We both nodded and walked over to them. "Hungry?" the female researcher asked with a tilt of her head.

We both nodded and replied, "Starving." We looked at each other and laughed at our alike thoughts.

"Well, let's go get you two something to eat," Victor said as he gestured us to follow.

We glanced at each other before following them down the hall. They led us to our room, where Angelica was waiting for us. They brought us some food before locking us in for the rest of the day.

We sat on their beds and talked about anything and everything. We laughed so hard we had tears running down our cheeks. For a while, we forgot we were experiments and just enjoyed each other's company. I found out that each of them had strengths in certain abilities. Alis got visions of the future, and Angelica could control fire; she could actually become fire if she wanted.

I asked Alis what she meant earlier by seeing me in her vision. "I've been having visions of you for a while. I keep hearing the words 'savior' and 'king' repeatedly in them. It gives me reason to believe that it means you will do extraordinary things."

"Are you sure?" I asked her with an arched eyebrow.

She nodded. "Yes."

"Interesting," I said thoughtfully.

"Lights out in 10," the guard in the black room said.

We all got up and went to get dressed. I went into the bathroom, while they got dressed in the room after the guard left to give them privacy.

I put on the gray sweatpants and white t-shirt before knocking on the door to make sure I could come out. They gave me the okay, and I opened the door.

They were both dressed in sweatpants as well and were already in their beds.

I climbed into my bed right before the lights turned off. I fell asleep soon after and didn't have any nightmares.

CHAPTER ELEVEN

The next day, Victor took me into the experiment room. I didn't even fight, knowing they would get me there either way. Dr. Rodriguez was waiting, and I sat in the chair without meeting his eyes. He seemed surprised, but didn't say anything as he hooked the IVs to my arms. He didn't even bother cuffing me to the chair.

They stayed in the room as the drugs took their effect, and the haze settled over my mind. Once all the liquid was inside me, they started telling me what to do and I would have no choice but to obey.

I was told to write things on the paper, point to things, and stay still when Dr. Rodriguez would beat me. The meds wore off after about an hour and they talked about how they would make it last for an entire day.

By that time, I was emotionally and physically drained. Victor helped me walk to the room, where the girls were waiting, and helped me onto the bed. I heard them whispering amongst themselves once he was gone, their voices laced with worry and concern. I hadn't told them what they were doing to me every day and planned on keeping it that way for as long as I could.

I fell asleep soon after and woke from a nightmare before dinner. "You're okay," Alis told me as she held me to her. "You're going to be okay," she repeated, although it sounded like she was trying to reassure herself that I would be okay.

Angelica wasn't around until after we ate, and she ate while we talked. "What are they doing to you?" Angelica asked me.

"I don't want to talk about it," I said without making eye contact with either of them. "They aren't doing good things though," was all I gave them.

They looked at each other, but knew better than to press on. "Do you think we will ever get out of here?" Angelica asked after a moment of silence passed between us.

"I don't know…" Alis said. "I hope to someday."

"We will get out of here," I told them. "As long as we have hope, we can do anything. I've heard that love is the most powerful thing, but I think hope is a close second."

"I hope you're right," Angelica sighed. She smiled and looked over at Alis. "I think we can trust him. Don't you?"

"Trust me with what?" I asked.

Alis looked me in the eyes, and I could see the concentration in her face. *Can you hear me, Christian?*

I widened my eyes and slowly nodded. She was talking in my mind?!

One thing we haven't told the researchers is that we can speak to each other in our minds. Telepathically. We wanted to make sure we could trust you before we told you.

I tried to focus on talking inside her mind. I focused on what I wanted to tell her and sent it over. *Can you hear me?*

Her eyes widened. *How did you do that so quickly? It took us a while to figure out how to send clear messages.*

I shrugged, but quickly realized something that worried me. *I really wish you hadn't told me.*

She cocked her head to the side. *Why?*

I focused on both of them. *Because what they are doing to me, they may somehow find out about it. They are trying to make me a weapon for the military. To do that, they are putting a drug in me that makes me obedient to them. They might ask me something about this and they will force me to answer.*

Then, we will accept the risk, Angelica sent. *Let's hope that they won't find out.*

Alis nodded in agreement and we all crawled back into our beds after saying goodnight. I thought about how this new information could help us escape. We could form a plan without them knowing and escape when the time seemed right. I decided to talk it over with the girls sometime before falling asleep.

CHAPTER TWELVE

A few days later, instead of taking me to the experiment room, Victor led me to the training room. I was confused, but kept my mouth shut as we walked inside. Dr. Rodriguez was waiting for us and I saw the IVs behind him.

I couldn't feel my powers, so I knew they pressed the button. I walked over to Dr. Rodriguez, making sure to keep my head down because he told me to the last time, after slapping me.

"I figured we would try our experiment in here today," Dr. Rodriguez told me. He made me put my hands behind my back and put handcuffs over my wrists. He then hooked the IVs up to me before standing in front of me, waiting for the drugs to make me into a puppet. His puppet.

As they took effect, my head slowly raised, and my back became stiff as it straightened. I looked ahead, unblinking and unmoving, as they unhooked the empty bags of the drugs that were now inside me. Victor removed the handcuffs from my wrists before stepping back.

"Summon your wings," Dr. Rodriguez ordered once he stood in my line of sight again.

I did as I was told and closed my eyes to summon them before opening them again. I looked back at him and he grinned.

"Fly around the room one time and land in the center of the room," he told me before stepping back to give me space.

In one powerful flap, I was in the air. I flapped my wings again, and I was almost to the ceiling. I flew around the room and landed in the middle of the room. I stood tall, looked straight ahead, and my wings stood tall at my back.

Dr. Rodriguez grinned wider. I wondered if he had any idea of what I would do to him if I had control of my own mind. "Wonderful." He turned to look back at Victor as he said, "Turn off the blockers."

Victor pressed the button, and I felt the force of my abilities hit as they screamed to be released. Through the drugs, I winced at the pain radiating though my body. It felt like pins and needles all over my body and my head instantly started pounding. Victor ran his hand through his hair. "Shit. Do you feel that?" he asked his father.

Dr. Rodriguez nodded and looked back to me. "He is very powerful. He's the only one who we can actually feel the power coming off of. He'll make a perfect weapon," he said with a wicked grin.

"You're not actually going to give him to the military, are you? You did say he was *mine*."

"Of course, I'm giving him to the military. Think about what he could do for us."

"But you said-"

Dr. Rodriguez interrupted him with a raised hand, silencing him. He turned to look at his son. "I know what I said. But he could do so much more; help so many people."

"By killing other people," Victor came back. "He will kill you if you make him do that."

"Luckily, he won't be able to. He will always be monitored and chained up when he isn't being used. And will be our obedient little weapon."

Victor glared at his father, but turned to me. "Let's just move on with the experiment."

Dr. Rodriguez stepped forward and told me to create an energy ball and throw it at the target behind me. The target was shaped like a human with a red dot by its heart.

I turned and created the ball in my hand before aiming for the dot. I threw it and hit my target right on. It sparked and smoked, but didn't get destroyed.

"Good job, Christian," he praised. "Now, put your wings away and walk to your cell."

Victor walked ahead of me, while Dr. Rodriguez walked behind. Victor unlocked and opened the door before I walked inside. Dr. Rodriguez walked in after me and whispered in my ear from behind, "Lay in bed and go to sleep until dinner time."

I walked over to the bed and laid down before closing my eyes. I heard them walk out and Alis and Angelica come over to me. *Can you hear us, Christian?* Alis asked.

Yeah, I answered. *But I'm going to fall asleep soon. I'm still obedient and was told to sleep until dinner.*

Okay. Just making sure you're alright. I heard them whispering as they went to lay on their beds. I soon couldn't fight the sleep settling over my mind and welcomed the darkness.

* * * * *

AFTER DINNER, I was told to follow one of the guards into one of the rooms I haven't been in. I did as I was told and walked into the room. Dr. Rodriguez was standing in the corner of the small room with a wicked grin. Two other guards stood on either side of him with expressionless faces.

I looked around and saw that the room was empty. The guard I followed closed the door once we were inside. I turned to look back at Dr. Rodriguez before asking, "What's going on?" with an arched eyebrow.

He didn't answer. He nodded to the guards and they all surrounded me. I was still feeling sluggish due to the drugs and knew whatever they were planning, I wouldn't be able to fight. I noticed something start to come down from the ceiling in the middle of the room. It looked like chains with cuffs on the ends of them.

I panicked. Whatever was happening, wasn't good. I turned in a circle and tried to look for an opening in the men surrounding me. There wasn't any. They had me completely surrounded and were ready to pounce on me at any second. They all came at me at once, and I fought the best I could, but wasn't fast or strong enough with the drugs still in me. One brought one of the cuffs over while the others tried to hold me. He fastened the cuff to my right wrist before getting the other one on my left.

The chains then started rising until my arms were forced up with little slack. I glared at Dr. Rodriguez, who was still standing in the corner to my left with his arms crossed and a satisfied expression.

"What the hell is wrong with you?!" I yelled at him. "What are you doing?"

He looked at the guards who were standing behind me and said, "Leave us."

Without a word, they left the room and closed the door behind them. Dr. Rodriguez came to stand inches from my face. I glared at him as he just stared at me.

Without warning, he punched me in the stomach so hard that I had trouble breathing for a moment. I sucked in a breath once I was able to and blinked to refocus my vision. However, he didn't give me much of a break and punched me again, harder.

I knew I had to have at least one broken rib by the force of his punches. He then aimed lower, aiming for my groin. My legs gave out, but the chains kept me up. He went behind me and pulled my shirt up to my eyes, covering them with it.

I heard him grab something from somewhere in the room and come back a moment later. He brought something down on my back and I knew it had to be a whip. I cried out at the searing pain it brought to my back. I felt my warm blood run down my back slowly. He did it over and over again, each slash more jarring than the last. I sobbed as I yelled out, cursing him every time.

Once I thought I couldn't take it anymore and started to whimper instead of yell, he stopped. He touched my back harshly, making me cry harder. He whispered in my ear, "Goodnight, Christian."

I thought he was going to knock me out and braced myself, but I heard him walk out and close the door behind him. *What the fuck?! He really just left me here for the night?!*

I took a deep breath, hoping to calm myself before I had a panic attack. My back felt as if it was on fire and the blood ran down it slowly. My arms ached from being up for so long and basically were holding my weight since my legs gave out. I thought about summoning my wings to ease the pain in my arms, but thought better of it because I didn't know how bad it would hurt my back. I just hoped the night would pass by quickly.

CHAPTER THIRTEEN

The night did not pass quickly. I dozed in and out for a while, but never actually fell asleep. I lost track of time quickly and kept praying the ordeal would end soon.

I was still dozing when I heard Victor's angry voice outside the room. It sounded as if he wasn't aware of what his dad did to me until he got here this morning. But I knew that even if he wasn't part of it, I still couldn't trust him.

He stormed into the room and rushed over to me. He lowered the chains, and I sank to my knees as soon as I was given the chance. He removed them from my wrists before pulling my shirt away from my eyes and over my arms. I lost feeling in my arms hours ago and they started tingling as the blood rushed into them.

I basically leaned my body forward and into Victor. He pushed me at arm's length to look me in my unfocused eyes. "It's okay. I've got you," he told me. He put my arm over his shoulders and wrapped his around my waist, careful not to touch my bleeding back, before standing us up.

He led us to the cell and asked someone to unlock the door as we approached. I was so tired; all I could think about was curling up in bed and sleeping the day away. However, he led me to the bathroom and sat me on the shower floor before turning the water on.

I hissed as the water hit my back and Victor cursed. "Sorry, Christian. But I have to ensure they don't get infected."

I only grunted in response as I curled in a ball on the shower floor. Someone knocked on the door and Victor called out, "You can come in!"

I heard the door squeak open and close a moment later. "What did you do?" Alis demanded.

"I had no part in this," Victor answered. "It's all my dad."

"Get out," she ordered in a stern voice.

"What? No!" he yelled. "I'll help him get dressed before I leave."

She sighed. "Fine. But only because you're a guy and it will be more comfortable for him."

"Can you ask the guard to get some clothes for him? Just pants and underwear. I don't think he should wear a shirt yet."

She left and Victor bent down next to me. "You okay with me helping you dress?"

I slowly nodded, but didn't look at him. At that point, I didn't care because all I wanted to do was get to bed. And if he helped, that would get me there sooner. Plus, I didn't think I had enough strength to dress myself.

Alis came back and asked, "Do you need help with anything?"

"Could you ask the guard to get Lisa while I dress him?" he asked her.

She left and Victor turned the water off. He got a towel and helped me out of the wet shower and onto the middle of the cold cement floor. He tried to dry me quickly when I started to shiver. He was careful with drying my back, but it still hurt like hell.

He helped me out of my wet pants and underwear while I closed my heavy eyelids. "This isn't my first time doing this," he told me. "So, don't worry."

He slid the new underwear up my legs and secured them around my waist before putting the sweatpants on me. He then helped me stand while I kept my eyes closed. "I'm trusting you not to let me run into anything," I told him groggily.

He laughed as he led me out of the bathroom. He helped me over to my bed and guided me to lay on my stomach. I heard Lisa come in and ask what was wrong.

"What can you do with whip wounds and possibly broken ribs?" he asked her.

"Did you wash the wounds?" she asked.

"With water, yes."

"Place some cool washcloths on his back and check them every hour," she said as she gently ran her finger along one of my slashes. "As for the broken ribs… I'd have to see them, but that will have to wait."

My breathing started to slow, and I felt them trying to find a way to feel my ribs without bothering me before I fell asleep.

* * * * *

WHEN I WOKE, I heard Victor and Alis whispering nearby. "You should really go get some rest," Alis said. "Angelica or I will be here with him at all times."

"No," Victor answered. "I want to be here with him. I don't trust my dad." He sounded exhausted, like he'd been up all night.

"He's been out for a while. I think you should at least close your eyes."

I tried focusing on Alis before saying, *Hey, Alis.*

I could tell she wasn't trying to show that she heard me as she replied, *Christian? Are you alright?*

I'm fine. How long have I been asleep?

About 16 hours, she answered after some hesitation.

I jerked up, fully awake. 16 hours?! No wonder Victor sounded so tired!

I looked over and saw Alis and Victor lounging on the beds. Alis pursed her lips as she tried not to laugh at my reaction, not wanting to give away our secret.

Victor jumped up and was at my side in an instant. He looked me over and seemed to be happy with my healing progress. "You mind if I take your temperature? We've been taking it every few hours."

I nodded, letting him know it was okay. He placed a thermometer under my tongue and waited for it to beep. He looked at the number and cringed. "It's still high. 102.2 degrees."

I laid my head back into my folded arms as I looked over at him. I shivered before saying, "I'm cold."

He nodded in understanding before pulling a blanket up to my shoulders. I knew he was only being nice to me to make me trust him more with his experiments, but could have gotten used to it.

"You thirsty?" he asked me as he picked up a glass of water from the floor beside my bed.

I nodded in my arms and he helped me sit up enough so I could drink from the glass of water. Once I drank the whole thing, I sighed before settling back down. I closed my eyes and fell back to sleep almost instantly.

CHAPTER FOURTEEN

I woke up a few hours later and was able to sit up on my own. I looked over at the beds and saw that Angelica was the only one in the room. She was reading a book and didn't notice me slowly stand up.

I walked over to her and sat on the bottom of her bed. She jumped, startled. She put her hand on her heart as she said, "Jesus. Don't scare me like that!"

I chuckled and asked, "What are you reading?"

She closed the book and showed me the cover. It was *Romeo and Juliet*. I raised my eyebrow in question, and she admitted, "It's what they gave me. Trust me, I would have never picked it."

I laughed. It felt good to laugh. I couldn't even remember the last time I actually had laughed.

"How are you feeling?" she asked me to change the subject as she closed the book.

"Better," I told her with a smile. "Much better."

She sat on her knees. "Let me see your back," she told me.

I turned around and she ran her hands gently down my back. I shivered at her touch. "It doesn't hurt anymore," I told her breathlessly.

"That's good," she told me. "There are still a few slight areas that aren't fully healed, but should be within a few hours."

I stood up and told her that I was going to the bathroom. I walked inside and shut the door behind me. I took care of my business before looking in the mirror above the sink. I was pale. Really pale. I had dark rings under my eyes even though I slept for over 16 hours.

I checked my ribs next, making sure they were healing. They were still slightly bruised, but not as bad as I thought they would be. I ran my hands over them and made sure they were healing properly. Angelica knocked on the door and asked, "Everything okay?"

"Yeah!" I called. I looked myself over one more time before opening the door. "I'm never going to get used to this speed healing," I admitted as I leaned against the door frame.

She laughed. "At least it's a perk," she pointed out. "Or else you wouldn't be standing right now. "

"True," I told her as I sat on her bed and she sat next to me.

She looked over at me with tears in her eyes. "I was so scared for you. I seriously thought you weren't going to make it at one point. I wanted to kill Dr. Rodriguez for what he did to you. I wish we could get out of here."

I pulled her to my side and tried to comfort her. "I've been in and out of foster homes all my life," I started. "I was beaten by my mother when I was eight and had to be sent to the hospital for weeks. I let all their hateful words get to me and pull me down. I didn't think it could get any worse, and now… it got worse. But I just keep reminding myself that I will get out of here someday, and that you and Alis will be with me. We will get through this. Together."

"I hope you're right…" she said as the tears leaked from her eyes. "Do you think Luke still thinks about me? Is he planning a way to get me out?"

I knew Luke had to be her boyfriend before she was brought here. "I don't know," I told her honestly. "But if he has given up on you, then he isn't the right guy for you."

She looked up and our faces were so close that they could touch. We both stopped breathing and slowly closed our eyes as we leaned closer. Our lips gently touched before she deepened it by wrapping her arms around my neck. She moved to straddle my lap and opened her mouth to give me access to her tongue. Our tongues danced with each other and we poured everything in the kiss. Our longing, loneliness, sadness, anger, and fears. However, something was off. I felt as if I was doing something wrong, as if I was cheating on someone. But I didn't have a girlfriend, so I didn't know why I felt that way.

After a moment, we both pulled back to catch our breath. She climbed off my lap and sat next to me once more. Her head rested on my shoulder and we sat like that for a while.

She broke the silence when she said, "I needed that. Thank you."

"Would it surprise you if I told you that was my first kiss in three years?" I asked her.

She lifted her head off my shoulder and looked at me. "You can't be serious."

I nodded. "I'm serious."

"You haven't had sex in three years then either?" she asked in shock.

I shook my head and my face heated in embarrassment. "I'm…I'm a virgin."

"What?!" she shrieked. "But you're so good looking!"

I laughed. "Doesn't mean I had sex!" I cleared my throat and asked, "So, what about you? Are you a virgin?"

She shook her head. "God, no! I lost my virginity to Luke when we were sophomores in high school."

"Well, you've officially beat me," I told her with a mischievous grin.

She slapped my arm playfully. "Why are you a virgin?" she asked after a moment of silence. "Religious views?"

"Sort of. I am religious, but don't think God will shame me for having sex before marriage. It's just that I never found the right girl," I told her with a shrug. "I mean, yeah, I've dated a few girls, but they only wanted me because I was the quarterback on the football team and one of the 'hottest' guys in school."

"I'm sure that's not true…" she told me.

"Then why did they always end it when they found out about my horrible life at home?" I asked her. "Or when they are finally popular in school?"

"Oh, shit," she quickly said. "Wow. That's low."

I nodded. "Yeah…"

"Have you met any girls that have caught your interest?" she asked.

"Umm…yeah," I said with an unsure nod. "I only met her once, though. An hour before I was brought here. She was so beautiful, and I felt an instant connection with her the moment our eyes met."

"Ooh, what's her name?" she sang as she bumped my shoulder.

"Eliana. She's actually part of the reason I'm here," I told her. She tilted her head in confusion and I explained, "Victor used her to out me. He pinned her against the wall to see if I would do anything to help. I pulled him away with my abilities and he called the military after running away. I was going to explain myself to Eliana after school, but… didn't get a chance to."

"So, she's not really 'part' of it," she told me.

I looked down at my hands in my lap. "Yeah…"

She hugged me and whispered, "I'm sorry, Christian."

"It's alright," I told her as I hugged her back. "I'll be okay."

The door unlocked and Victor stepped inside. He smiled at me and said, "Good to see you awake."

He handed some food and water to both of us before sitting next to me. Angelica and I ate in silence, and Victor sat there until we were done. "What does your dad have planned for today?" I asked as I took a sip of water.

He sighed and gave me a guilty look, one that told me I wouldn't like whatever it was. "You're not going to like it…"

"As long as it doesn't include hurting me, I think I'll be okay with it."

He hesitated before telling me, "It doesn't harm you physically…but mentally, it might."

"More Project Obedience?" I groaned.

"No," he said quickly as he shook his head. "We're working on improvements for that. He plans to…keep you locked in a room with no human interaction for a while."

"How long's 'a while'?" I asked him curiously.

He shrugged. "Who knows with dad? Don't tell him I gave you food because I wasn't supposed to."

He stood up and gestured for me to follow. I sighed. "Now?"

He gave me a surprisingly apologetic look. "Yeah…"

I stood up and Angelica stood too. She gave me a hug and wished me luck. She even gave me a quick kiss on the lips before letting me go. I followed Victor out and down the hall.

"So, you and Angelica are a thing now?" Victor said with a smirk.

I shrugged. "I don't know. We are both really lonely right now, so I think we are just trying to get a little comfort from each other."

He nodded in understanding. "Makes sense."

He opened the door next to Lisa's room and we walked inside. It was small, significantly smaller than the cell. There was nothing but concrete floors, walls, and ceilings. Even the 'bed' was made of concrete. I noticed a camera in the middle of the wall in front of me. There was also a small tube underneath the camera, and I figured I would know what it was for soon enough. There was a door on the wall to my right, and I assumed it led to a bathroom. Dr. Rodriguez stood in the middle of the room and had a stern expression on his face.

"This room is where you will be staying for the next two weeks," he started. "You will not have any human interaction or be given anything except for food and water through this pipe," he told me as he gestured to the pipe. "We will be watching you slowly go mad through the camera."

"Why are you doing this?" I asked him.

"Because it's part of an experiment," was all he said. He gestured for Victor to follow him out and called over his shoulder, "See you in two weeks."

He closed the door and I heard him lock it from the other side. I cursed before looking around the room. It was dark, the only light came from the crack underneath the door and the red dot on the camera. I knew they were doing this because I told them that being alone was one of my biggest fears. I had to take a few deep breaths to calm myself down.

I walked over to the door that I assumed was a bathroom and opened it. Sure enough, there was a toilet in the very small space. No shower. No sink. Not even a mirror. I closed the door and walked over to the camera.

I saw that it was focused on me and gave whoever was watching the finger. *Christian?* Angelica's voice asked.

I jumped and tried to make it look like I felt something crawling on my leg as I answered, *Hey.*

What are they doing to you? she asked with a worried tone.

I'm locked in a room for the next two weeks. No human interaction during that time.

That sucks! she exclaimed. *Which room?*

The one to the left of Lisa's room, I told her as I sat on the 'bed'.

I'm going to kill Dr. Rodriguez when we get out of here someday.

Jump in line, I told her with a chuckle attached to the thought. *Talk to me when you are able to, okay?*

Okay. I'll let Alis know too.

I laid down and closed my eyes. I prayed that I could fall asleep, and that the next two weeks would go by quickly.

CHAPTER FIFTEEN

I was fed through the tube. Food literally came out of it three times a day…at least, I think it was three times a day. I didn't have much sense of how much time was passing. The food was always in small portions and never had much taste. It was always mushy and smelled like… bad hospital food. I couldn't see what I was eating, due to the darkness, but wasn't sure I wanted to.

Alis and Angelica took turns talking to me whenever they could, and I was glad we could talk telepathically. Although, it didn't help me from going mad. I slept most of the time, but when I was awake, I felt like banging my head against the wall. So, I did. And instantly regretted it. My head throbbed and started bleeding. I went and grabbed a small piece of the little toilet paper I had. I put it up to my head and the bleeding stopped after a few minutes.

At one point, I started singing out of boredom. And I *never* sang unless forced to. I was told I had a really good singing voice, but never really used it much. I felt like a caged animal. The only thing I had grown to like was the tube that provided me food and bottled water.

I paced when I grew anxious and restless, slept whenever I could, and talked to Alis and Angelica when we were able. At times, I felt as if the walls were closing in on me and that I was suffocating.

"Please, let me out of here!" I yelled one day when I couldn't take it anymore. Of course, there was no answer.

Christian, Alis' voice sounded when I was drifting in and out of consciousness. *How are you holding up?*

Absolutely terrific, I replied sarcastically. *How long have I been in here?*

About a week and two days. You have five more days.

I groaned out loud, knowing the people watching would only think it was out of boredom. *I am slowly going insane in here.*

I bet. But I know you can push through it. You are one of the strongest people I know.

I smirked at her comments. *Thanks, Alis.*

I heard something come out of the tube and looked over at it. I sat up and walked over to it. At first, I didn't feel anything under it and thought I imagined it. Until I kicked something a few feet away as I was walking back to the bed. I let out a giddy chuckle when I bent down to pick it up. It was round and fuzzy, and I knew it was a tennis ball.

I grinned like a kid on Christmas morning as I tossed it from hand to hand, glad to have something to do, and bounced it a few times. I sat on the floor with my back pressed against the cement block of a bed, and bounced it off the wall across from me. I smiled when I caught it and kept doing that for a long time. I didn't know if it was part of their plan to give me it, or if someone snuck it in for me. I didn't care, I was just happy to have something to entertain myself with.

* * * * *

THE BALL KEPT ME entertained for a while, but I eventually grew bored once more and laid on the floor. It wasn't different than lying on the bed. I curled in a ball and cried for the first time since I was whipped.

I wished my life could go back to normal. I missed my friends, going to school, and football practice and games. I missed everything. I missed my freedom.

"Christian?" I heard a female ask from above me. I looked up and saw Linda standing over me.

I jerked upwards and she laughed as she bent down in front of me. I wiped my eyes and whispered, "Mrs. Peters?"

She smiled and sat next to me. "You're okay. You'll make it through this," she told me as she put her hand on top of mine.

However, I didn't feel it. I couldn't feel her touch. I choked back a sob when I realized I was hallucinating. She wasn't real. She was a figment of my imagination, but I was surprised when I realized I

92

didn't care. I didn't care that she wasn't real. I was happy to have someone to talk to, even if she was a made-up figure in my mind.

"I miss you," I told her as my body rocked with another sob.

"We miss you too," she told me. "But we have to have faith that we will be reunited again soon."

"I hope," I said with a sigh. "Will you wait for me?"

"Of course, we will. We will always wait for you. And I told you you would be extraordinary. Look at you," she said as she gestured to me.

I shook my head. "I'm not extraordinary. I'm a guy with a messed-up life and am now being held captive because of what makes me 'extraordinary'. I'm…worthless," I told her as I hung my head.

"Don't say that. You are not worthless. You are a miracle. You may not see it yet, but you will do many great things for this world."

I looked up at her with tears in my eyes. "You really think so?"

"I know so. Now, why don't you get some sleep," she told me.

I closed my eyes and laid back on the floor. "Goodnight, Linda."

"Goodnight, Christian," she whispered before I fell asleep.

CHAPTER SIXTEEN

I heard the door unlock and open when I was dozing in and out of consciousness a few days later. I hadn't had anything to eat or drink for the last two days because I wanted to die. God, I wanted to die right then and there. I kept my eyes closed and remained still. *Maybe they will think I'm dead if I don't move,* I thought.

"Christian," Victor whispered as he shook my shoulder. "Wake up."

I remained still, not caring that I was finally able to get out of the room of boredom. I think I was actually in shock, not sure what to do.

"Christian?" he asked, his voice laced with worry. When I still didn't move, he began to panic. I heard him rush out of the room and knock on the door next to the room to get Lisa. "Lisa! Christian is not waking up!"

I heard her open the door and they rushed back into the room. They bent down next to me and Lisa checked for my pulse by pressing her fingers to my neck. "His pulse is weak. Help me carry him to my room," she told Victor.

She grabbed my legs, while Victor grabbed me from under my arms. They carried me to her room and placed me on the medical table. She flashed a light into my eyes as she pulled back my eyelids. "I think he's in cardiogenic shock," she told him as she wrapped a blood pressure cuff around my arm. I felt it tighten around my arm for a few seconds before slowly releasing. "His blood pressure is very low."

"What does that mean?" Victor's voice rose in panic.

"I need to get an IV started on him," she said. I heard her rummage through drawers and gather what she needed before coming over to me. She felt my arm to find a good vein and cleaned it before sticking the needle in. I felt the drug drip into my veins and felt my body and mind slightly relax.

"Is he going to be okay?" Victor asked her after a moment.

"I think so," she sighed. "Luckily it didn't happen that long ago, and I think we caught it in time."

"Thank goodness," he said with a relieved sigh. "I hope he gets better soon."

"You and me both."

* * * * *

I JERKED AWAKE a few hours later. It was dark inside the room, most likely because I was in the dark for the past two weeks and they didn't want me to be blinded by the sudden light. Lisa stood up from her chair quickly and was at my side in an instant. She pushed my bangs back and I closed my eyes and leaned into her touch. I missed human contact so much. She removed her hand and I instantly felt cold and alone again.

I opened my eyes and saw her staring down at me in worry. I picked up my hand and grabbed hers while looking at her with fearful eyes. I was scared to be left alone again. I didn't want her to leave. Her eyes softened in understanding and she gave me a soft smile. "I can't imagine what you just went through," she whispered with tears in her eyes.

"I'm okay now," I told her with a forced smile. She gave me a look and I sighed. "Alright, maybe I'm not okay, but I will be."

"I understand completely. I don't think I could go without human contact for a day, let alone two weeks."

Victor walked into the room and his eyes lit up when he saw me awake. "Thank God, you're okay."

"Since when do you care about my health?" I asked him with a smirk, but I was generally curious.

"I don't wish a near death experience on any-one," he told me with a guilty expression.

I rolled my eyes, but said nothing. He just needed me alive so he could continue his experi-ments, right? That seemed to be the only reason I could think about. Lisa took my vitals and told me everything appeared to be okay now.

"Thank you, Lisa," I told her as she took the IV out of my arm and helped me stand. My legs were weak, and she held onto my arm until I was able to regain my balance.

She told Victor to take care of me and to tell his dad to take it easy on me for a few days. He nodded and told her he would. He opened the door and I squinted at the sudden light in the hallway.

He gave me a worried glance and remembered the light. He grabbed my arm. "I'll lead you while you adjust."

I nodded as he led me out of the room. It took me a while to adjust to the light, but I was finally able to open my eyes when we reached the cell. Angelica and Alis were in the room and jumped up when they saw me. They gave me hugs and told me they missed me.

"Missed you too," I told them with a smile.

"Well, I'll leave you guys to get reacquainted," Victor said before leaving and locking the door.

"Are you alright?" Alis asked me.

I slowly nodded. "I will be. I'm in desperate need of a shower though..." Two weeks without a shower made me feel so gross and dirty.

"Go ahead," Angelica said. "You do stink," she joked as she fanned her hand over her nose.

"Haha," I replied sarcastically as I asked the guard in the room for a change of clothes. He handed them to me and I walked passed the girls and into the bathroom.

I turned the water on and took my clothes off before stepping in. I scrubbed my body with soap three times, wanting to get rid of the horrible memory of the last two weeks.

Once finished, I dried myself off and got dressed in the t-shirt and pants. I looked at myself in the mirror and was surprised I didn't look as bad as I thought I would. My eyes had dark rings under them, but other than that, I looked like the regular me.

I stepped outside and jumped when I saw Dr. Rodriguez standing in front of me. "Hello, Christian," his deep voice boomed. "Feeling better?"

I eyed him wearily. "As good as anyone would be without two weeks of contact with others," I answered smartly.

He only grinned. "So, a few days ago, I was watching you. I noticed you appeared to be talking to someone. Did a ghost visit you or something?" he said with a chuckle.

I pursed my lips angerly before responding, "I was hallucinating. Don't worry about it."

"I thought I heard you say something like Mrs. Peters. Isn't that your friend's mom?"

"Yeah. She's like a mother figure to me."

"Oh..." he said, and he seemed to lose interest after that. "Want to go unleash some of your magic? No drugs. No tricks. Just you."

I nodded and followed him out of the room and down the hallway. He opened the door and I walked in. I instantly dropped to my knees at the sudden tightness in my chest and the onslaught of a migraine. My magic was begging to be unleashed and started to take control of my body.

I started shaking as my magic unleashed itself. The air picked up around me and blew every which way. I couldn't control it as my magic swirled around the room. I started to glow. Literally glow bright blue as it surfaced.

I screamed. At least, I think I did. The force was so powerful that I thought the building could collapse. The few items in the room, chairs, tables, and many other things, flew across the room and hit the wall. I protected my head as the lights began to spark and rain down on me.

Then, as fast as it started, it stopped. I cowered, curled in a ball, for a while. I was scared to move because I was worried it would start back up again, but it didn't. I slowly raised my head and looked around.

The chairs and tables were scattered all over the floor, all broken. The lights still flickered, but stopped sparking. I couldn't believe that I did all of that. It was like a scene from a sci-fi movie.

I looked behind me and saw Dr. Rodriguez watching me with wide eyes. He appeared to be as shocked as I was. "In my many years of working with people like you, I've never seen anyone do that," he told me as he recovered. "You are very powerful, Christian. Very powerful."

I slowly stood up and faced him. "I couldn't control it. It took over my body."

He shook his head. "I can't believe you have all that power inside you. What does it feel like?"

I shrugged. "It feels…like pins and needles going through my body. The pressure builds up the longer I don't use them, and it begs to be released. But once it settles, it feels like a blanket. A blanket that comforts and protects me. I'm not sure if that makes sense, but I don't know how else to explain it."

"Do you feel different when you don't have access to them?"

"Yeah… it makes me feel weak. And that makes me feel scared and alone," I told him. I wasn't sure why I was telling him all of this, but it felt good to tell somebody what I felt.

"Wow," he said with a shake of his head. He walked away without another word.

I didn't care where he was going. I was happy to be able to use my abilities again. I turned towards the targets on the wall across from me. I formed a blue ball of energy in my hand and aimed for the bullseye. I threw it and hit the red dot right on.

I did that a few times before trying fireballs. However, my fireballs were blue. The more I thought about it, the more I began to realize a lot of my visible powers turned out to be bright blue. I threw them at the target, and it caught on fire, but the sprinklers over the target went off and put it out. I then turned to one of the pieces of a chair and tried to lift it with my mind. I focused on it and lifted my arm and it followed. I made it come closer and let it float in front of me.

"Having fun?" Angelica asked from the door, making me jump and drop the piece. I turned and saw her casually leaning against the door frame.

I nodded. "Just testing what I can do."

She walked over and looked at the target. She made a bright orange fire ball in each hand and threw them both at the targets, hitting both in the bullseye. I turned to her and smirked. "Showoff."

She threw her head back and laughed. She made another flame in her hand and turned to me. "Try to put it out before it gets to you."

She didn't give me any time to react before throwing it at me. I flinched and threw my hand up. I waited for the pain of burns, but felt none. I opened my eyes and saw her smirking in front of me.

"Well, you put it out," she told me. "But we have to stop the flinching."

"You're saying that I put it out?" I asked in shock. "But I wasn't even trying!"

"Your magic reacted on its own and put it out when you held your hand up," she explained. "Let's try again."

She did it again, and I flinched…again. She kept doing it until I didn't flinch anymore and just flicked my wrist to put out the flames being hurtled at me.

"Good job," she told me.

"Thanks," I said with a smirk. "Now, let's see you do it," I told her jokingly.

"Haha. Very funny," she told me. "You're just lucky you can do almost anything and aren't stuck with only one power."

I laughed and put my arm around her. "Let's just be glad we aren't Alis, who had the ability to see the future. I mean, it's a cool power, but not as fun as playing with fire."

She giggled. "Very true."

I looked down at her. "I missed you these past two weeks. Both of you."

She gave me a sad smile. "We missed you too." She stood on her tiptoes and placed her lips on mine for a second. "I missed doing that too," she told me before walking past me and out of the room.

I stood there for a moment until she was gone. I didn't know how to react. I kept getting a weird feeling every time she kissed me. It felt so…wrong. I just wished I knew why.

CHAPTER SEVENTEEN

They found a new and faster way to make me 'obedient'. Instead of hooking me up to IVs and waiting for it to take its time entering my body, they now could insert a needle into my neck and inject the drug in me with a syringe. It took effect just moments later.

They took me into the training room after injecting me with it. A person who was handcuffed to a chair was sitting in the middle of the room. I gave Victor and his father a confused look as we approached the man in his late twenties. His skin was chocolate brown and he had big brown eyes that were full of fear.

"Christian, this is Henry. Henry was caught trying to sneak in here, even though it says that trespassers would be arrested on sight. Since he wanted to see what we do here, we figured we'd show him."

The man, Henry, gave me a pleading look. "Look, kid. I didn't do anything," he said. "Why is someone your age working here anyway?"

I couldn't speak, due to the drugs, but tried to with my eyes. I tried to tell him I was sorry for what they were about to make me do.

Dr. Rodriguez put his hand on my shoulder. "Well, you see, Christian here is one of our experiments."

The man's eyes went wide as he looked at me. He whispered to me, ignoring Dr. Rodriguez's presence. "Whatever they are doing to you, I can help. I can help you."

"Why don't we show him a few tricks, hmm?" Dr. Rodriguez said. He turned the chair around and told me to throw something at one of the targets.

I formed a ball of blue fire in my hands. I tossed it back and forth a few times before releasing it towards the target. It burst in flames until the sprinklers put it out.

"Holy shit!" the man exclaimed. "I don't know what I was expecting, but it wasn't that!"

"Now, Christian," Dr. Rodriguez started, "we are going to teach Henry a lesson."

"What the hell is he? Was he created in this lab?!" Henry asked fearfully.

"No," Dr. Rodriguez quickly said. "He lived a normal life until a few months ago."

He leaned as far as the cuffs would let him and glared at Dr. Rodriguez. "What did you do to him?"

"He came into abilities on his 18th birthday," he explained with a shrug. "Now we're training him to become a weapon for the military."

Henry glanced at me. "Listen, kid. I can help you. I have no idea what he did to you, but you don't have to listen to him. You don't have to be afraid of him."

I wanted to speak so badly and fought the obedience. My jaw tightened and I fought long enough to say, "I can't fight it."

Dr. Rodriguez smacked me on the back of the head. "Stupid boy."

"Hey!" Henry yelled at him. "Let him talk!" He looked back at me. "You can't fight what?"

I started shaking as I fought the drugs again. "The obedience."

"We have to make some more changes on the drug," Dr. Rodriguez told Victor. "We can't allow him to do this when we hand him over to the troop." He turned back to me and said, "Now, electrocute him until I say stop."

I fought it. God, I fought it like hell. But couldn't fight it long enough. The next thing I knew, my hand was on Henry's shoulder. I was focusing on making energy flow from my hand and into his body. He screamed and tried to move away as he was shocked. Sparks flew off where I was holding him. I closed my eyes, wishing Dr. Rodriguez would put an end to it already.

His screams of pain were almost unbearable to hear, but I couldn't stop. My hand gripped his shoulder and the energy flowed into him fluently.

"Stop," Dr. Rodriguez finally said.

I instantly pulled my hand back and blinked a few times to clear the tears that started to form. I looked down at Henry, furious at myself for not fighting harder.

Henry breathed heavily for a while before saying, "I don't blame you, kid. Like you said, 'you can't fight it'."

"Stop talking to him!" Dr. Rodriguez yelled. "He's not allowed to talk. So, don't talk to him!"

Henry ignored him. "You are a good kid, I can tell. Don't let them make you think otherwise. They are controlling you; you are not in control of yourself. Don't blame anyone other than them."

"Very touching speech," Dr. Rodriguez said sarcastically. He turned to me. "Again."

I put my hand on his shoulder and closed my eyes as I shocked him again. I couldn't stand his moans in pain anymore. I fought the obedience and pushed into his mind to make him go unconscious. I figured it would make it look like he passed out from pain and it would end.

His screams stopped and he slumped in the chair. "Stop!" Dr. Rodriguez said. He walked over to Henry's limp body as I backed away. "Damn it! Stupid man. Why does he have to pass out now?!"

I started to feel lightheaded. *I must have used too much of my energy,* I thought before staggering back. Even though I was still obedient, I don't think it stopped me from passing out.

"Dad," Victor said. Dr. Rodriguez held up his hand to tell him to give him a moment. "Dad!" he exclaimed again, with a more urgent tone.

"What?" Dr. Rodriguez said with annoyance as he turned around. I blinked and swayed as spots started crowding my vision and he realized something was wrong. "Shit!" He came over to me. He slapped my face so hard that I saw more spots.

"DAD!" Victor yelled. "That won't help! He's used too much of his energy."

Dr. Rodriguez sighed and pinched the bridge of his nose. "Take him to his cell before he passes out."

Victor grabbed my arm and pulled me gently. I followed him willingly, wanting to get Henry's limp body out of my view. "You alright?" he asked me once we were out of the room.

I couldn't speak. The drugs still had effect on me and I wasn't allowed to talk yet. I looked over at him and tried to make him understand with my eyes.

"Oh, right. You may speak," he told me.

I let out a sigh in relief before saying, "I'm *really* lightheaded." The black spots were dancing around my vision and I soon couldn't see past them. I managed to say, "I think I'm going to faint," before falling to the ground. My ears started ringing and I heard Victor yell my name.

He took hold of my arm and placed it around his shoulder. The last thing I remember is him slowly carrying me to the cell before I lost the last bit of energy keeping me semi-conscious and blacked out entirely.

CHAPTER EIGHTEEN

When I awoke, I knew something was off. I heard muffled voices and beeping noises around me. I groaned when I felt a headache coming on.

"He's waking up," a woman's voice said. "Should I give him more anesthetic?"

"Give him a small dose," Dr. Rodriguez answered. "We're almost done."

I felt someone place a mask over my nose and mouth and I took a breath of some kind of medicine smelling vapor. I felt my mind slow down and myself relax as it took effect. I tried to open my eyes and managed to after a moment of struggling.

I first saw the bright light above me. I had to squint because it was shining directly down on me.

I turned my head to the right and saw people with surgical masks on looking down at me. They didn't seem to notice that I was awake as they worked on me.

I had no idea what they were doing, but didn't feel any pain. Victor was standing back and watching them perform whatever procedure they were doing on me.

He's the one who noticed I was awake. He walked over so he was standing over me and he brushed my bangs out of my eyes as he whispered, "You okay?"

"What's happening?" I asked.

"We're taking a few samples," he told me calmly. "We'll be done soon." He looked down at what they were doing before looking back at me. "Are you feeling any pain?"

"Not at the moment," I said.

"That's good," he said.

"Do you want me to give him some anesthesia?" a girl in her twenties asked from behind him.

He looked at her and nodded. "Yeah."

He moved out of the way and she moved to take his place. She held up a mask and held it onto my face. "Okay, Christian. I need you to take deep breaths and count backwards from ten."

I took a deep breath of the anesthesia and counted, "Ten. Nine…eight.. seven…..six…" My eyes slowly closed and I fell asleep before I got to five.

CHAPTER NINETEEN

"Christian," Alis' voice sounded from nearby. "Wakey, wakey, sleeping beauty."

I moaned and pulled the blankets over my head. I did not want to get up. "I don't wanna," I whined.

She laughed and I opened my eyes to see her kneeling next to my bed. She gave me a sad smile and helped me sit up. I winced when I felt pain in my right side. I looked down and pulled my shirt up to reveal an area a few inches long that had been stitched up.

Alis gently ran her fingers along it. "At least they stitched you up. Sometimes they don't and leave us bleeding out because they know we can heal at rapid rates."

I wiped my face, trying to get rid of the sleep still settled around my mind. "God, they are really fucked up, huh?"

She giggled. "Yeah…they are."

I suddenly got really nauseous and got up to run to the bathroom before throwing up in the toilet. Alis came up behind me and rubbed my back as I continued vomiting the little contents in my stomach.

When I couldn't throw up anymore, I dry heaved until Alis put her hand on my forehead, checking for a fever. "Christian," she breathed. "You're burning up."

I leaned my back against the wall to my left and moaned. "Is this a normal thing after they take samples?"

She shook her head. "No. I mean, yeah, we're miserable for a while, but we never get fevers or throw up that much. I'm going to tell the guard to get someone who can help. Be right back."

She left me sitting next to the toilet and went to talk to the guard in the dark room. I put my head in my hands to stop it from spinning. She came back a moment later and sat next to me. She wrapped her arm around my shoulders and pulled me close. I rested my head on her shoulder and let the tears flow.

"What's wrong?" she asked me, her voice laced with worry.

"I'm starting to lose hope that we'll get out of here," I told her as I cried. "We're going to die in here, aren't we?"

"Don't say that," she told me quietly. "There is always hope. Hope is what keeps us alive. It's what keeps us moving forward. Without it, we wouldn't survive."

"I hope you're right," I told her honestly.

Victor and Lisa rushed inside and Alis moved to let them get to me. They bent in front of me and asked what was wrong.

"He has a fever and just threw up everything in his stomach," Alis answered for me. "That's never happened to Angelica or I."

Lisa put her hand on my forehead and agreed that I was running a high fever. "Do you feel any pain or discomfort?"

"My head hurts really bad," I told her with a wince. "And my side hurts a little," I added as I felt a sharp pain in my side. It was like someone was holding a knife up to it and just pierced the skin.

She pulled up my shirt and examined my side. "They might've hit your appendix," she said. She looked back at Victor. "We might have to get him into surgery. Contact your father now."

Victor rushed out of the room while Lisa examined my side. She put a little pressure on it and I winced. "Definitely the appendix," she confirmed.

I started to tear up again as the pain worsened. "It hurts," I told her as my lip quivered.

"I know it does, hun," she told me as she gently pulled me towards her. "You're so incredibly brave, though."

I smiled, although I'm sure it came out as a grimace. "At least I will get a few weeks off after this surgery. "

She laughed for a second before getting serious. "You will need lots of rest, though."

I sighed and rested my head back against the wall. "Sounds good to me."

She smiled. "That's what I like about you, Christian. You know how to make any bad news turn into good news. You see the positive side in everything."

"He's not going to be happy, is he?" Alis asked. I knew she was talking about Dr. Rodriguez.

"No," Lisa answered. "But it's not Christian's fault. It's on his surgeons; the ones who took the samples."

As if on cue, Dr. Rodriguez came into the room with a sour expression on his face. If looks could kill, everyone in the lab would be dead. Alis stood up and blocked him from getting to me. "I won't let you hurt him," she told him boldly. Her fingers curled into tight fists.

"I don't plan to," he answered through his clenched teeth. "I'm just mad that the stupid surgeons messed up everything! I fired them right when I got the news."

"Who's doing the surgery then?" Lisa asked as she looked back at him.

"I contacted one of the labs nearby to see if they could send some surgeons. They should be here in two hours."

"Two hours?!" Lisa screeched. "Do you realize how serious this is?! How much pain he's in?!"

"I'm going to sedate him!" he yelled back. "Give him a high dose of morphine," he said as he looked over at Victor, who stood to his left.

Victor nodded as he walked past Alis and over to me. He uncapped a needle from his pocket and looked me in the eye, waiting for my okay.

I nodded and he stuck the needle in the vein in my right arm. I barely flinched as it pierced my arm; barely felt it over the pain in my side.

I instantly felt sleepy. My eyelids got heavy, and muscles relaxed as the pain went away. I sat there, in a daze, while they talked around me.

"You okay?" Victor asked while Alis, Lisa, and Dr. Rodriguez argued above us.

I blinked and looked over at him. I couldn't talk, but knew he understood that I was more relaxed at the moment.

He gave me a small smile. "You'll be better soon enough."

I looked up at the craziness happening above us. They were so loud, and it didn't help my headache.

Victor somehow understood and stood up. "Guys!" They all stopped and looked at him. "If you're going to continue this argument, leave the room. In case you don't remember, Christian has a headache."

They all looked down at me, but I zoned out and was staring out into space. I was in my own little world and didn't worry about anything for a moment.

I jerked back to the present when Victor put his hand on my shoulder. I looked up at him after realizing everyone else was gone and we were the only ones left in the cell. He gave me a weak smile and helped me up. He guided me out the bathroom, to the door, and down the hallway. I stumbled a few times, but he kept his grip on my arm to keep me from falling.

"Help me?" he asked one of the young female workers as she came up to us.

She nodded and put my left arm over her shoulders. "Where are you taking him?"

"Room 104 to prep him for surgery," Victor answered. "I can't believe you girls actually did it. You handled it so well. Good job."

"Thank you," she said. "I'm kind of regretting it right now, though."

"Don't. It will help things for a little while."

I thought about what they could have been talking about as we continued walking. I pieced together the details and figured out that they somehow burst my appendix on purpose. But why? Maybe as an experiment of some kind? But why didn't Dr. Rodriguez know?

We reached the room and they helped me onto the hospital-like bed. They started talking about which medication to give me and started preparing IVs. They inserted the needles into my arms and told me I would fall asleep soon.

They whispered amongst each other as I slowly became surrounded by the darkness.

CHAPTER TWENTY

Something was beeping near me. It sounded like a heart monitor. I felt IVs in my arms and an oxygen tube in my nose.

I slowly peeled my eyes open and looked around the small room I was in. There was a window! That was the first thing I noticed. I hadn't seen the outdoors in weeks, maybe even months. It was sunny and the landscape was full of giant brown rocks and sand. There was fencing and military towers outside, but it still excited me to see the outdoors.

I blinked and looked away when a young female voice snapped me out of it. "Who are you? Are you sick?"

I looked over and saw a young girl at the bottom of my bed. She couldn't have been older than 10 with bright red curly hair that went to her mid-back, green eyes, and freckles peppered over her nose and cheeks. "I'm Christian. Who are you?"

"Doesn't matter," she said with a shrug. "Are you sick? You must be really sick if you are here."

"No, I'm not sick," I told her with a shake of my head. I went to move my arms, but realized my left arm was handcuffed to the railing on the bed.

She looked down at it before asking, "Then, did you do something illegal? Are you a bad guy?"

"No. I'm not a bad guy." I hesitated. How do you explain this to a child? "I'm different than other people. They want to figure out why."

"How are you different?"

I looked around before whispering, "Can you keep a secret?"

She nodded eagerly.

"I have superpowers," I whispered to her.

Her eyes widened. "Really?"

I nodded. "Yep."

Victor walked into the room and stopped when he saw the girl. "Poppy," he sighed as he pinched the bridge of his nose. "Didn't dad tell you not to come in the rooms that were occupied?"

She put her hand on her hip as she faced him. "I was bored. I saw Christian start to wake up and thought he might want someone to talk to."

"Well, you don't work here, Poppy!" he told her. "If any of the guards, or even dad, caught you, do you know what would have happened?"

She hung her head. "You're right. I'm sorry."

"Go wait outside," he ordered her while pointing towards the door.

She walked out of the room with her head hung low. Once she was gone, Victor sighed. "Sorry about that."

"Who was that?" I asked him.

"My sister. Well, my half-sister. Same dad, different mom. She sometimes comes here when her mom gets off work late."

"She wasn't bothering me," I told him with a shake of my head. In a way, she reminded me of my foster brother, Alex. Forgotten in the family, not cared for, wanting a friend.

"She's not supposed to be in here. If dad found out, he would most likely punish her. No matter how much she gets on my nerves, I don't like seeing her get punished for only being curious." He cleared his throat. "Anyway…how are you feeling?"

"I'm okay. Just tired."

"That's understandable," he said with a nod. "You will be for a while."

"So, I get a break?" I asked hopefully.

He smiled and nodded. "Yep. You do. At least a week or two off from experiments."

"Thank goodness," I said as I leaned back in the pillows.

He laughed. "I'll go get Lisa," he said before walking out of the room.

I sighed and closed my eyes until she came into the room a few minutes later. "How are you feeling, hun?"

I opened my eyes and looked over at her. "I'm pretty good," I told her with a content sigh.

"That's good," she said with a smile. She checked my vitals and took the oxygen tube out of my nose. "I think you should be good to go back to your room, if you're up to it."

I hesitated. I really didn't want to go back to the 'room' at the moment. Knowing that I would be stuck there for who knows how long, scared me shitless.

She gave me a sad smile. "I understand if you don't want to yet."

I forced a smile to my face as I replied, "Can I stay here for a little longer?"

She nodded and placed my hand in hers. "Of course, you can," she told me. "Want me to stay with you?"

I nodded. "Yeah."

She let go of my hand to pull a chair over to the bed. She placed my hand back in hers after she sat in it.

"How's your granddaughter?" I asked her after a moment.

She seemed surprised that I remembered, but smiled as she answered, "She's good."

"How old is she?"

"16. Almost 17. I wasn't lying when I told you that she would be all over you. You're definitely her type," she explained with a cackle.

"She have a boyfriend?" I asked with a raised eyebrow.

"No. Says she has a crush on this one guy. She says he has blonde hair and bright blue eyes, like you."

"Oh? Which school does she go to?"

"Lincoln High School. She's still getting adjusted because we just moved to the area a few weeks ago. Actually, I think we moved here the week before you came here."

I widened my eyes. "You do know that I'm from Lincoln High too, right?"

She shook her head. "No, I didn't. In fact, I don't know much about you."

"Does your granddaughter happen to be named Eliana?"

She nodded. "Yeah. Do you know her?"

"I met her a hour before I was brought here," I told her while I tried to wrap my head around the fact that Eliana was Lisa's granddaughter. "It may seem weird… but I felt a connection with her the moment our eyes met."

"Really?" she asked. "Well, now that you mention it, she did say she met a guy who had piercing blue eyes the day you were brought here. I didn't think anything of it when she mentioned she most likely would never see him again because he wasn't going to school anymore. But now I think she was talking about you."

"You're not saying… she likes me too?"

"I think she does," she answered with an amused smile. "She is going to be very shocked when she finds out that I'm not testing rats, but you."

"I feel like a rat in this place," I admitted quietly while down casting my gaze to my lap.

"Oh, honey," she said as she stood up and hugged me to her. "You are so much more than a rat, you are an angel. Literally and figuratively. You have such a big heart and care about others more than yourself."

"Where has that gotten me, though?" I asked her. "I always try to be kind to others, but they never are in return. I think I should give up being the good guy and start giving them a taste of how I feel."

"No," she told me sternly, like a mother chastising her child. She held me at arm's length to look me in the eyes. "Don't let them change who you are, no matter how bad they may be. That's what they want. If they change you, they win."

I thought about that for a moment. I knew she was right, letting them make me into something I'm not would give them what they want; it would make me the weapon they were trying to create. And I would rather die than let that happen.

CHAPTER TWENTY-ONE

A few days passed, which were thankfully quiet because Dr. Rodriguez couldn't do any experimenting until I was healed. I spent most of the time in the cell, but did go to watch the girls train a few times. I also unleashed some of my pent-up magic while sitting in the corner watching them.

I was doing just that when Dr. Rodriguez walked in. He walked over to me and stood behind me, watching the girls. Angelica was throwing fireballs at the targets, while Alis was flying overhead.

I looked over my shoulder nervously, unsure of how to handle his close proximity to me. I hadn't seen him in a few days; he'd been working on improvements with the drugs for Project Obedience, according to Victor.

Without looking down at me, he asked, "You been flying recently?"

I was taken aback by his question, but answered, "No. Not since…" I trailed off. I couldn't remember the last time I'd flown. "I can't even remember."

"Your wings are probably aching to be un-leashed," he told me as he looked down to meet my eyes.

He was right, they were. My back ached more with each passing day of not unleashing them. However, as I looked at him, I noticed something I hadn't noticed before. Was it pain? Longing? I couldn't tell, but it seemed that he was missing something. He blinked and his features turned hard once again, no trace of pain.

I slowly nodded, shaking off the weird feeling. "They are."

"Why don't you release them then? At least stretch them out."

I shrugged. "I can't with this shirt, it doesn't have slits in the back." They gave each of us shirts that had slits for our wings to slide out of, but I chose not to wear one because I hadn't flown in a while.

"Take off the shirt then," he told me. "The girls have to keep shirts on, but you don't."

He was right. However, I still raised an eye-brow. "You sure?" I asked.

He nodded and I stood from the chair. I shrugged my shirt off and placed it on the seat. I closed my eyes and willed my wings to emerge from my back. Once I felt them, I opened my eyes and al-most sighed in relief. I flapped them a few times, stretching them out. It felt so good to have them out.

Alis came over and gracefullylanded in front of me. "Hey," she said, out of breath. "You up to do some flying?"

I shrugged and smirked. "I guess I could do a few laps."

She grinned. "Let's go."

We took to the air with one powerful flap of our wings. We both smiled and flapped them two more times to reach the ceiling. I still couldn't get over the fact that I had wings and could fly with them.

We did a few laps around the room before landing next to Angelica, who was still aiming her fireballs at the target. She stopped and turned to face us.

"How are you feeling?" she asked me.

I rolled my eyes; I was getting very annoyed of hearing that question. They asked me at least five times a day. "Please stop asking me that," I groaned. "I'm fine."

"Dr. Rodriguez is watching you closely," she whispered as she looked over my shoulder.

"Probably trying to see if I'm okay to be experimented on again," I whispered back.

"Probably," Alis agreed with a nod.

I turned to peer over my shoulder in his direction in time to see Victor walk in the room. He walked over to his father and they whispered amongst each other, so quiet that I couldn't hear them with my super-hearing.

They looked over at us and Dr. Rodriguez motioned for me to come over. I made my way over to them as I retracted my wings. I walked over to the chair next to them and grabbed my shirt off it. "You need me?" I asked as I shrugged it on.

"We are now on a very strict timeline and need Lisa to look you over," Dr. Rodriguez answered as he crossed his arms over his chest.

I raised an eyebrow. "A strict schedule?" I asked, unconvinced.

"Some of my most trusted men now know about Project Obedience and want to evaluate to see if they want you."

"What?! You want to hand me off to a troop? Like a slave?" I hissed.

Victor cringed as Dr. Rodriguez answered, "You are so much more than a slave, Christian. You are a weapon that will help us win the wars in other countries. Don't you want to help people, men, from our country win the war?"

"Yeah, but not like this," I replied through my clenched jaw.

"Don't worry, it will be a while until we actually send you to train with the troop. They only want to evaluate and see what they might be receiving."

He turned to Victor. "Take him to Lisa's, I want to see if he is ready."

He nodded and I reluctantly followed him out of the room. "He's really doing this?" I asked him.

He sighed. "Yeah."

He led me to Lisa's room and left after telling Lisa that Dr. Rodriguez wanted to know if it was okay to experiment on me yet. I sat on the bed after he closed the door.

She shook her head at Victor's abruptness before turning to me. She motioned for me to lie down on the exam table and pulled my shirt up to reveal the area they stitched up. "Let me know if you feel any pain or discomfort," she told me.

I nodded and she placed her cold hands onto my stomach. She put pressure on different areas as I asked, "Can I ask you a question?"

"Hmm?" she hummed as she continued examining me.

"Do you know anything about my friend, Connor Peters? Like is he okay?"

"I don't, but I can find out," she told me. She stopped examining me and said, "I think you're good to go. I'm not sure if that's a good or bad thing, though..."

I laughed nervously. "Me neither..."

She went over and wrote something on a piece of paper before coming back over. "I'll be back in just a minute," she told me. She slipped the paper on the counter and left, closing the door behind her.

I sat there for a moment, but curiosity got the better of me and I got off the bed and picked up the paper.

Cameras are off today. My phone is in the top drawer. Call your friend. I'll keep the Dr. away for as long as I can.

I stood there a minute, in shock, before ripping up the note and throwing it in the trash. I didn't want Dr. Rodriguez to find out what Lisa just did. I walked over to the drawers and opened the top one. I found her phone and picked it up. Heart racing, I dialed Connor's number from memory and prayed he would answer.

He picked up on the second ring. "Hello?"

"Connor? It's Christian."

"Christian? Is it really you?"

"It's me," I answered him as I tightened my grip on the phone.

"Dude! I've missed you!" he exclaimed. "How are you calling me?"

"One of the nurses snuck me her phone," I told him.

"Oh. Where are you? How are you? Are you okay? Are you alone? Will I ever see you again? Will you-?"

"Woah, woah, woah. Slow down," I told him with a chuckle. "I'm at a military base, but don't know where. I don't know if I will ever see you again or not, but hope to. Sadly, I am not okay."

"What? Why are you not okay?" he asked.

"Because they are doing some fucked up shit to me."

"What do you mean?"

"They are-"

I was cut off when the door opened, and Dr. Rodriguez walked in. "What the hell?!" he yelled when he saw me on the phone.

CHAPTER TWENTY-TWO

He marched over and ripped the phone out of my hands. "How did you get this?" he asked angerly.

I didn't want Lisa to get in trouble, so I lied. "I was curious and looked through the drawers and found her phone. I'm sorry, but I had to tell my friend I was okay."

"You are in big trouble," he said as he jabbed his finger at me. "You're lucky I can't do anything until tomorrow, but you will be punished!"

"I didn't tell him anything," I tried to tell him. "He knows nothing."

"Doesn't matter. You still took the phone and called someone."

Lisa walked in and stopped short when she saw him standing over me. "What's going on?"

"I walked in on Christian using your phone. He told me he found it in a drawer," Dr. Rodriguez said as he handed it to her.

She seemed surprised that I took the blame, but hid it well. "Oh my. That's not good."

"No, it's not," he agreed. "He will be punished for his actions tomorrow."

"It's my fault," she blurted out. "I should have taken my phone out of the drawer or never have left him alone."

Dr. Rodriguez shook his head. "You are not in trouble. I am just thankful that I walked in when I did."

I glared up at him as he called Victor to the room. He came in a moment later and was told to take me to my cell. However, as I pushed myself up and stood, Dr. Rodriguez got an idea. "Actually, take him to the isolation room," he told him.

My heart sank. The isolation room had to be the room I was alone in for two weeks. He wasn't serious, was he? I followed Victor out and he looked over at me with concern as we walked to the room next to Lisa's.

"What did you do to make dad mad?" he asked me.

I sighed. "He caught me with a phone."

His eyes widened in surprise. "How did you get a phone?"

"I found it in a drawer in Lisa's room," I lied again, "and called Connor."

"What did you tell him?" he asked.

"Didn't get to say much," I told him truthfully. "He asked so many questions all at once. I only got to tell him that I'm at a military base and that I'm not exactly okay before your dad walked in."

"Yikes," he said as he sucked in a breath. "Well, luckily this is only for one night." He opened the door to the cell and I walked inside.

He closed the door and locked it behind me, leaving me in the dark.

* * * * *

A FEW MINUTES, OR HOURS, later, Lisa came into the room when I was laying on the concrete bed. I sat up and she walked over to me. She sat on the bench next to me as I swung my legs, so they were hanging off the side.

"Why?" she whispered while looking down at her folded hands in her lap. When I didn't respond, she looked up at me and added, "Why did you not tell him I told you where the phone was? Why did you take the blame?"

I tilted my head as I answered, "Why would I want you to get in trouble?"

"But your punishment is going to be far worse than what I would receive. I would most likely get yelled at and fired for my actions. You on the other hand…" she choked back a sob. "You're going to be beaten or worse."

"I don't want to see you get fired," I told her softly. "You're the only person I like around here, other than Angelica and Alis, of course."

She wrapped her arm around my back and rubbed by left arm. "Now I understand. You don't want me to get fired because they might hurt you more, right?"

I slowly nodded and swallowed back my tears. "Yeah."

She pulled me to her and hugged me the way my mother never had. "Out of all the angels I've met in my years of working at these bases, you're my favorite. You're different than the others, and not just your wing color, but in your personality and ways of thinking."

"How many angels have you met?" I asked her curiously.

"You would be the sixth one I've met. The third male."

"Where are the other ones?" I asked her.

"At other bases. One female in Virginia and the other two males in New York," she answered. "I came here when they offered me the job. I said yes because I felt it would be best for Eliana. I was ready to quit after the first few weeks, after seeing how Dr. Rodriguez treated those two precious girls. But then you came the day I was going to put my resignation in, and I felt something in me change. I don't know what or how, but I got this overwhelming urge to stay. I have to believe that some big force told me to stay and take care of you guys. I'm not sure what it was, maybe God, maybe something else. I don't know," she told me with a sigh.

We sat there in silence for a moment, lost in thought. I was surprised that Lisa decided not to quit because of me. Maybe not exactly all because of me, but something changed her when I showed up.

"Do you think I will die here?" I asked her as a few tears escaped.

"I hope not," she whispered back. "I hope you will be able to be free again. Not worrying about being caught or constantly looking over your shoulder in fear."

"I hope so too," I responded. "So, am I allowed out of this room of torturous boredom?"

"Yes," she told me. "I've come to take you back to your regular cell, but wanted to have that talk first."

I nodded and stood up. She led me out of the room and down the hallway. We walked to the cell, where the guard opened the door and I walked in.

I saw the girls waiting on their beds and turned to face them after the door locked behind me. We talked about what happened today before getting dressed for the night and going to sleep.

CHAPTER TWENTY-THREE

The next day, Dr. Rodriguez had permission to start experimenting on me again, and he didn't waste any time. He came into the cell early that morning and practically dragged me out of bed, telling me it was time for my punishment.

He brought two guards in with him, and they fastened metal cuffs on each of my wrists before I was fully awake. The cuffs each had chains connected to them, and Dr. Rodriguez pulled me behind him, like an animal.

He led me to the room he whipped me in weeks ago and I stopped walking before he pulled me through the door. My heart beat frantically and my breathing quickened as I started to panic.

The guards behind me shoved me inside the room before closing the door, locking the four of us inside. Dr. Rodriguez handed them each a chain and they connected them to the walls on either side as he went over to what looked like a furnace in the corner of the room.

Soon, I was chained with my arms out to my sides and my feet were cuffed to the floor. Dr.

Rodriguez grinned as he looked over his shoulder at me. "Oh, I am going to enjoy this."

I glared at him as he picked something out of the fire. My eyes widened when I realized what it was. It was a branding iron. The symbol was round, with what looked to be the capital building and had the words, 'PROPERTY OF THE U.S. GOVERN-MENT' glowing orange around it.

He took his time, eyeing up my side as if strategizing where to put it. He then brought it up to my left side, just above my navel, and pressed it against my skin.

I screamed and cried out when he held it there. The pain was like nothing I'd ever experienced before. It felt as if my whole side was on fire and the skin was melting away. It hurt like hell and back.

Black spots crowded my vision as he finally moved it away. He put down the iron and came over to inspect his work. He ran his fingers over it and smiled when I hissed and tried to move away.

I wrinkled my nose in disgust when I smelled the charcoal like aroma of my burned skin and couldn't bring myself to look at it, not only due to how bad it might look, but also because it was a freaking brand! Telling the world that I belonged to the government.

"Take him to his cell," Dr. Rodriguez told the guards who watched by the door.

"Yes, Sir," they said quietly as they walked over to me and started unhooking the chains. They put my arms over their shoulders and carried me back to the cell. They were careful not to bump the area of skin that was just burned as they helped me lay in bed.

Before they walked away, I heard them whispering amongst each other. "Dude, this just doesn't feel right, ya know?"

"Yeah, I agree. But what can we do? He's government property."

"True, but that doesn't make it right."

"Whatever. We still have a job that pays well, let's try to keep it," he answered as they opened the door and walked out.

However, one of them came back in and draped a fuzzy blanket over me before leaving me alone.

I curled myself into a ball, careful not to touch the burned flesh and cried once I knew they were gone. The girls weren't in the room, so I let out all my emotions. My anger, sadness, loneliness, and most importantly, pain. I was in so much pain, physically and emotionally.

I lost my hope and will to survive. I lost the will to continue fighting. As I laid there, I prayed to die. I wanted to die because I didn't see a way out of this situation and would rather be dead than here.

* * * * *

I FELL ASLEEP AT ONE POINT and was woken up when Victor nudged my shoulder. I was laying on my right side, my back to him.

I looked back at him with sleepy eyes as he sat on the edge of the bed. He tilted his head in concern. "Were you crying?"

I didn't answer, just turned back so I was facing the gray brick wall. "Shit," he breathed. "What did dad do this time?"

"Don't you already know?" I snapped without looking at him, my voice husky from crying.

"Look, you and I are on the same side. I don't know what he did, but have a feeling it wasn't good."

I turned my head to glare at him. "Same side? I doubt that. You were the one who sent me here, just so you could experiment on me. We are not on the same side, not even close." I turned back around.

He sighed. "What I did, I wasn't just doing it to benefit myself. I was doing it for you too. If you weren't brought here, who knows what would have happened? When you came into your wings, alone and afraid? In *pain*? What if you lost control of your abilities and got yourself into trouble? You wouldn't be able to do anything; wouldn't have anyone to talk to because no one, not even Connor, was trustable. If I would have known dad's plans, I would've taken you in secretly. Helped you through gaining your wings, controlling your abilities, in secret.

"But I was selfish," he admitted. "My dad promised me that I would be able to experiment on my own angel if I found one. So, when I found you, I got excited and didn't think it through. I should have and I'm sorry about that, man. Really, I am. Just," he sighed in frustration, "just tell me what he did, please?"

I slowly moved to sit up and removed the blanket covering me. He sucked in a breath and I looked over at him with tears in my eyes. "Is it bad?" I asked him.

He met my eyes. "You haven't looked at it yet?" he asked in disbelief.

"He only did it this morning and I…cried myself to sleep afterwards," I confessed.

He stood up and told me he would be back before walking out of the room. I mustered up enough strength to look down at the scar on my stomach. I sucked in a shaky breath as my body started shaking out of panic and fear.

The skin was raised and clearly said 'PROPERTY OF THE U.S. GOVERNMET' in a softball sized circle. It was an ugly red color and I felt like the pain got worse once I saw how bad it really looked.

I quickly looked away, not able to look at it any longer. Victor came back into the room with something in his hand.

"You okay?" he asked as he sat on the edge of the bed once again.

I nodded, but was still shaking badly. I tried to take deep breaths to calm myself and Victor breathed with me until I stopped shaking and my breathing returned to normal.

"You okay?" he asked again.

I nodded. "Thanks."

"I brought some therapeutic salve to put on it," he told me as he uncapped the small container of the white lotion like substance.

He looked up at me, his green eyes meeting mine. "You want to apply it, or do you want me to?"

"You. I can't look at it anymore," I told him honestly.

He nodded and motioned for me to lie down. I propped myself back on my elbows as he dipped his fingers into the salve. "This may sting at first," he told me before dabbing it onto the burn.

I hissed at the stinging sensation that jolted through my entire body. However, it quickly turned into relief. I slowly relaxed as he continued dabbing the salve on until he declared it good enough.

"I'll leave this with you," he told me as he handed me the container after putting the lid on.

"Thanks," I told him as I took it and put it by my right side before I sat up once again.

"I brought some lunch too," he told me as he handed me a bag from Chick-fil-a.

I raised an eyebrow. "Your dad okay with this?"

He chuffed. "Who cares? It's food. I hope you like the Chick-fil-a sandwich."

I nodded. "Thanks."

He opened a bag of his own and we both ate in silence for a moment. "You have no idea how much I miss fast food," I told him once I finished.

He laughed and offered to take my trash. I handed it to him and he walked out to throw it away before coming back inside. "You want me to stay here or do you want to be alone?"

I sighed. "I honestly don't know. I mean, I don't want to be alone, but also want to just go back to sleep."

"I could stay here with you until you fall asleep, or when the girls come back," he suggested.

"Are you sure?" I asked. "You don't have to stay."

"Christian," he started as he looked me in the eyes. "I want to."

I slowly nodded and he went to lay on Alis' bed. He crossed his ankles and folded his arms behind his head with a sigh. "You're not going to get your phone or anything?" I asked.

He opened his eyes. "Why would I?"

I shrugged. "Aren't you going to get bored?"

He looked perplexed. "Why would I use my phone in front of you when I know you can't? That would just be rude of me. Plus, I think I can willingly give up my phone for a few hours since you unwillingly gave up yours for…a while."

"You would really do that?" I asked, unconvinced.

He nodded. "Of course I would."

I stared at him for another minute before laying back down and rolling onto my right side. I closed my eyes, but didn't fall asleep quickly.

I waited.

Waited for Victor to leave me when he thought I was asleep, but he didn't. Even as my breathing slowed, he stayed. He stayed because he…he cared about me. I realized that then. He was doing what he was told because he was afraid; he was afraid I would be punished for his actions.

He came over and pulled the blanket up to my shoulders before going back to lie on the bed once more.

I fell asleep soon after I came to terms with the fact that Victor had somehow changed. That Victor was now on my side.

CHAPTER TWENTY-FOUR

I woke up when I heard someone rustling around the next morning. I slowly opened my eyes and looked over my shoulder to see Victor's silhouette as he stood from where he was laying…on the floor?

He stayed the night? On the floor next to my bed? I was surprised, considering it was a weeknight, which meant he had school.

He somehow noticed I was awake in the dark. He bent next to me and whispered, "I have to go to school, but will be back as soon as I can. Hopefully, dad won't do too much damage."

I nodded, but grabbed his hand before he walked away. He turned to look at me. "Can you somehow tell Connor something to lessen his worries?" I whispered. "You don't even have to talk to him. Just sneak a note into his backpack when he isn't looking or something."

He hesitated before saying, "I'll try."

"Thank you," I told him before he walked out of the cell and locked the door behind him.

I rolled back over and closed my eyes, letting myself drift off once more.

* * * * *

I WOKE UP AGAIN WHEN Dr. Rodriguez walked inside. The girls were already gone and my heart beat frantically at the thought of what he had planned for the day.

He told me to get dressed as he handed me some clothes. I gave him a puzzled look, but did as he said and walked into the bathroom.

I brushed my teeth and fixed my hair before stepping out to meet him. He simply nodded in approval and motioned for me to follow him before walking out. He led me to the training room and inserted a needle into my neck before I could even react.

I instantly felt the effects of the drug and my muscles became strained. Within a few minutes, I was unmoving and staring straight ahead, waiting for his command.

He came into view and said, "As you can already tell, our improvements are going well. We now can get the drug to take effect almost immediately. Now we will see how long it lasts."

I stood there, waiting, because that's the only thing I could do. He brought his hand up and slapped me across the face. I didn't even blink, but knew I would have a red handprint on my cheek.

He then kneed me in the groin, and I winced slightly, but stood still. "Now, fly around the room 20 times," he told me.

I summoned my wings, realizing that he gave me a shirt with slits for my wings to emerge from. I took to the air and started doing laps around the room. I got dizzy about halfway through, but couldn't stop until I reached 20 laps.

Once I landed in the center of the room, I wobbled a bit and thought I might have been sick. "Good," Dr. Rodriguez said as he walked over to me. "Form a ball of electricity and throw it at the target over there," he ordered me as he pointed to a target on the wall to our left.

He stepped back and I formed a softball sized ball of blue electricity and threw it, hitting the bull-seye.

"Again," he said from behind me.

I did it again and again; over and over until he finally stopped asking. He ordered me to do many things for hours, and the drugs didn't wear off. I was growing tired and frustrated after not having control of my own body for such a long period of time.

He ordered me to walk over to him and checked to make sure the drugs were still working. They were. He then handed me a sword. A real fucking sword! "It is required for my troops to learn how to defend themselves if they were to be captured by the enemy. I figured a sword would fit you well."

I took it and weighed it in my hand. It was heavy, but not terribly heavy. He came behind me and placed his hands over mine. He showed me some basic moves, slicing through the air. My movements were rigid at first, but became more fluent when he told me to relax my muscles and move into the movements.

He told me the names of each move as he guided me to do them. "Have you ever held a sword before?" he asked as he continued guiding me through some moves. He gave me permission to speak after asking.

"No," I answered with a shake of my head. "Never."

"Okay," he told me as he looked at the clock on the wall. "The drugs have been in your system for about five hours now. Are they still working?"

I swallowed before responding, "Yes."

He let go of my hands and stepped back. "Practice the moves I just taught you," he told me as he stepped in front of me, out of reach from the sword still in my hand.

I slowly did the several different moves he showed me. He told me to do them faster each time I went through them, and soon I was moving the sword quickly and gracefully, but most importantly, at deadly speeds and forces.

He grinned at my progress and told me to stop. He asked me how the drugs were holding up and I was forced to answer, "They are now weakening." *Finally*, I thought.

He nodded and took the sword out of my hand. I knew I would be sore for the next few days due to using muscles I haven't used since football practice, some maybe never before.

He placed the sword in a cabinet by the door and told me to follow him out of the room. He led me to the cell, where the girls were already sitting on their beds, and ordered the guard to open the door.

He leaned down to whisper, "You may act normal once you walk inside."

I walked inside the cell and he closed the door and locked it behind me. I blinked a few times, finally able to have control of my body.

The girls waited patiently, allowing me to adjust again. When I looked over at them, Angelica patted her bed, offering me to sit next to her.

I smiled and walked over. I sat next to her and laid back so my head was resting in her lap. She smiled down at me as she played with my hair. I sighed in contentment, finally able to relax.

"What did he make you do today?" she asked.

"The effects of the drugs lasted almost six hours," I told them as I closed my eyes. "They are still having an effect on me. He made me do so much that I think I will sleep for a week. My muscles ache because he's teaching me how to use a sword."

"What do you mean?" Alis asked.

"He says that he requires everyone in his troops to learn how to defend themselves, in case they get captured, and thinks I will do good with a sword. He started teaching me the basics today."

"Oh," they both said.

We talked for a while, but I grew more tired by each passing minute and found myself slowly closing my eyes. My breathing slowed and I drifted in the void between consciousness and unconsciousness.

I heard the door open a few moments later and Victor ask, "Is he asleep?"

"Yeah," they whispered back.

"Fell asleep a few minutes ago," Alis told him.

"Do you want me to move him?" he asked.

"No, I'm okay right now," Angelica answered. "I don't want to disturb him; he's had a long day."

I imagined him cringing as he asked, "What did my dad do today?"

"He told us that the drugs had an effect for six hours," Alis explained, "and that your father wouldn't give him a break. He was teaching him how to use a sword, so he told us he's pretty tired and sore."

He sighed in frustration. "He's getting ready to hand him over to a troop then."

"How do you know?" Angelica asked.

"I just know," he growled.

I felt someone start lifting my shirt and heard Alis ask, "What are you doing?"

"Checking to make sure the brand is healing," he answered.

"The what?!" they both said loudly.

He sighed. "He didn't tell you, did he?" He paused and I assumed they shook their heads. "Dad branded him yesterday. That's why I was so worried all day and night."

He lifted my shirt, so the brand was visible and they both gasped. "Why would your father do that?" Alis asked.

"Because my dad is 50 shades of fucked up," he answered bluntly. "Like I said, he's getting him ready to hand over to a troop. Wouldn't surprise me if it happened in a week or two."

"Does that mean we would never see him again?" Angelica asked, sounding terrified at the thought.

"I don't know," he honestly responded. "All I know is that I'm running out of time for figuring out how to fix my mistake."

"You'll figure it out," Alis told him. "I know you will."

CHAPTER TWENTY-FIVE

The next few days, Dr. Rodriguez continued teaching me how to master sword fighting. I was getting better with each passing day and on the third day of training, he brought his own sword to spar with me.

He started slow, telling me what to do in different situations. Block, hit, swipe, lunge, duck, jump, you name a move and he probably called it. He corrected my stances by stopping me and showing how to stand, where to put my feet, and how to maneuver gracefully and yet deadly.

"Good," he told me when I ducked at his blow and lunged at him. He stopped and said, "You're getting much better. Tomorrow, I want to spar with you. No corrections, no slowing down, nothing. Just you and me." *And the drugs*, I thought.

He took my sword and placed both in the cabinet. He motioned for me to follow him out, but instead of leading me to the cell, he took me to Lisa's room. He knocked on the door and she told him to come in.

We walked in, but I stopped when I saw a young girl sitting on the medical bed. She looked up and her bright blue eyes met mine. My heart flip-flopped. Eliana.

She looked as surprised to see me as I was to see her. Her lips were slightly parted in shock and I found myself wondering how they would feel against mine.

"Two pints today, Lisa," Dr. Rodriguez ordered, snapping us both out of our shock.

"Okay," she said gently. He shoved me inside the room, making me lose my footing, before closing the door and leaving the room.

Lisa sighed at his aggressiveness before placing a smile on her face. "Well, I guess we should get to work before he comes back. Eliana, could you please move off the bed so Christian could sit?"

She slowly slid off the metal bed, her eyes never leaving mine. "Grandma? What's-"

"I'll explain in a minute," Lisa interrupted. "You," she said as she pointed to me. "Sit."

"Yes, ma'am," I told her with a smirk. I sat on the bed and she started getting the materials ready.

As she rummaged through drawers and got what she needed, she explained, "I know you thought I was testing rats and things like that, but that wasn't the truth."

Eliana and I looked at each other as she continued, "In reality, Christian is the experiment here, along with two other girls. I am only the nurse at the facility and Dr. Rodriguez is the boss. He is in charge of everything around here, including how they…care for Christian. I don't agree with anything they do here, but stay for Christian and the girls."

"Why are they experimenting on him?" she asked as she finally broke our eye contact.

Lisa began feeling for a vein and cleansing it. "I'll let him explain," she responded as she looked at me.

"Umm. Well, when I turned 18, I came into…abilities," I started as she tied the rubber band around my upper arm. "To say I was terrified would be an understatement. I practiced with them when I was alone the next day and was kind of getting the hang of it. But then I went to school the next day." I winced as she stuck the needle in my arm, but kept explaining, "By last period, I felt as if I was drowning due to not using my abilities and went to the bathroom to try to get myself under control. That's when I heard you."

Her eyes lit up when she realized I remembered her. Remembered helping her.

Lisa, on the other hand, looked confused. So, I explained, "I saw Victor on you and your eyes locked on mine. I knew I had to do something. So, I used my abilities to pull him off you and made him run away. However, it was a trick. He used you to out me and then called his dad, *Dr. Rodriguez*, to tell him."

"I'm going to kill that boy," Lisa muttered.

I looked over at her and said, "Trust me, I wanted to too. But he isn't the same anymore. He explained everything to me, and he feels so bad that he's trying to help now."

She switched bags after the first pint-sized bag was full and attached a second to the tube. "Why did he have to drag Eliana into it, though?"

"Grandma, it's fine," Eliana said.

A few moments of silence passed by and Lisa finished taking my blood and gave me a cloth to stop the bleeding. Luckily, it stopped after a moment, thanks to my fast healing.

"I'm going to take this to the lab. I'll be right back," she said before leaving us alone in the room and closing the door behind her.

Eliana looked at me and stood up. "Ever since I laid my eyes on you, I haven't stopped thinking about you," she told me as she wrapped her arms around her middle. "I thought I would never see you again, but here my grandma was with you the whole time."

"She had to keep it a secret, for yours and her safety," I told her as I pushed myself off the bed and threw my paper towel in the trash. I turned to look at her. "Dr. Rodriguez is a monster. He won't chance the secret of what he's doing getting out of this facility."

Lisa came back into the room and asked, "Are you feeling any discomfort or pain from…the past few weeks?"

I thought about it. "Actually, my side has been hurting today." I hadn't looked at it and knew it was the brand. I was slightly embarrassed to show it in front of Eliana.

"What do you mean?" Lisa asked with a scrunched-up brow. "Is it from your surgery?"

"Not that…" I said with hesitation. I eventually gave in and lifted my shirt to show her the brand.

They both gasped and Lisa asked, "When did he do that to you?"

"A couple days ago," I answered with a shrug. "Hurts like hell right now," I admitted.

"It looks infected," she said as she rummaged through her drawers. "Why didn't you tell me about this?"

"I haven't seen you since he did it," I responded. "Victor gave me some ointment to put on it and I've been putting it on every morning and night."

"He really branded you?" Eliana asked, in shock.

I looked her in the eyes as I said, "Like I said, he's a monster. He did this not only as a punishment, but because he is going to hand me over to the military. They're making me a weapon and I can't control it."

She looked at me in horror. "Why would he do that?"

"Because he's fucked up," I told her bluntly as Lisa started washing the brand.

She looked like she could cry at any moment as she said, "I wish I'd known sooner. That way I could have helped figure out a way to get you out of here."

"I wish you were here sooner, so I had a chance to talk to you more. To get to know you more."

"You sound like a dying person," she said as her tears finally escaped her eyes.

I shrugged. "Maybe I am."

"What do you mean, hun?" Lisa asked.

"I'm saying that if I get my hands on a gun at the camp or in war, I will not hesitate to kill myself."

"No, honey," Lisa cried as she stopped cleaning the brand and went to hug me to her.

I leaned into her touch as I closed my eyes. I let a few tears slide. Her embrace comforted me, almost like a mother's.

"You can't kill yourself," Eliana whispered.

I pulled back from Lisa and looked at her. "How will I be able to live with myself if I kill people? Innocent people. I would rather kill myself than let hundreds die because of me."

"But you're not in control of that," Lisa told me. "You were put on this earth for a reason, it's up to you to figure out why."

"But I wouldn't be able to live with myself when it happens," I countered. "The only person I would be willing to kill is Dr. Rodriguez."

"Then, if you get your hands on a gun, kill him," Eliana argued. "Don't kill yourself."

"If I did that at the camp, I would be immediately punished severely. And he won't be at the battlefield, so that wouldn't work."

"Please, just don't kill yourself," she cried. "Grandma, please tell him not to."

Lisa looked speechless, like she didn't know what to think or say. She met my gaze and I could tell she was silently telling me to not do it unless absolutely necessary. But she also wouldn't be able to stop me, and she knew that.

Dr. Rodriguez barged into the room and took one look at Eliana's tear-streaked face. "What's wrong, dear? Did Christian hurt you?" he asked as he shot a deadly glare in my direction.

"No. No," she said as she wiped her cheeks. "My boyfriend just broke up with me this morning and it's just now setting in," she lied. "Christian was just giving me advice on what to do now."

He looked over at me and Lisa to make sure it was true. We both smiled and nodded, playing along. He seemed suspicious, but changed the subject. "I want Christian in room 107 in five minutes," he told Lisa.

She nodded and he walked back out, closing the door behind him.

"Have I been in room 107?" I asked Lisa. I didn't know the room numbers, just their names and what happens in them.

She shook her head. "Not that I know of. I don't even know what's in that room."

My heart sank in my chest at what that could mean, and my face must have shown my fear because Eliana looked concerned. "What's wrong?"

"It's just… I haven't had good experiences in many of these rooms. I doubt this one will be any different."

"Well, let's go," Lisa said with a sigh and went to open the door.

Eliana must have sensed my hesitation and rising panic because she took my hand and squeezed. "I'll come with you."

I looked over at her and nodded before we walked out of the room, hand-in-hand. We walked down the hall and Lisa pointed to the door to our left with the number 107 next to it.

"You okay?" Lisa asked me, her brows creasing in worry.

I nodded and she opened the door. We walked inside, Eliana still holding my hand, and took in the room together. There was glass separating the back half from where we stood. A chair was in the middle behind the glass with wires connected to it. On the side we were in sat three chairs and multiple wires and buttons.

Dr. Rodriguez was talking to a man in a white lab coat a few feet away. Eliana squeezed my hand, trying to keep me calm, as he turned to face us with that malicious grin of his. His gaze landed on Eliana and his smile disappeared when he saw our interlocked hands.

"Lisa," he said without looking away from us. "I'll need you in here with us. Your granddaughter may want to leave, she may not like this experiment, and we don't need any interruptions or distractions."

"I'll stay," Eliana said as she took one step towards him. "I won't be a distraction."

He sighed. "Fine." He turned to Lisa and said, "If she causes any commotion, it goes along with a punishment."

Her face went pale, and she glanced at me before nodding. "I understand."

"What punishment?" Eliana asked with her free hand on her hip.

Lisa sighed. "Eliana, please. We'll talk later, okay?"

She slowly nodded and backed up.

"Dr. Patterson will tell you what to do, while I get Christian ready," he told Lisa.

The man in the lab coat stepped forward and shook hands with Lisa before leading her away. Dr. Rodriguez watched them for a moment before telling me to follow him.

Eliana kept hold of my hand as he opened a hidden door in the glass and walked through it. He looked at us over his shoulder and told Eliana to not go in with me.

She hesitated before letting go of my hand. She stayed at the door as I walked inside the other half of the room.

Dr. Rodriguez told me to sit in the chair in the middle of the room. I eyed it wearily as I did so. I noticed the cuffs on the armrests only seconds before he grabbed my arms and fastened them to the chair, locking them in place.

I only glared at him, knowing yelling and cursing would do nothing. He hooked different wires and monitors up to me, on my arms, chest, and head.

"You better do the things I ask, or you will be punished severely," he hissed in my ear. With that, he walked out and closed the door behind him. I watched him walk past Eliana, who was frozen by the glass, and over to Lisa and Dr. Patterson.

I looked over at Eliana and caught her gaze. She looked scared, terrified, as her eyes traveled down to the cuffs around my wrists.

"It's okay," I mouthed to her once her gaze flicked to my face again. Although everything wasn't okay, I didn't want her to be frightened. I felt a shock run through my body, almost like the first time I saw her, and knew there was some kind of connection between us. I just didn't know what it meant.

CHAPTER TWENTY-SIX

"Okay, Christian," Dr. Rodriguez said a few minutes later, drawing my gaze away from Eliana. "We are going to do a few tests today. We're going to start with the painless one. Could you form one of those electricity balls in front of you?"

I raised an eyebrow. "How can I do that without access to my abilities?"

"Oh, right!" he said before pressing a button on the panel in front of him. I felt my abilities return and start coursing through my veins. "There."

I focused in front of me, concentrating on forming a ball of electricity in front of my face. The sparks started at my fingertips and rose to create a bright blue ball of electricity at eye level. I held it there, not knowing if I could stop or not.

"You can stop now," he told me when I started to tire.

It vanished as I released the breath I didn't know I was holding until then. I moved my concentration from it to Eliana, who was now looking at me in wonder. Her eyes were large, lips slightly apart, and her head was tilted slightly to the side. She saw me watching her and quickly snapped out of her shocked stupor.

She gave me a soft smile and I returned it. She looked over her shoulder when Lisa asked her something and started blushing as she glanced back at me. I found myself wondering what Lisa asked her.

"Okay, Christian," Dr. Rodriguez said, drawing my attention to him. "Now try holding it until you can't anymore."

I nodded and did the same as the last time. I held it for several minutes before tiring and having to drop my concentration and take deep breaths due to holding it for so long.

"Good job, Christian," Dr. Rodriguez praised. "You held it for 5 whole minutes."

I glanced over at Eliana, who was still watching me, before focusing on Dr. Rodriguez. He was speaking to Dr. Patterson and Lisa, but I couldn't hear what they were saying. Somehow, they could control when I could and couldn't hear them.

"Um, guys?" I said after a few minutes. They turned to look at me after stopping mid conversation. "How long am I going to be here like this?"

Dr. Rodriguez pressed a button before saying, "Why? You got something better to do?"

"Not exactly. But I do have to use the bathroom, so could we hurry this up?" I asked as I shifted as much as I could in the chair. I saw Eliana smirk in the corner of my eye.

Dr. Rodriguez and Dr. Patterson shared a look. "We'll skip the other stuff and go right to the test," Dr. Patterson told him after a moment.

Dr. Rodriguez nodded in agreement and turned off the speakers as they prepped everything. I focused on Eliana, knowing she was the easiest to read as she listened to what they were saying. Her complexion paled as she listened and she got a panicked look in her eyes. I knew whatever they were planning wasn't going to be good because of her reaction. Even Lisa glanced up at me with a worried expression.

I mouthed to Eliana, 'What's going on?'

She only shook her head in response before Dr. Rodriguez turned the speakers back on. "Okay," he started. He looked over at Lisa and Eliana. "Do not intervene. I do not want to put a punishment on top of this," he warned.

They quickly nodded, but still looked worried.

"Just do a test," he told Dr. Patterson.

The man nodded and pressed a few buttons. I heard it before I felt it. The electricity started running through the wires connected to the chair I was in, snapping as it fought to meet the chair. I was shocked. Not just a small shock, but one that made my entire body feel like a taunt wire, paralyzing me. It was quick, only about three seconds, but scared the living hell out of me. I sat there for a moment, frozen in fear, as I stared at Dr. Rodriguez.

He was grinning as he looked back at me. "Well, it definitely works." He turned to Dr. Patterson. "Do it for 15 seconds."

He pressed a few buttons before I heard the cracking of the angry electricity rushing towards me. Once it made it to my chair, it felt as if I was being struck by lightning and it wouldn't stop. I think I screamed, but couldn't be sure as it ran through every inch of my body, from the tips of my hair to my toes. I started seeing spots; black, white, yellow, and red danced around the outside of my vision.

As fast as it started, it stopped. My ears were ringing, and I blinked to get rid of the spots crowding my vision. My breathing was staggered and rushed, and I tried to slow it down. I didn't know where to look, so I focused back on Eliana.

She was looking around in panic, but when she noticed me looking at her, her features softened. We just watched each other and everyone else around us seemed to fade away. There was only me and her. My breathing slowed and I felt myself calm down as our gazes stayed locked onto one another.

I only snapped out of it when Dr. Rodriguez said, "30 seconds."

I didn't get much time to prepare myself before the electric current was running through my body again. The spots crowded my vision about halfway through and my eyes closed. Once it finished, my head hung low, and I kept my eyes shut as I focused on breathing. I probably looked unconscious to them by how limp I was, and I planned on keeping it that way.

"What's his heart rate at?" Dr. Rodriguez asked.

"130 beats per minute," Lisa answered. "You should stop now, or he may have a heart attack, or even die."

He sighed, but agreed that they should stop the test. I heard him open the door and walk over to me. He removed the cuffs around my wrists and asked Victor and Eliana to help me back to the cell. However, I noticed that he said the 'new' cell. What did that mean?

They came over as Dr. Rodriguez walked back out. "Christian?" Eliana whispered to me. "You still here?"

"I'm here," I mumbled as I opened my eyes slowly to see Eliana crouched in front of me, and Victor standing behind her.

"Can you walk?" Victor asked.

I shook my head. "My legs are still paralyzed."

They put my arms over their shoulders and helped me stand. I put slight pressure on my feet, but that's all I could do at the moment. We slowly made our way out of the room and passed the three adults in the other half of the room to get to the hallway.

"What new cell was he talking about?" I asked as we made our way down the hall.

"You caught that, huh?" Victor asked. "He doesn't want you sharing a cell with Alis and

Angelica anymore. He thinks you three have gotten too close and doesn't like that. So, he had another room renovated for you."

"What did he expect? We were obviously going to get close when he put us all in the same cell."

"You will still see each other during training sessions," he added.

We passed the cell I was held in for the past few months, which was thankfully empty, and he opened the door next to it. The cell was about the same size as the isolation room, but had an actual bed instead of a concrete slab.

The wooden door was replaced with a window door, so I could see out and they could see in. "He's making you stay in here?" Eliana asked as they helped me sit on the bed. "Alone?!"

"This is an upgrade compared to the isolation room," I told her with a shiver at the memory.

She looked over at Victor and asked, "Do I want to know?"

He shrugged. "Probably not." He turned to leave after saying, "I'm going to go do some things. You are allowed to go to the training room once you feel up to it," he told me.

We both watched him leave and Eliana sat on the bed next to me. She crossed her legs so she was sitting Indian style and we sat in silence for a few minutes, content with each other's company.

She started picking at the tag of the blanket on the bed as she asked, "So, you really have no idea where you are?"

I was a little surprised by her question, but shook my head. "No. They won't tell me."

She raised her eyebrow. "Any guesses?"

"A lab somewhere in the country," I answered, not knowing where she was going with this.

"Christian," she sighed, "you're at Area 51."

CHAPTER TWENTY-SEVEN

"You mean, *the* Area 51?!" I asked. I shouldn't have been too shocked. I mean, we were in Nevada, where Area 51 was located. But to think that I was an experiment at the infamous Area 51 was surreal.

"Yeah…" Eliana said. "Did you have any suspicions?"

"No. It never even crossed my mind," I answered honestly. I sighed in frustration as I ran my hand through my hair. "This changes…a lot. I thought that if I got the opportunity, I could attempt to escape. But it will be very difficult to at a heavily guarded and secured base."

We sat in silence for another moment, lost in our own thoughts, before she asked, "What's this training room Victor mentioned?"

I tentatively put pressure on my feet, and once I realized I could feel them, I stood. "You want to go see?" I asked her with my hand outstretched towards her.

She smiled and took my hand. I led her out of the cell and to the training room. Alis was flying around the room and Angelica was sitting on the floor in the middle of the room as she played with fire in her hands.

"Wow," Eliana breathed as we walked in together.

"There he is," Alis said when she saw me. She flew over and landed in front of us gracefully. "Who's your friend?" she asked as she nodded towards Eliana, who was still holding my hand.

"Alis, this is Eliana, Lisa's granddaughter. Eliana, this is Alis."

"Well, aren't you cute," Alis said as she smiled at her. "Be nice to Christian," she joked. "He's like my little brother."

I rolled my eyes as I replied, "I'm not that much younger than you guys."

"I don't know… 8 months is a lot younger than ya think. Ain't that right, Angelica?" she called over to Angelica.

Angelica was watching us from where she was sitting and nodded with a slight smile. She seemed to be uncomfortable with Eliana in the room. I knew she was quieter than Alis, but she was definitely quieter than normal today.

"Well, I've got bad news," I told them. "Rodriguez is not letting me be cellmates with you ladies anymore."

"What?!" Alis shrieked. "Are you for real? Why?"

"Because he doesn't want us to be close anymore," I said with a shrug.

"Bullshit!" she exclaimed. "Well, might as well hang out when we can. What do you want to do?"

"Anything," I answered.

"Want to fly around the room first?" she asked.

I nodded and let go of Eliana's hand to remove my shirt. All of their eyes went to the brand, but I pretended not to notice. I closed my eyes and willed my wings to emerge from my back before opening them.

Eliana was looking at me with an awed expression. She looked from my wings to Alis' and back to mine. "Why are yours white?" she asked after a moment.

"I don't know," I said with a shrug. "I was told they would be black, but they came in white. Alis told me that it means I'm destined for greatness or something like that, but I don't know what to think of it."

"And you can fly? Like Alis?"

I nodded and flapped them, so I raised a few feet off the ground to show her.

"Wow," she said again. "I wish I could fly, always have."

I scooped her in my arms, making her squeal in surprise, before flapping my wings so I almost reached the ceiling. "Now you can," I told her as I grinned at her shocked expression.

She wrapped her arms tightly around my neck as she looked at the ground below. "Just don't drop me," she told me.

"I promise I won't drop you, angel," I whispered in her ear.

She shivered against me and looked back at me. Her gorgeous blue eyes sparkled with joy and excitement as I started to circle around the room. She looked back down and started to slowly loosen her grip on my neck as she relaxed more and more.

After a few minutes, I slowly descended until my feet hit the ground. I gently put her down, so her feet were on the ground. She smiled as she let go of me, only to wrap her arms around my waist. "Thank you," she said into my chest.

I hesitated a moment before hugging her back. "No problem."

She pulled back and continued beaming with excitement. "What else can you do?"

"He can do almost anything," Victor said from behind me.

We both turned to look at him and I realized Alis and Angelica weren't in the room anymore. He had his hands in his pockets as he walked towards us. "Anything you can imagine, he could probably do," he said once he reached us.

"Yeah, I-" I started, but couldn't finish before I got a blinding migraine and fell to my knees as I held my head. It took my breath away and I started seeing black spots.

They were talking to me, but I couldn't even comprehend what they were saying over the pain. The black spots crowded over my vision and I fell over as the darkness swallowed me whole.

CHAPTER TWENTY-EIGHT

I was in a small one-story home. I looked around, confused as to where I was exactly. I saw a black leather couch in the room across from me with the TV on above it. I was in a small kitchen next to the living room with a hallway to my left and the front door to my right.

A door opened in the hallway and I saw Eliana rush out with tears in her eyes. I stepped in front of her and asked her what was wrong, but she didn't seem to see me. I realized I must have been in a vision of some sort and knew I was seeing it for some reason.

"You're not going anywhere," John, one of my teammates, called as he chased after her. "We're going to have a good time." He pushed her onto the couch, ignoring her pleas for him to stop.

She tried to push him off her, but he pinned her wrists above her head. She started screaming and fought harder as he used one hand to pull her dress up to reveal her underwear and flat stomach.

He punched her in the stomach, so hard that I knew there would be a bruise. "Stop squirming, bitch!"

He pulled his phone out of his pocket and started recording. I looked away from them when he pulled her underwear down and pulled his own pants down.

I heard her cry as he raped her. She sobbed and pleaded for him to stop. After what felt like forever, he finally stopped and pulled his pants up.

I looked over at Eliana when he walked out of the room. She laid on her side with silent tears running down her face. I wanted to comfort her so badly it hurt.

She eventually pushed herself off the couch and moved to grab her things before hurrying out of the house as the tears pooled from her eyes.

* * * * *

I CAME TO WITH a deep intake of air, almost as if I was holding my breath. I opened my eyes and saw that I was laying in the middle of the training room with Eliana, Victor, and Alis all around me. I sat up with Victor's help and groaned at the headache.

"You okay?" Alis asked. She gasped when she saw the look in my eyes. "I know that look. You had a vision!"

I nodded and glanced over at Eliana, who was sitting to my left. She was looking at me with a worried expression. "Let me see your stomach," I told her after I remembered that she should have a bruise there if it already happened.

"What? Why?" she asked, clearly confused.

I gently took her hands and looked her in the eyes. "Please."

She looked at the others, who were watching us, but slowly nodded. She lifted her shirt and I sucked in a breath at the sight of the purple bruise just below her navel.

"What happened?" Victor asked.

She looked uncomfortable as she pulled her shirt back down to cover it. Tears started building up in her eyes as she looked up at me with pleading eyes.

"Do you guys mind if I talk to Eliana alone?" I asked them quietly.

They nodded and left the room without a word. Victor closed the door behind them, and I nodded in appreciation.

Once they were gone, Eliana broke into sobs. I wrapped my arm around her shoulders and pulled her to me. "You're okay," I whispered to her.

"Did you see it?" she asked into my shirt.

"Yeah," I told her. "I'm so sorry, Eliana. He's a jerk that needs to be put in his place or arrested. Does Lisa know?"

"No!" she exclaimed. "She can never know. She wouldn't let me out of her sight if she knew."

"When did it happen?"

"Three days ago," she cried, and my heart broke for her. "We were supposed to be studying at his place when he tried to kiss me. I tried to run out, but he caught up to me and…" She choked back a sob.

"You don't have to keep going. I saw it already," I told her.

"Right," she whispered to herself.

"What can I do for you?"

"Just hold me," she told me quietly.

I bundled her into my arms and hugged her to me as she put her arms around my neck. She sobbed into my shoulder as I rocked her back and forth.

"He took my virginity," she cried, making my heart shatter into a million pieces. "Something I have been saving for marriage was taken from me within minutes."

"I'm sorry. Believe me when I say that if I wasn't trapped here, I would kill him myself."

"I know you would." She let out a content sigh after her crying slowed. Her breathing started to slow, and I knew she fell asleep as her grip loosened on my neck.

I slowly and carefully stood up as I held her to me. I carried her out of the room and Victor was waiting in the hallway. He took one look at Eliana and whispered, "What happened?"

"Tell you in a minute," I told him as I walked past him and into my new 'cell'. I laid her on my bed and sighed as I ran my hand through my hair. I turned to Victor, who was standing in the doorway, and cursed. "John McKinley raped her three days ago. Took her virginity like it was nothing."

"Shit," he swore. "Is she okay?"

"I don't know. I wish I could kill John myself," I said with an angry shake of my head. "Who knows how many times he's done this?"

"I'll take care of him," he told me with a clenched jaw. "Trust me, I will." He looked at Eliana again. "Want me to get Lisa to take her home?"

I shook my head. "Just tell Lisa she's staying here tonight."

He nodded. "You okay with that?"

"Yeah. As long as Lisa is okay with her staying, it's not a problem."

He nodded and closed the door behind him on his way out. I sighed as I looked back at Eliana, who was sleeping on her side with her face facing me. I went to the bathroom, which was surprisingly slightly bigger than the last. It had a small closet in the corner, and I opened it to find three shelves of towels, toiletries, and clothes. I pulled out sweatpants and a t-shirt and put them on before brushing my teeth.

Once finished, I walked out of the bathroom. I watched Eliana for a minute. She looked so peaceful and young when she slept that my heart broke even more at the thought of anyone hurting her. I carefully slid onto the small bed with her, and she snuggled into my side in her sleep. She sighed in contentment when I put my arm around her, and I closed my eyes. I smiled softly to myself at how normal it felt to do this with her.

A few minutes later, I heard Victor and Lisa whispering by the door. "See? They're fine," Victor told her. "I would've never left them alone if I didn't trust Christian completely."

Lisa sighed. "It's not that I don't trust Christian. She's been keeping something from me these past few days, but I don't know what. I'm just worried."

"She probably has a lot on her mind. New school, new friends, new state."

"You're probably right," she said as she slowly walked over to us. I felt her drape a blanket over us before she ran her hand through my hair in a way I imagined a mother would do. "I wish I could do more to help," she whispered as she continued to mess with my hair.

"Trust me you're probably the best person here and you help him so much," Victor told her softly. "He's never really had a mom and Linda did what she could, but you are like a motherly figure to him here. And you have taken care of Eliana her whole life. There is so much you don't realize you've done until you step back and take in the effect you have on others."

"I know," she replied softly. "Thank you."

They left the room, and I adjusted my position before settling in and falling asleep.

CHAPTER TWENTY-NINE

The next morning, I woke up to Eliana starting to stir in my arms. Sometime in the middle of the night, she moved so her head was laying on my chest. I opened my eyes and looked down at her. She was looking up at me with those big blue eyes and smiled.

"Morning," she whispered. "It is morning, right?"

I chuckled and responded, "Yes."

"How do you know?" she asked as she slowly sat up.

"The lights in the hallway are brighter and the researchers are more active," I answered as I tilted my head and used my super-hearing to hear the tapping of shoes, the papers being shuffled, and the soft whispers of ideas and theories being discussed in the area.

"Oh," she said. She pulled her hair, so it was over her left shoulder before looking back at me. "Where's the bathroom?"

I pointed to the door over my shoulder. "Take your time," I told her. "You can use one of the toothbrushes in the closet if you want."

She stood up and smiled. "Thanks." She walked into the bathroom and closed the door behind her.

I slowly sat up and stretched my arms over my head. I swung my legs, so they were hanging off the bed and bent over with my elbows resting on my knees as I waited.

Dr. Rodriguez came in a minute later. "A group of teens were found trying to break in early this morning. I need your help interrogating them."

I raised my eyebrow. "Do I have to?"

"Of course, you have to!" he yelled. "Get dressed."

I nodded and looked down at my hands as I fiddled with my thumbs.

"Now!" he ordered.

"I…I can't," I told him, unsure of how to respond.

He walked over and grabbed my hair harshly. "What do you mean you can't?" he spit in my face as I cried out. "I gave you an order."

The bathroom door opened, and Eliana took in everything happening in front of her. "What the hell are you doing?!" she screamed as she marched over. "You're hurting him. Let go," she ordered Dr. Rodriguez.

He let go of my hair and I rubbed my head. "Eliana," he said, seeming speechless. "What are you doing here?"

"I spent the night," she answered sternly. "Wanted to make sure Christian was okay after what you did to him yesterday. Clearly you are taking good care of him," she sarcastically remarked. "If you think I'm oblivious to things, you're wrong."

He seemed speechless and glanced at me before turning on his heel and walking out. We watched him and once he was out of sight, I quietly said, "Thank you."

"No problem," she told me as she sat on the bed next to me. "He's an ass and needs to be put in his place."

"I should go get changed." I stood up and walked to the bathroom, but turned to look at her before walking inside. "Seriously, thank you."

She gave me a soft smile and nodded before I closed the door and got ready for the day.

* * * * *

DR. RODRIGUEZ CAME TO GET ME a few minutes after I finished changing. When Eliana took my hand and followed, he didn't stop her. He led us to the training room where five teen boys were handcuffed to chairs.

He turned to Eliana. "This may not be something you want to see, but knowing you, you'll stay anyway."

"Well, look at you. You're already learning," she said with a smile.

"As long as you stay here, we should be fine." He motioned for me to follow him and I let go of Eliana's hand before doing so. He stopped in front of the teens and I stopped next to him.

I studied each of them and realized that I knew them. They went to my school and were in my graduating class; they were my football teammates.

Their eyes widened when they saw me too. "Christian?" Kyle asked in shock.

I knew better than to speak, so I remained silent as Dr. Rodriguez spoke with authority in his voice. "You boys were caught trespassing on government property. You're lucky my men didn't shoot you dead. Christian will assist me in your interrogation." He turned to me and pressed a needle into my neck.

I didn't even flinch.

He continued speaking as the drugs took effect, "This drug, makes Christian obedient to my every command. He won't listen to you. He's not going to be your friend now." He looked over at me. "Show them something."

I willed my wings to come out and flapped them once. They widened their eyes and gasped. "What the hell?!" Nick yelled. "What did you do to him?!"

"I didn't do anything," Dr. Rodriguez said firmly. "He came into them when he turned 18." He told me to stand behind Nick's chair as I put my wings away, and once I did, he explained, "Now, this is how this is going to work. I'm going to ask you some questions and if you don't answer, Christian will electrocute you guys one at a time. He will check to see if you are lying and will tell me."

He studied each of them before asking, "Why are you boys here?"

"The reason everyone else comes," Brayden said, "to see the infamous Area 51."

Dr. Rodriguez's eyes flicked up at me and I realized he wanted me to try to detect if they were lying. I focused on Brayden and slipped into his mind. He was thinking so many things that I had to push through the thoughts to find out if he was telling the truth or not.

I found a shaky thought and listened to it. *It's partially the truth, right? I mean that is one of the reasons we came, but not the main reason. Crap! What's taking so long? Does Christian really know?*

I pulled out and said, "It is the truth." That technically wasn't a lie because he wasn't fully lying.

Dr. Rodriguez nodded and asked, "Then why did you go past the gates?"

"Because we were curious," Noah answered. "We wanted to see what would happen."

I focused on him and heard his thoughts. *Stupid. Why lie about that? Christian's going to know. Why is he here anyway? Shit! He's watching me. He knows I'm lying.*

I pulled myself out of his head and said, "Lie."

"Shock him," Dr. Rodriguez told me as he nodded to Noah.

I walked over to him and put my hand on his shoulder. He looked up at me, clearly confused. I tried apologizing with my eyes, and he seemed to understand. I closed my eyes and let energy flow into him, making him yell in pain. He tried to pull away, but I kept hold of him.

"Stop!" I heard Eliana yell as she ran over. She pleaded with Dr. Rodriguez. "Please, stop. Christian doesn't want to do this, and these are his friends! You have to stop!"

Noah continued screaming and I continued shocking him, not able to stop until I heard Dr. Rodriguez's command, which I hoped came soon.

A few seconds later, Dr. Rodriguez sighed and finally said, "Stop."

I quickly stopped and took my hand off him. His breathing was heavy and irregular as he hung his head. "Shit," he swore after a minute.

"You alright man?" Jacob asked.

"I'll be fine," he answered. "Just don't lie."

"Let's try this again," Dr. Rodriguez started. "Why did you boys go past the gate?"

"We saw Victor, a friend of ours, go past with no problem," Nick blurted out.

We both knew that it had to be true, so I didn't even bother checking. Dr. Rodriguez and I shared a knowing glance before he cursed Victor under his breath. "Victor works here," he told them. "He's allowed here."

"What?" some of them whispered in shock. "He works with you?" Nick asked.

"He does," he answered. He turned to Eliana, who was standing next to him silently. "Go get Victor for me, dear."

She looked over at me before nodding and walking out of the room.

"Does she work here?" Brayden asked.

"No. Her grandmother does. Eliana just came for the first time yesterday."

"Can you please let Christian talk?" Kyle asked. "It's kind of creeping me out how he is just standing behind us."

Dr. Rodriguez pinched the bridge of his nose and sighed, clearly annoyed. "Fine. You may speak, Christian. I'm going to see if she found Victor yet. Watch them for me," he ordered before leaving the room.

"Dude!' Nick exclaimed. "What's that guy's problem?"

"Trust me, he has lots of issues," I said with a clenched jaw.

"I can tell. Does he…hurt you?" he asked, his brow creasing in worry.

They all craned their necks to look back at me and I lowered my gaze to my feet as my face heated in embarrassment. "Yeah."

"Dude, if you're embarrassed, don't be," Jacob told me. "That guy is obviously an ass. How bad does he hurt you?"

"Very bad," I answered as I looked up to meet his gaze. "As in, every day he finds a new way to hurt me."

"What's the worst?" Noah asked.

"Umm. Well, the first really bad one happened about a week after they brought me here. He took me to a room, chained me up, and whipped me. He then left me there all night until Victor found me in the morning."

"Jesus, that's messed up," Brayden said with a shake of his head.

"What else did he do?" Jacob asked.

"He did this a few days ago," I told them as I pulled my shirt up to reveal the brand.

"He did that?!" Noah asked. He was the closest to me and could see it perfectly.

I nodded as I pulled my shirt back down and Dr. Rodriguez walked in with Victor and Eliana following. Victor widened his eyes when he saw the five guys handcuffed to the chairs. He looked up at me and I shrugged helplessly.

"These boys tell me they saw you come in and followed you," Dr. Rodriguez told his son.

"And how is this my fault?" he asked with a raised eyebrow.

"You should be more aware of who is near you when coming here," he stated as though it should have been obvious.

"I was!" he yelled. "They must have gotten here before I did, and I didn't see them when I drove past the gates."

"Well, now what do we do with them?!" Dr. Rodriguez yelled back. "They snuck in because they saw you! I'll let you call the shots!"

"I'll make sure they don't talk," Victor argued. "Just let them go."

"I think Christian should erase their memory of this," Dr. Rodriguez told him.

"Wait, what?" I asked. "How do you know I can even do that?"

"Stop talking," he ordered me. "Eyes down."

I lowered my gaze to my feet obediently.

"You really think he can do that?" Victor questioned his father.

"He can do almost anything," Dr. Rodriguez started. "Why wouldn't he? But first, let's ask a few more questions. Christian!" He snapped his fingers. "Look up."

I looked up at him and noticed that everyone was watching me, even Noah was craning his neck to look back at me.

"What did you expect to find here?" he asked them.

"I don't know," Kyle said with a shrug. "Aliens?"

Dr. Rodriguez looked over at me, waiting for my verification. I focused on Kyle and confirmed it was the truth a moment later. He then asked, "Is what we are actually doing better or worse? Each of you go down the line."

"Worse," Nick answered without any hesitation.

"Worse," Kyle agreed.

"Definitely worse," Noah told him.

"Everything you are doing here makes me sick," Brayden answered with a glare.

"Worse than anything I've seen before," Jacob added.

"Why?" Dr. Rodriguez asked.

"Because you're hurting Christian!" Brayden yelled. "Why would we want that?!"

He looked over at me and his eyes flared. "Go down the line and shock them until they lose consciousness. Then, erase their memories of everything that happened here today."

I fought the obedience, but my legs were already moving me towards Nick. I knew he was doing this to punish me because I told them he hurt me. He knew this would cause me emotional pain. I held back as long as I could, but my hand eventually ended up on his shoulder and I started shocking him.

He yelled and screamed in agony as I continued to let the energy flow into him. I closed my eyes and prayed it would end. It hurt me internally as much as it did him physically. He finally passed out after a few minutes and I stopped.

His head slumped forward so his chin rested on his chest as I took his left hand and closed my eyes. I focused on the strand of memories from the past few hours and made them vanish. However, before I pulled away, I got an idea.

Dr. Rodriguez never told me I couldn't do anything else, so maybe I could add something. Like a message, or plea for help. I focused on creating an image of me, with my wings out and sword on hip, asking for help. I implemented it into his mind before letting go.

I moved down the line of my friends and did the same for each of them. I shocked them until they slumped over, erased their memory of the day, and sent the same plea to each.

"Good job, Christian," Dr. Rodriguez praised. "Now, you may go back to your cell."

I nodded and walked past him and Victor. The sooner I got out of there, the better I would be. Eliana was waiting in the hall; she must have left sometime while I was obedient. She pushed herself off the wall when I walked out of the room.

I walked right past her, not because of the obedience, but because I needed to be alone for a while. I walked into the cell and straight into the bathroom. I turned the shower on and pulled my shirt over my head. I didn't even bother taking my pants off before stepping under the hot water.

I braced my hand on the wall and broke down. My sobs were muffled by the running water and I turned to slide my back against the tile until I was sitting on the shower floor. I pulled my knees up to my chest and cried.

CHAPTER THIRTY

After what felt like forever, Eliana knocked on the door. "Christian?" she asked softly. "You okay?" When I didn't reply, she sighed. "You better have clothes or a towel on because I'm coming in in 3...2...1..." She opened the door and stopped when she saw me sitting in the shower.

She walked over and turned the water off before kneeling in front of me. She put her finger under my chin and gently tilted my head, so I was looking at her.

The tears still silently pooled from my eyes, but blended with the water running from my hair.

She got up and walked over to the closet to get a towel. Once she found one, she came over to me and ran it through my hair as I sat and silently watched her. She patted my back with it once my hair wasn't a soaking mess. She then took my hands and helped me stand up.

I stood silently as the last few tears escaped and she started to dry my chest off. She blushed when she realized what she was doing. I offered a small smile as I stopped her by taking hold of her wrist. She looked up at me with those gorgeous blue eyes and her blush deepened.

"You don't have to do that, angel. I got it," I told her. My voice was husky from crying, but I tried to lighten it with a small chuckle.

She smiled and I took the towel from her. I dried myself off and she gently ran her fingers over the brand once my upper body was mostly dry. "Does it still hurt?"

I watched her as she slowly traced it with her pointer finger. "A little," I breathed. "But not nearly as bad."

She looked up and met my gaze. "That's good," she whispered.

We both stopped breathing when we realized how close our faces were. If she stood on her tiptoes, our lips would meet. That's exactly what she did. She slowly closed her eyes and I closed mine before our lips met. The kiss started out gentle, but she deepened it after I kissed her back. She snaked her arms around my neck, and I put my hands on her hips. This was the first kiss that actually felt right to me. I didn't feel as if I was cheating on someone like when Angelica kissed me. It felt…like we belonged together.

After a moment, we eventually pulled back, but didn't move away from each other. She smiled up at me and blushed when she noticed me smiling down at her.

She seemed to then remember that I was still in my wet pants and stepped away. "I'm just going to…um… let you get changed. I'll be outside when you…um…finish."

I chuckled at her stuttering and nodded as she walked out and closed the door behind her. I then pulled out a pair of sweatpants and a sweatshirt because I was freezing and wanted comfort for a day. Once I finished, I opened the door and saw Eliana sitting on the bed.

She looked up at me as I made my way over and sat next to her. She rested her head on my shoulder and I wrapped my arm around her shoulders, pulling her closer. We sat there in silence for a few minutes, content to be with each other, until I quietly asked, "What's today's date?"

"February 12th. Why?" she replied as she lifted her head to look at me.

My mind reeled. That meant I had been there for almost four months. I couldn't believe how much time went by since I was brought here. I looked at Eliana with wide eyes as I said, "I didn't know how long I've been here. Has it really been four months?"

She looked sad as she nodded. She removed my arm from her shoulders and brought my fingers to her lips. "I'm so sorry," she cried as she kissed the tips of them.

I closed my eyes, her featherlight kisses soothing and comforting me. I opened my eyes and saw she had her eyes closed too. I stopped her by bringing my other hand up and tucking the strand of hair that fell into her face behind her ear.

"Why me?" she whispered after she opened her eyes to look into mine and dropped my hand.

"Because when I'm with you, everything feels okay," I told her honestly. "With you, it feels…right. But I could ask the same thing, why me? I can't be a normal boyfriend. Not as long as I'm here."

"Because I've been thinking about you ever since that day at school. I can't stop thinking about you. And this past day, you've shown much more compassion towards me than most guys do in a year. You're right, it won't be easy, but I'm willing to try."

I swallowed before taking her hands and replying, "I'm willing to try too, angel."

She tilted her head. "Why do you call me that?"

"Because even though you don't have wings, you're an angel in my eyes," I answered honestly.

Her eyes filled with tears as she whispered, "Really?"

I reached up to wipe the tears from her eyes with my thumbs as I said, "Of course."

She leaned over and kissed me, surprising me. I quickly snapped out of my shocked stupor and kissed her back. We didn't go as gently as the last kiss. She got up on her knees without breaking contact and wrapped her arms around my neck. She moaned when I pressed my tongue to her lips, giving me access to hers. Our tongues danced around each other, and I moved so she was on her knees between my legs.

She brought her hands up and pulled my hair gently. I moaned against her and she bit my bottom lip before pulling back. We rested our foreheads against each other as we tried to normalize our breathing.

We eventually pulled back and settled down onto the bed. She laid next to me and I wrapped my arm around her to pull her closer. She pulled the hem of my sweatshirt up and traced the outline of my abs in slow circles.

"I know I can't get you anything. But Valentine's Day is in two days and I was wondering if you'd be mine?" I asked her.

"I wouldn't want anyone else," she told me as she smiled up at me.

Lisa then came in and we both lifted out heads to look at her. "You want to come home, Eliana?" she asked with an amused smirk. "You have school tomorrow."

"Do I have to go to school?" Eliana groaned against me.

"Yes," Lisa answered with a cackle.

Eliana tilted her head to look at me and I chuckled at her pout. "Go. I'll be fine."

She slowly pushed herself into a sitting position and looked back at me. "I'll see you tomorrow?"

I sat up with her and nodded. "I'll be here."

She climbed off the bed, but turned to give me a quick kiss before walking out. Lisa looked at me with a shocked expression before following her granddaughter out of the room.

I laid back down and stared at the ceiling for a moment before Dr. Rodriguez came inside. I looked over at him without getting up. He stood there for a moment before saying, "We have a long day tomorrow. Get some sleep."

"What's happening tomorrow?" I asked.

He walked over to my side and bent down next to me. "Tomorrow we are going to a boot camp nearby to show you off," he told me quietly. He brushed my bangs back and stuck a needle I didn't know he had into my neck. "Go to sleep," he whispered as I went limp under his touch and was surrounded by darkness.

CHAPTER THIRTY-ONE

Dr. Rodriguez woke me the next morning, and it was as if nothing changed. He was bent down next to the bed with his fingers running through my hair. When I opened my eyes, his face was in front of mine. "Hey, buddy," he whispered in an almost too friendly tone. "Time to get ready. I set some clothes in the bathroom for you. Be ready in 15 minutes," he told me before standing up and leaving the room.

I laid there for a moment and worried my bottom lip. Where was he taking me? Was he going to leave me there or was he just showing me off? How was he showing me off? Would he beat me or just order me to do things?

Eventually, I just got up and walked into the bathroom. He set clothes on the closed toilet seat and I picked them up. A pair of black combat boots were on top of the pile, green camo pants with a black belt, and a black t-shirt. I got dressed in everything except the boots and brushed my teeth before opening the door.

I sat on the bed as I waited for Dr. Rodriguez and started lacing up the boots. He came in as I finished lacing up the second. He nodded in approval as I stood and walked over to him.

He was holding something behind his back, and I was scared to know what it was. I didn't have to wait long before he brought the cuffs connected to chains into view. I backed away, but he quickly took hold of my left wrist and connected one of the cuffs to it. He pulled the chain connected to it and I jerked forward. He put the other one on my right wrist and held the chains together.

"Be good today, okay?" he said as if I was a child. He pulled me behind him and down the hall to the right. We walked past Alis and Angelica's cell and I saw they were still asleep. He turned down the hall to the left and led me to the door on the end. I looked around and realized it was another hallway, full of doors.

He opened the first door to the left and pulled me into a large garage. About 15 cars, trucks, and jeeps were inside. He led me to a SUV with tinted windows and made me climb into the passenger seat before closing the door and going around to the driver's side.

I adjusted my hands, so the chains connected to the cuffs were between my knees and on the floor by my feet. He started the car and backed out of the garage.

The weather was gloomy. It appeared as if it had been raining for the past few days due to the puddles on the ground. The sky was covered with angry-looking gray clouds that looked as if they could unleash their wrath at any given moment.

I noticed the military towers around the base and men with guns on top of them. There was fencing around the entire parameter and guards were walking along them with dogs on leashes.

Dr. Rodriguez drove towards the main gate and a guard stopped us. He put the window down and said, "Hey, David. Just taking Christian to one of the camps nearby to see if they want him."

David nodded and looked at me. I recognized him as the guard who carried me back to the cell after I was branded, the one who questioned what Dr. Rodriguez was doing. He gave me a small smile before saying, "Good luck," and opening the gate.

We drove out of the fenced area and on the dirt road for a few miles. He turned left and we stopped at another guarded gate. This gate I recognized as the one that everyone posted pictures of when they decided to 'see' Area 51 in person. I repositioned my hands and rested one elbow on the armrest and propped my chin in my hand as I peered out the window.

Dr. Rodriguez told the guards the same thing and they opened the gates. A few people with cameras were in front of the gates and taking pictures as we drove by. They looked at me as we drove past, and I knew they were taking notice to the chain connected to the cuff on my wrist.

Good, I thought. *Maybe they'll bring it to the media's attention, and I could get out of here.*

We drove a few more miles before he took a slight right and headed down a gravel road. The base came into view and men in uniforms were outside training. Some were running laps, some were on a shooting range away from others, and some were sparring.

They looked over at us as Dr. Rodriguez put the car in park and got out. He came around to my side and opened the door before taking hold of the chains and pulling me out. He pulled me close and whispered in my ear, "Keep your eyes down unless told otherwise."

I nodded as I lowered my eyes to the ground.

"What did you bring us today?" a man asked as he walked over to us.

"This one is classified for now. Is Kirkwood in his cabin?"

"Yeah," the man answered. I felt his eyes on me, trying to figure out what I was doing there.

Dr. Rodriguez pulled me behind him and started walking towards some cabins. I looked up as we walked, so I could see where I was going, and saw he was heading towards the cabin on the end of the walkway.

He knocked on the door before opening it and led me inside. I noticed a tall man sitting behind a wooden desk in the small room. Three younger men were in chairs along the wall to the right. They were wearing the same uniforms as me, so I assumed they were recruits.

"There he is!" the man, who I assumed was Kirkwood, said as he stood up. He was wearing all camo; camo pants, camo shirt, camo shoes, and camo hat. "Recruits, this is Commander Rodriguez," he told the men sitting in the chairs as he gestured to Dr. Rodriguez. "He is my boss and supplier of weapons."

"You got that right," Dr. Rodriguez replied with a chuckle. "I'm assuming these are your most trusted."

"Yes, Sir. Handpicked them myself."

He grinned. "Wonderful." He turned to them. "You may be wondering why we called you here. I am trusting you with the care and training of our newest weapon, Christian," he told them as he gestured to me.

They looked at me curiously, wondering how I could be a weapon. "Him?" the one asked.

"Yes," Dr. Rodriguez answered.

"What does he do?" another asked. "He's just one kid."

"He does a lot," Dr. Rodriguez answered. "If he didn't have these cuffs on, he wouldn't be silently standing there." He looked back and I realized that I broke the rule of keeping my eyes down. He whacked the back of my head and ordered, "Eyes down."

I slowly lowered my gaze to my black boots and the red carpet I was standing on. He started talking again, "He obviously has a few quirks, but we're still trying to break him. With a little bit of scopolamine, a drug that makes people obedient to any command, he listens like an obedient dog."

"Who wants to go see what he can do?" Kirkwood asked. "I know I do."

They all nodded and agreed to go to a more open, but private spot. Dr. Rodriguez pulled me out and we walked out of the cabin. He purposely tugged on the chain, making me lose my footing and almost fall to the ground. One of the recruits, who has caramel colored skin, caught my arm, and steadied me.

I looked up and met his chocolate brown eyes. He had so many questions swirling around in them, but didn't ask any. Instead, he asked, "You okay?"

I nodded as Dr. Rodriguez pulled again. "Come on, Christian," he called as if I were a dog.

The recruit stayed next to me the rest of the way. We walked into a building on the other side of the camp, and it was about the same size as the training room back at the lab.

Once the door was closed, Dr. Rodriguez pulled me next to him as he turned to face them. He took a deep breath before explaining "Now, first, before you do anything with him, you always want to inject him with this drug." He pulled a syringe from his pocket and told them, "You will inject it into his neck," as he did so. "You then wait a few minutes until he is standing tall, and his eyes are focused forward. His pupils usually dilate, so that's another way to tell if it's working."

"How long does it last?" one asked.

"We've gotten it to last up to six or seven hours depending on what we have him do," he answered as he stepped back. "And once they aren't as strong, he gets very tired."

They watched as my muscles became strained and my gaze focused in front of me. I saw the recruit who helped me standing behind Dr. Rodriguez with a worried look on his face. He looked as if he could have been sick at the sight of me becoming obedient.

"Alright," Dr. Rodriguez said as he rubbed his hands together. "Looks like he is ready." He took the cuffs off my wrists and I felt my magic return. The others around us gasped and Dr. Rodriguez turned to them. "What you are feeling right now is Christian's abilities. He is the only one we have in our care that we can actually feel it radiating off him. The longer he doesn't have access to them, the stronger that feeling becomes. No, he cannot control it, so you will have to get used to it."

"Can they try controlling him?" Kirkwood asked. "Since they are the ones who will be in charge of him."

"Let me show them what he is capable of. Then, they can practice for a little while." He turned to me and told me to take my shirt off before summoning my wings.

I did as he ordered and handed him my shirt after removing it. I then willed my wings to emerge, and everyone gasped.

"Fly around the room," Dr. Rodriguez ordered me.

I flapped my wings a few times before flying around the room once and landing in front of them once more. He then walked over so he was standing in front of me. "That's not all. He also doesn't react to pain when the drugs are in his system." He proceeded to punch me in the gut and even though it hurt, I didn't flinch.

"So, he has wings," one of the recruits asked with his arms crossed. "Is that all?"

Dr. Rodriguez shook his head as he stepped away from me. "He can do a lot more. Almost anything." He turned to look at me again and ordered, "Make a ball of fire in your hands."

I concentrated on making a bright blue ball of fire in between my hands and once it appeared, they all gasped. I held it for a few seconds before letting it fizzle out and returning my hands to my sides.

"Amazing," the Sergeant breathed.

"Make a glowing ball and throw it at the wall," he said as he pointed to the wall across from us.

I nodded and made a ball of electricity in my hands and tossed it back and forth for a minute. Then, I turned towards the wall and threw it as hard as I could towards the wall. It connected with a snap and sparks flew everywhere, but didn't leave any damage.

"Holy shit!" the recruit with caramel skin exclaimed. "Remind me to stay on his good side."

Dr. Rodriguez grinned proudly before saying, "You guys play with him while I talk to Sergeant Kirkwood."

He walked over to the sergeant and they whispered amongst each other as the recruits glanced at each other. They slowly approached me and one with red hair whisper-yelled, "This is insane!"

They ran their hands down my wings as I stood still. However, the caramel skinned recruit stood in front of me with his arms crossed. He looked into my eyes as if trying to read my thoughts through them. *What are you thinking?* he thought as I tapped into his thoughts. *Can you even think with these drugs in your system? Can you feel pain?*

I blinked, trying to send some kind of message. "You okay if I touch them?" When he realized I couldn't speak, he said, "You can speak."

I shrugged as I answered, "Sure."

He walked behind me and ran his hand over my right wing. "I'm Derek," he told me as he stood in front of me again.

I nodded in greeting. "Christian."

"This is Robbie and Ben," he said as he gestured to the other two, who were still stroking my left wing. I looked back and they waved. Robbie has bright orange hair with pale skin and green eyes, while Ben has tanner skin, not as dark as Derek's, and brown hair with green eyes.

They walked over to stand next to Derek and asked, "Should we try something?" Robbie asked.

"Can you make yourself invisible?" Ben asked me.

I nodded. "I think so."

They all watched me, and I realized they were waiting for me to do it. I closed my eyes and imagined myself invisible. They all gasped, and I assumed it worked. As I opened my eyes, I looked down and realized I couldn't see myself, not even my clothes!

"Wow," Robbie breathed. He ran his hand along the area I was standing and whacked me in the head.

"Ow!" I claimed as I smacked his hand away. "Just because I'm invisible, doesn't mean I'm not here."

He chuckled. "Sorry."

"How do you make yourself visible again?" Derek asked.

I closed my eyes and willed myself to be visible to them, and myself, again. I opened my eyes and looked down to see myself again. They all laughed and jumped up and down like kids on Christmas morning. "This is so cool!" Ben exclaimed.

"Can you read minds?" Derek asked curiously.

I nodded. "Yeah. I actually read yours earlier when I still couldn't talk."

"What was I thinking?" he asked with a raised eyebrow.

"You were wondering what I was thinking and if I could feel pain," I answered.

"What am I thinking right now?" Robbie asked excitedly.

I tapped into his head and focused on what he was thinking. *ABCDEFGHIJKLMNOPQRSTU-VWXYZABCDEF…* I pulled back with a wince.

"You're singing the alphabet, *loudly*," I told him.

He laughed and looked at his friends. "This is insane!"

"How's it going over there?" Dr. Rodriguez called over.

They all turned to look at him and excitedly said, "This is so cool!"

Dr. Rodriguez walked over to us and asked, "What did you figure out so far?"

"He made himself invisible and read our minds!" Robbie exclaimed.

Dr. Rodriguez laughed. "I'm deeply concerned about this generation. You guys get excited over the smallest things."

"How do you like him?" Sergeant Kirkwood asked. "You boys willing to work with him and get him ready for war?"

"Totally!" Ben exclaimed as the others nodded.

"Alright," Dr. Rodriguez said. "We'll have him ready to go by the end of the week. In the meantime, I need you boys to move into a cabin together to be more private. No one can know about this. Once you settle, review these papers on our study and how things work." He handed each of them binders full of papers. "My son, Victor, will stay with you when I bring him and will oversee your progress and training."

They nodded and looked over their shoulders at me. "We can't wait to get to know Christian and will be honored to train him," Derek told him.

Dr. Rodriguez shook hands with each of them as he said, "It's a pleasure to do business with you boys."

They said their goodbyes and Dr. Rodriguez told me to retract my wings and put my shirt back on before putting the cuffs on my wrists. He pulled me behind him and to the car.

The rain let loose as we walked back and we both were almost instantly soaked. It was as if the Gods above knew what had just happened and were letting their anger known as a bright flash of lightning flashed through the sky. The loud bang of thunder sounded a few seconds later and shook the ground with the force.

Dr. Rodriguez cursed as we started sprinting to the car. Once we were both inside and heading down the road, he put his hand on my leg. "You did good, Christian. Very good."

That's all that was said as we made our way back to Area 51.

CHAPTER THIRTY-TWO

I got a warm shower once we returned and dressed in sweatpants and a sweatshirt before sitting on the bed as I waited in my cell for Eliana to come from school. I was so nervous to tell her the devastating news; that I was going to be trained for war. As I waited, I fidgeted and ran my hands over my thighs.

Her and Victor must have left school together to come because they both came into the cell. They instantly knew something was wrong and both asked, "What happened?"

"I'm going to the camp nearby in less than a week," I told them. "They're going to train me for war."

"What?" Eliana asked in disbelief as she sat next to me.

"Dr. Rodriguez took me to the camp today. He formed a small group of recruits to train me in secret to be their newest weapon."

"Why didn't he tell me?" Victor asked.

"I don't know. He plans on having you come with me to oversee my training."

"What?! What about school?" he asked. "He didn't even think about my life."

Suddenly all of my pent-up anger rushed to the surface. "You never thought about *my* life when you turned me over! I haven't gotten to see any friends, go to school, or do anything without being monitored over the past few months. Don't you *dare* say what he is doing to you is unfair when you are able to go to school while I'm being beaten by your father here! He drives me insane! It drives me nuts how he finds a new way to hurt me every day! You don't even know half of what I've been going through because you're doing everything I can't do."

He hung his head. "I know, man. I'm sorry. It's just, my dad has been controlling my life since day one. He never thinks about how I will feel before he does something."

I felt guilty for lashing out at him and said, "I'm sorry. I shouldn't have lashed out at you. I just have a lot of pent-up anger that needs to be un-leashed and I let it out on you."

"It's cool. Everything you said is true," he said with a shrug. "Want to unleash some of that anger in the training room? Preferably not on me," he added with a chuckle.

I looked over at Eliana and agreed. I took her hand as we stood and walked to the training room. Once we walked in, I let go of her hand and formed a ball of energy in my hand. I threw it at the wall with all my might and it sparked with a crack. I sighed in relief and said, "That felt good."

"Want to practice sword fighting?" Victor asked from behind me. "That usually helps me get rid of my anger."

I widened my eyes at him. "You know how to use a sword?"

He laughed at my reaction. "Yeah. Dad started giving me lessons when I was 12."

"I've got to see this. Let's do it."

He grabbed two swords from the cabinet and handed one to me. Since it was the first time I wasn't obedient while using a sword, I had some fun swinging it around and getting a feel for it.

Eliana stood back and watched as Victor and I faced each other. I swung my sword in my hand before getting ready to spar. I stood in the fighting stance and raised my sword.

Victor made the first move and I blocked it easily. The sound of metal on metal echoed off the walls. We pulled apart and he made a swipe for my head, but I ducked before it made contact. I swiped at his feet and he jumped.

We kept going for a while, neither one of us getting the upper hand. We were both getting tired and were sweating and breathing heavily. He went to take a shot at my chest, but I anticipated the move and blocked him. I swiped my leg under his feet, making him fall over. I quickly got up and put the tip of my sword to his chest, claiming victory.

"I win," I told him with a smirk. I took my sword away from him and offered him my hand to help him up. We put our swords on the floor and complemented each other's skills.

Clapping sounded from the doorway and we turned to see Dr. Rodriguez pushing off the door frame. "Well done," he said as he walked over. "My two best sword fighters sparring together. Ain't that a dream come true?"

I glanced over at Eliana and she had a slight panicked expression on her face. I gestured for her to come over and once she did, I wrapped my arm around her waist and pulled her close as he stopped in front of us.

"What do you want now?" Victor snapped.

"I saw you two sparring on the cameras and had to see it in person." He looked over at me. "I'm impressed. You beat Victor, who has been training since he was in middle school."

I kept my face expressionless as he looked at Eliana, who was pressed into my side. "Looks like you two are getting comfortable with each other," he said with a grin.

I growled at him, warning him not to lay a finger on her, and he laughed. "Oh, don't worry, Christian. I don't plan on harming her…not unless I have a reason to," he told me with a malicious look in his eyes. He was warning me not to do anything; not to act out or he would hurt Eliana.

"Are you sure you want to do that?" I asked. "Because I will bring hell fire upon you if you even look at her wrong."

He tsked his tongue, but turned to Victor. "I have some things I would like to go over with you."

"You mean going to the camp?" Victor asked as he stepped up to his father.

Dr. Rodriguez shot a glare towards me. "He told you, didn't he?" He didn't even wait for a response before hitting the back of my head. "Stupid boy."

I had to hold myself back from saying, or doing, something to him. I tried to call my magic to at least give him a warning, but quickly realized that he blocked them sometime when he came inside.

"It's not his fault," Victor intervened. "I asked him what was wrong and what happened today. Don't blame him for telling me something I would have found out anyway!"

"I will talk to you, privately," Dr. Rodriguez told him before turning and walking towards the door. "Now!" he called when Victor didn't follow.

We shared a look before he picked our swords from off the floor where we left them and ran after his father. He put the swords in the cabinet and followed him out of the room.

"Well, that went…well," Eliana said after a moment.

I threw my head back and laughed. It felt good to laugh, really laugh. I let go of her and walked over to the center of the room. I summoned my wings and flapped them a few times to stretch them out before motioning for her to come over.

She smiled as she quickly made her way over to me. I caught her as she barreled herself into me, wrapping her arms around my neck and legs around my waist. I chuckled before flapping my wings and lifting off the ground.

She nuzzled my neck, making me moan. "Who would have ever thought that my boyfriend would be an angel? Literally an angel."

I chuckled. "You're so cute."

She giggled against my shoulder. "You're mine," she said as she pulled back to look me in the eyes.

"And I always will be, angel," I told her before she leaned forward and kissed me passionately. I kissed her back and our tongues met after she gave me access. Our tongues danced around each other as she moved her hands up to my hair. She pulled slightly, making me moan into her mouth.

We eventually pulled back and she looked into my eyes. "You are amazing at that," she told me as she bit her lip. She put her hand on my cheek. "*You* are amazing. Extraordinary."

She glanced back at my wings, which were occasionally flapping to keep us up in the air and reached over my shoulder to stroke my left one with her fingertips.

I shivered at the delicacy of her touch. It didn't affect my flying, but I slowly descended to the floor to ensure it wouldn't. She planted her feet on the ground, but continued to lightly stroke my wing as she kissed my neck.

"I guess I can finally say that I've found my guardian angel," she whispered in my ear.

"I will always be your guardian angel. You have my word."

She pulled back to look at my face and I noticed tears in her eyes. "I'm going to miss you when you go to war."

"I'll miss you too, angel," I told her as I wiped the tears that escaped away with my thumbs. "Can I try something? I promise it won't hurt, I'm just curious."

She gave me a puzzled look. "What?"

I focused on her mind and sent, *Can you hear me?*

Her eyes widened and I knew it worked. "Yeah," she whispered.

I didn't think this would work. But now I can always be with you.

"Can I send stuff back?" she asked curiously.

"You could try," I told her with a shrug. "But since you are human, I'm not sure if it will work or not."

"How do you do it?"

I concentrate on who I want to send the message to and it just works. Hard to explain.

She took a deep breath before getting a cute look of concentration on her face. Her nose wrinkled up and she closed her eyes. After a moment, when she looked like she was about to give up, I heard her. *I'm trying so hard.*

"I heard you!" I told her as I took hold of her hands.

She opened her eyes and squealed as she jumped up and down. "Really?" she asked once she settled slightly.

I grinned and nodded. "Yeah. You're cute when you get excited."

She blushed and tucked her hair behind her ear. "Let me try again."

She wrinkled her nose in concentration again and I had to hold a laugh back. *Is it working?*

Yes, angel. It's working.

Oh my gosh! This is so cool!

Now, if you ever want to talk to me, you can. Like I said, I'll always be there for you, no matter where I am.

I am still going to miss you, she said before standing on her tiptoes and kissing me.

"Christian," Alis said from the doorway.

We both shifted to look at her as she made her way over. Eliana pulled away from me, but didn't leave my side. "I heard you are being sent to the camp," she said.

"How do you know that?" I asked.

She smiled. "I have my ways." Her face fell before she said, "We'll miss you."

"I will too," I replied. "Where's Angelica?"

"She'll be here soon," she answered. "I suggest no PDA when she's here. She doesn't like it."

I had a feeling there was something more to it, but kept my mouth shut. Eliana simply said, "I should go check on grandma anyway. I'll see you later."

I nodded and she walked out the door. Alis and I watched her before looking back at each other. "What's really going on with Angelica?" I asked her. "She hasn't been herself lately."

She hesitated before responding. "She thought there was something between the two of you, but then Eliana came, and she was caught off guard."

I was shocked by this information. "I had no idea she felt that way. I thought we were just messing around with each other due to loneliness and boredom."

"She didn't," was all she said before summoning her wings and flying up to the ceiling.

I flew up with her and asked, "Did you have someone before you were brought here?"

"I had a girlfriend," she told me quietly. "She made me so happy." I saw the hint of a smile. "Kylie. Her name is Kylie. We were together for about a year before…" She looked up at me with tears in her eyes. "We didn't even get to say goodbye."

"I'm sorry," I told her.

"Can I ask you something?" she asked.

I nodded. "Of course."

"If…if something happens to me, will you take care of Angelica for me? Like, if you escape, would you take care of her?"

I nodded. "Of course, I would. But nothing is going to happen to any of us."

"You never know," she told me with a sigh.

"Hey," Angelica said from the doorway.

We both turned and she made her way to the center of the room as she looked up at us. I swooped down to land in front of her and retracted my wings. "Hey," I replied as I crossed my arms over my chest.

Alis landed next to me, but left her wings out. "What's up?" she asked.

Angelica looked me over as she said, "I heard you are going to boot camp soon."

I nodded. "Dr. Rodriguez took me today to show me off."

"I'm sure Eliana was sad to hear that," she replied dryly, making me cringe.

"Angelica!" Alis gasped in disbelief.

"I'm sorry," I told her. "I didn't know you felt that way about me. If I had, I would have explained to you how I felt."

She looked at me with tears in her eyes and just whispered, "Yeah."

I had no idea what that meant, and she didn't go on to explain before turning and throwing a fireball at the target to the left. It burst into flames and the fire extinguisher put it out a second later. She seemed to be ignoring me and I decided to leave it be for the time being.

"She'll get over it," Alis whispered to me. "She just needs time."

I nodded and she flapped her wings to fly around the room. I watched her as I mumbled, "But I don't have time," to myself before walking out of the room without another word.

CHAPTER THIRTY-THREE

The next day was Valentine's Day and I hoped that Dr. Rodriguez would let me have the evening off.

I woke up and took a shower before getting dressed in shorts and a t-shirt. When I walked out of the bathroom, I jumped when I saw Dr. Rodriguez standing right in front of me. He was so close that I had to crane my neck to look him in the eye. I knew he was tall, but standing that close to him made me realize that he towered about a half a foot over me.

"We're taking some samples today," he told me.

"Of what?"

"Of some skin, bone marrow, and blood," he replied. "Follow me," he ordered before turning and walking out.

I followed so I wouldn't be punished later, and he led me into a room I hadn't been in, as far as I knew. He let me go in first and I noticed that three other people were standing in the room with surgical masks and coats on. A hospital-looking bed was in the middle of the room and Dr. Rodriguez shoved me towards it.

I clenched my jaw tightly, not wanting to get myself in trouble, and laid down on the bed without a fight.

The surgeons all waited for Dr. Rodriguez's order before doing anything. He nodded as he walked over to my side. "You may proceed."

They started getting equipment ready and one told me she was going to put an IV in my arm. I nodded and she cleaned my arm before sticking the needle into it and starting the IV.

Another put a mask over my nose and mouth before telling me to count down from 10.

"10..9..8…7…6….5……" The drugs took over and I slipped into darkness.

* * * * *

I WAS BACK IN MY cell when I woke up again. I had no idea what time it was and was completely disoriented. I assumed that it wasn't after four o'clock because Victor and Eliana weren't back from school yet.

I looked around, trying to get my bearings, before slowly sitting up. I hissed when I felt the searing pain jolt through my right shoulder.

I pulled the neckline of my t-shirt down to reveal a gauze covered area from where they took their samples. I pulled it back and saw the inside was filled with dried blood, but the bleeding had stopped. I pulled the gauze off the rest of the way and examined the area. It appeared as if they sewed it up for a few minutes, until I healed, and then took the stitches out before I woke up.

It was sore, but not unbearable as I got up and went to the bathroom. Once I relieved myself and washed my hands in the sink, I walked out. Dr. Rodriguez was waiting by the door and nodded when he saw me. "We're going to train some more."

He turned and walked out, and I sighed before following him to the training room. He blocked my abilities and grabbed the swords out of the cabinet. Before handing me my sword, he stuck a needle into the side of my neck and waited a moment.

Once I was obedient, he told me, "You may act completely normal. Just don't injure or kill me."

I blinked and my muscles loosened before he handed me the sword. I swung it around in my hand in a circle to warm up.

He told me that we were going to spar, like Victor and I did yesterday, to see if I was ready.

We faced each other, standing about six feet apart, and stood in our fighting stances. We raised our swords in front of us with one foot in front of the other.

"Begin," he said before stepping towards me. He brought his sword up to my chest and I blocked him easily. The sound of metal on metal reverberated throughout the room as our swords clashed. I pushed him and he pushed back against our swords.

He pulled back and prepared to thrust his sword at my chest, but I ducked and swiped at his feet, which he jumped over. I backed up before he could make another move and took a second to right myself. I then brought my sword up and swiped my arm out quickly, missing him by mere inches when he backed up at the last second.

He didn't wait to thrust his sword at my chest. I blocked it quicker than he expected, and knocked his sword out of his hand. I didn't hesitate to push the tip of the sword into his chest. I silently wished I wasn't obedient because I could have killed him then and there.

Despite his loss, he grinned. "Bravo. You've beat the teacher."

I pulled my sword away and he took it out of my hands before grabbing his off the floor. He walked over to the cabinet to put them away, but grabbed a long black box out of it. He brought it over and handed it to me.

I gave him a puzzled look. "What's this?"

"It's yours. You've earned it," was all he said.

I lifted the lid to reveal a beautiful custom-made sword. It had a blue iridescent hue to the sharp metal and a shiny silver hilt. The hilt had small engravings of stars and moons on it, and the end of the handle had angel wings. Even the sword itself had shooting stars etched into the metal. It probably cost a fortune. If it wasn't a deadly weapon that I would most likely use in war, it would have been perfect for decoration.

I looked up from it to look him in the eye. "This is mine?"

He grinned and nodded. "All yours. Custom made to your height, not too heavy or light, and just sharpened."

I ran my hand over it as I breathed, "It's beautiful." I cleared my throat. "It's hard to imagine using it and dirtying it with blood."

"It will get its use, but cleans very easily," he explained, seemingly unaware of how disgusted I was at the thought of using it to…kill people. "Go on. Take it out and get a feel for it."

I took hold of the handle and lifted it from the box before he grabbed the box from my hand. I weighed it in my hand and had to admit it was much lighter than the other sword but still had some weight to it.

"Do you like it?" he asked after a moment.

"Yeah," I answered. "But why did you get it for me?"

"I figured you would need one for when you go to war. So, I got it made when I was teaching you so you would be able to train with it." He walked over to the cabinet again and put the box down before grabbing something else.

I saw that it was some kind of strap as he walked back to where I was still standing. "This is a sheath for it," he told me. "It goes over your head and over one shoulder," he explained as he helped me put it on, so the strap was resting on my right shoulder and went down to my left hip. "You sheath it to your back when you aren't using it." He helped me by guiding my right arm up, so the sword went behind my head and helped me slide it into the sheath.

"It will take some practice, but you'll get the hang of it." He stepped away and met my gaze as he put his hands on my shoulders. "You leave in two days," was all he said before walking out of the room.

I staggered back as my heart dropped. *Two days?!* I suddenly got dizzy and started seeing spots dancing around my vision. I had to sit down. I staggered towards the wall and rested my back against it as I slid down.

Taking the sword out of the sheath allowed me to rest my back and head against the tiled wall. I bent my legs and tried to control my breathing. I picked up the sword from the floor next to me and rested it between my legs as I slowly spun it by the hilt. Tears slowly pooled down my cheeks and I made no effort to wipe them away.

I don't know how long I sat like that, watching the light reflect off the blue metal, before Victor and Eliana walked in. They stopped when the saw me sitting against the wall to their right.

"Christian," Eliana breathed before rushing over. She kneeled in front of me, but I didn't take my eyes off the sword. "What's wrong?" she whispered as she reached over and wiped the tears from my face with her thumbs.

"I..." I swallowed and cleared my throat. "I leave in two days," I admitted before meeting her blue eyes.

She pulled her hands back from my face and sat to my left. "We knew this was coming," she said after a moment.

"I know," I told her as I pursed my lips. "It's just… now that I know when I'm leaving, it's starting to sink in that I may never see you, Alis, Angelica, or Lisa again. I had hope that I would get out of here, but don't think it will be as easy when I'm surrounded by trained men with guns."

"I swear I will figure something out," Victor said.

Eliana and I both looked up at him as he continued, "I promise you will see everyone again, even Connor and his family. I got you into this mess, let me get you out of it." He noticed the sword in my hands. "What's that?"

I looked down at the sword. "Your dad gave it to me after I beat him in a sparring match. He had it custom made for me. It's so nice that it's hard to imagine killing people with it."

"Let's hope you never have to use it," he told me. He looked around nervously before saying, "Look, when we go to boot camp, I won't be the nicest. I most likely will be extremely rude to you, but I have to be in order to ensure they don't suspect me helping you. Just don't let it get to you, okay?"

I nodded. "Thanks for the warning."

"I'll leave you two alone for a little while," he told us before walking out of the room.

I looked over at Eliana and saw her looking back at me. "Happy Valentine's Day," I told her with a smile.

She choked back a laugh before cupping my face in her hands. "Happy Valentine's Day." She leaned over and kissed me softly. She pulled back and whispered, "You're my guardian angel."

I smiled. "And you're my angel."

For the rest of the day, we stayed in the room together. Talking, laughing, and occasionally kissing until it was late at night and the lights started dimming, signaling that it was nighttime.

Lisa found us when we were experimenting with my abilities. I was making a sparkly snowflake in my hands. Eliana was watching with wide eyes because she was the one who requested it.

"Eliana," Lisa said. "You ready to come home?"

"Victor offered to take me home," Eliana told her.

"He's getting ready to leave too."

She sighed. "Okay."

We all walked out of the room and Eliana and I said goodbye in front of my cell door. "I'll see you tomorrow," she told me.

I nodded and she kissed me one more time before going down the hall to catch up with Lisa. I opened the door and walked inside my small room. Laying down on the bed, I let out a sigh and fell asleep without even getting changed.

CHAPTER THIRTY-FOUR

Dr. Rodriguez made my last day at the lab a living hell, claiming he 'wanted me ready to train' as soon as possible. He first made me train with the sword for three hours before making me practice with my abilities for another hour.

He then took me into the room of my worst fears. The room where he whipped and branded me. I had to control my breathing and focus to keep myself from shaking in fear.

He closed the door once we were both inside and walked over to the button on the wall. I knew that button, that button made the chains come down from the ceiling.

I was still obedient, so I couldn't really do anything and that scared the crap out of me.

"Come here," he ordered.

I had no choice but to obey.

"Arms up," he commanded. I did and he connected the cuffs to my wrists. "I hope you'll understand that I do this for a reason. It may seem cruel now, but it will help you in the future."

"How the fuck does this help me?" I spat as he raised the chains to ensure I didn't have any slack.

"It gets your body used to healing harsh wounds, so you'll heal faster when you seriously need to. If you were severely wounded in war, your healing will be quicker after getting used to situations like this." He lifted my shirt over my head and covered my eyes with it.

I knew where this was heading and braced myself for the searing pain. He brought the whip down on my back and I tried not to give him the satisfaction of hearing me yell, so I pressed my lips tightly together and yelled without opening my mouth.

He brought it down again and again, each one faster and more jarring than the last. The familiar feeling of warm blood trickling down my back and on and into my pants came soon after.

Once I thought I couldn't take the pain anymore, he stopped. He came over and unlocked the cuffs around my wrists. They were the only thing holding me up and my knees buckled to the floor, causing pain to course through my body at the impact on the cement floor.

He pulled my shirt away from my eyes and back down. It stuck to my back like Velcro and made me curse. I opened my eyes and had to crane my neck to look at him standing above me.

He bent down and said, "Now go to your cell and lay in bed until Victor and Eliana come."

I obediently stood and winced with every movement as I stumbled back to my cell. I laid on my stomach and laid my head into my folded arms as the tears flowed out of my eyes. The pain was excruciating, and I wished I could take my shirt off without causing more pain, but decided to wait.

My tears made my eyes heavy and droopy, so I allowed myself to fall asleep, knowing that I wouldn't be in pain when I did.

* * * * *

I FELT THE BED DIP DOWN as Eliana whispered, "Christian. Wakey, wakey."

There was a pause and I felt her touch my back. I hissed and flinched away at the sharp pain that came with her touch. She quickly pulled her hand back and lifted the hem of my shirt. She gasped and breathed, "Oh God."

I heard her rush out of the room and come back with Victor a moment later. "His back is covered in blood," she cried as they rushed inside.

He lifted my shirt slightly. "Fuck!" he swore when he saw how bad it looked. "Dad did this. He had to."

"Should we take his shirt off?" Eliana asked.

"Yeah. Let's hope it isn't infected already." He paused. "I just don't know how to get it off of him."

"I can do it if you help me," I groaned into my arms.

"Are you sure about that?" Victor asked.

I turned my head to look at them. Victor was looking down at me with concern and was obviously angry with his dad. Eliana had tears in her eyes as she looked at me. "Help me sit up," I told Victor.

He grabbed my upper arm and helped me as I pushed myself up. I winced with every movement and my shirt pulled at the gashes, making the pain even worse.

Once I was sitting, Victor simply said, "Arms up," and I obeyed, knowing I wouldn't be able to take it off myself. He slowly pulled it off, but it was almost like ripping off a Band-Aid, only 100 times worse.

I cried out and hissed in pain as I felt every inch of my back become unstuck from the shirt. Eliana tried helping him pull it off my back, but nothing could ease the pain until it was off. "Just rip it off already!" I yelled through my clenched jaw.

They hesitated before pulling it off quickly. I screamed as they did, and I put my head in my hands as I rested my elbows on my knees afterwards.

"I'll go get some washcloths," Victor said before going into the bathroom.

Eliana sat next to me and rubbed my arm. "What happened?"

"He whipped me. Chained me up and whipped me," I told her, embarrassed at how weak I must have sounded.

"You're not weak," she told me as if she was the one who could read minds. "You are one of the strongest guys I know. Most wouldn't make it a week in a place like this, let alone four months. Even guardian angels need rescued some days."

I looked over at her. "You think so?"

She gave me a sad smile. "I know so."

"Okay," Victor said as he walked out of the bathroom with his hands full of washcloths. He handed a handful to Eliana as he instructed, "Dab these on his back to clean it."

She nodded and they started to blot my bloody back with the wet cloths. I let myself relax because their gentleness didn't hurt me at all. My eyes started to get heavy again and I had to force myself to stay awake and in the hunched over sitting position I was in.

"You alright, man?" Victor asked after a few minutes.

"Yeah," I drawled out groggily. "Just tired. It's been a long day." *Or a long four months*, I thought.

"I understand," he told me softly. "You know you can lay down, right?"

Eliana noted my hesitation and said, "Lay down, Christian." She didn't wait for my response before helping me lay on my stomach. They both kept dabbing my back with the washcloths and my eyes slowly started closing.

After a few minutes, my breathing slowed, and they assumed I was asleep. "He's never going to have a normal life, is he?" Eliana asked Victor.

Victor sighed. "No, he's not. Even if I did figure something out, he won't be able to live the rest of his life normally."

"I love him," she whispered so softly I barely heard it. "Even though I hardly know him, I love him. I won't be able to live with myself if anything happens to him. Victor," she choked on a sob, "promise me you'll take care of him at the camp. Be the one person he feels he can go to when he is in need."

"I promise I'll try," Victor whispered. "But why do I get the feeling that there's a reason you're telling me this?"

She hesitated before telling him, "Because he told me that he will kill himself if he ever gets the chance," as she cried. "He would rather die than kill others."

"Kill himself?" he asked, clearly alarmed to learn this. "I knew he would do anything to prevent my dad from turning him into a weapon, but...kill himself?!"

I adjusted my position, trying to get more comfortable, and they paused their conversation. "Let's let him rest," Victor said as he stood from the edge of the bed. "If today was hard on him, these next few weeks are going to be a shock."

They both left and I heard the door shut behind them. My heart sunk at the thought of what the next few weeks would be like; at the thought of them being worse than today. *What could possibly be worse than being tortured every day?* I thought to myself before the darkness claimed me.

CHAPTER THIRTY-FIVE

Victor and Eliana woke me up a few hours later with food in their hands. They helped me sit up and seemed happy to see that my back was starting to heal and would most likely be finished by nightfall. They both sat on the small bed with me, in a small circle, and smiled.

"We figured that since this is your last 'normal' day, you deserved a treat," Victor told me as he opened the box of pizza from Pizza Hut.

The wonderful smell of freshly baked pizza filled the cell and my mouth watered. We each took a slice of cheese pizza and bit into it at the same time. We all moaned as our tastebuds were hit with the flavorful cheese and tomato sauce.

"Pizza Hut is without a doubt my favorite pizza," Eliana said once she swallowed.

Victor and I moaned in agreement.

They picked up cups and bottles of soda from the floor and we poured ourselves drinks. "I feel like we should make a toast, but don't know what to toast to," Eliana said with a smile.

"To Christian," Victor said. "Because he has taught me the true meaning of hope and friendship."

I smiled as we raised our red solo cups in a toast before taking a sip. "And to you two, for giving me that hope and friendship."

We raised our cups again before Eliana smiled and leaned her head on my shoulder. "And to the best boyfriend ever, my literal guardian angel."

I kissed her head and we both tapped our cups together while Victor grinned at us.

"Grandma told me I can stay the night tonight," Eliana said after a moment. "If that's okay with you." She lifted her head to look at me.

I wrapped my arm around her and squeezed. "Of course."

"I'm spending the night too, but won't stay in here," Victor said. "I'm not going to school anymore and dad wants to leave early in the morning, so I figured I would stay here tonight."

I nodded. "Makes sense."

After we all finished eating and our stomachs were full, I got up to take a shower. I felt disgusting with the dried blood on my back, pants, and even in my pants.

I took my pants and underwear off before looking at my back in the mirror. It looked worse than it was now. Thanks to the fast healing, the blood was almost the only thing left.

I stepped into the shower and turned the water on hot, enjoying the last hot shower I would have for who knew how long. I washed my hair and body before turning off the water and stepping out.

I put on sweatpants and a t-shirt after examining my back one more time. There were scars, but it barely hurt and didn't look nearly as bad. After I walked out of the bathroom, Eliana walked into it with an overnight bag to change into her pjs.

Victor was no longer in the room and I sat on the bed before pouring myself another cup of soda. I took a sip as I waited for Eliana.

It didn't take her long before she stepped out of the bathroom in heart covered pants and a matching pink shirt that had the words 'kiss me, I'm cute' on it. I laughed at her embarrassed blush as she came over. I pulled her to me by her hips and she straddled my lap as she wrapped her arms around my neck.

"You're very cute, angel," I said before kissing her. She kissed me back and I moaned into her mouth. She took the opportunity to snake her tongue into my mouth and swirled it around mine.

She ground her hips against me, and I groaned in pleasure and longing. Pulling at the hem of my shirt, she lifted it enough to slide her hands underneath and press them against my stomach.

I pulled back and nuzzled her neck with my nose, making her moan. I opened my eyes enough to see Angelica standing by the door and looking through the glass at us-at me. She looked shocked as her eyes met mine before scurrying away from the door.

I looked at the spot she was standing for a moment, feeling slightly guilty. Eliana sensed my pause and pulled back to look at me. "What's wrong?"

I stared at the door for another second before looking at her. "Nothing. Everything's fine," I told her with a forced smile.

"You sure you're okay?" she asked as she took one of her hands from under my shirt and to my cheek.

I nodded. "Everything's fine."

She kissed me one more time before getting off my lap and sitting next to me. "Did Lisa leave already?" I asked her.

"No, she would have checked in if she did."

As if on cue, Lisa knocked on the door before opening it. She smiled when she saw us in our pjs and said, "I'm leaving. Just wanted to make sure you two were okay."

We both nodded and told her we were fine. "See you tomorrow," Eliana told her grandmother.

Lisa lingered at the door, a flash of sadness and guilt crossed her face when she looked at me. I tried to smile, to show her I was okay, but she saw right through my lie. I was not okay; I was in pain, angry, and sad I had to leave my new friends tomorrow.

She watched for one more minute before closing the door and leaving us alone for the night.

Eliana rested her head on my shoulder and sighed. "I'm tired, but don't want to go to sleep yet."

"What do you want to do then," I asked as I put my arm around her, pulling her closer.

"As long as I'm with you, anything," she said honestly.

I let my wings come out, remembering that I had a shirt with slits on it. I curled my right wing around her and she gasped in surprise before gently stroking the delicate feathers resting on her shoulder.

"I love you," I told her as I watched her.

Her head jerked back to look at me. "What?"

I laughed and kissed her head. "I love you."

She smiled and blushed, seeming surprised and happy to hear me say those words. Little did she know, I heard her say those words when she thought I was asleep.

She looked up at me as her eyes glistened. "I love you too."

I kissed her nose before we settled on the bad and she rested her head on my chest as I wrapped my arm around her. Our legs tangled together and we both sighed in contentment.

"I don't want to say goodbye tomorrow," she told me as she traced circles on my chest.

"Me neither."

We talked late into the night, not mentioning the dreaded day ahead of us, until both of us fell asleep from exhaustion.

CHAPTER THIRTY-SIX

Dr. Rodriguez was standing silently by the door when I finally opened my eyes the next morning. He was leaning against the doorframe, making me assume he had been standing there for a while. He noticed me watching him and pushed himself up.

"Time to get ready," he said after clearing his throat. "I left clothes in the bathroom for you."

Eliana stirred in my arms and looked up at me once she awoke. "What's happening?" she asked groggily.

"Christian has to get ready to leave," Dr. Rodriguez told her as she turned to look at him. He stood there for another moment before saying, "Be ready in ten," and walking out.

Eliana and I slowly sat up and stretched out our achy muscles before I got out of bed. "I'll be ready in five minutes," I told her with an expressionless face.

She nodded and I went into the bathroom. The same clothes from the day he took me to the camp were folded and sitting on the toilet seat. I changed into them, tied my boots, and brushed my teeth within five minutes, as I said.

She looked up when I opened the door and broke down into sobs when she saw me in uniform. I went over to her and hugged her to me. I rubbed her back and kissed her head as she cried into my chest. She wrapped her arms around my waist, hugging me tightly.

"Don't go," she said into my shirt.

"I don't have a choice. If it were up to me, I wouldn't be going," I told her softly.

"Time to go," Dr. Rodriguez said by the doorway. Eliana started crying harder and he sighed as he rubbed the back of his neck. "I guess you could come along to drop them off," he told her.

She pulled back from me and wiped her tears as she turned to face him. "Really?" she asked with a sniffle.

He nodded.

"Can you give me a minute to change?"

He nodded again. "You have five minutes."

She hurriedly made her way to the bathroom and closed the door behind her.

"Alis and Angelica want to say goodbye. Let's do that while we wait for her."

I nodded and followed him to their cell next to mine. "Say your goodbyes," he told me after he opened the door.

I walked inside and saw Alis standing in the middle of the room, waiting, while Angelica laid on her bed and wouldn't look at me.

Alis came over and hugged me. "We'll miss you," she told me. "You're like a baby brother to me, so be careful."

"I'll try," I replied with a smile.

And remember to stay in touch, okay? She telepathically reminded me with a smirk.

I nodded and made my way over to Angelica, who still wouldn't acknowledge my presence. Sighing, I sat on the edge of the bed next to her.

"You going to make me leave without a goodbye?" I asked.

No response.

"Look," I sighed. "I'm really sorry. I never meant to hurt you. I admit that I made the mistake of misjudging how you felt about me. I should have made it clear that I didn't see it the way you did. Can you please forgive me?"

Her eyes slid over to me and locked onto mine. "I'll try. It just...might take time," she told me honestly.

"Can I at least get a hug before I leave?"

She gave me a small smile and nodded. I leaned over and wrapped my arm around her. She leaned into me and rested her head on my shoulder as she hesitantly wrapped her arms around my middle. "No matter how mad I am at you, I will still miss you," she whispered in my ear.

I let go of her and pulled back to look her in the eye. "I know. How could you not?" I told her with a grin.

"Cocky bastard." She laughed and punched my shoulder.

I laughed with her before standing up and heading towards the door. I said goodbye to Alis one more time and walked out the door to meet Eliana and Dr. Rodriguez.

He had the cuffs and chains in his hands, and I put my wrists out to him. He seemed surprised, but locked them on my wrists.

"What are those for?" Eliana asked.

"These chains block Christian from using his abilities. They also ensure he won't escape on us."

"Oh," was all she said before we started heading towards the garage.

Victor was leaning against the black SUV with his arms crossed over his chest as he waited. He pushed himself off when he saw us, and his eyes immediately went to the chains connecting me to his father. His eyes traveled back up to mine and I shrugged as if to say, *What can I do?*

He looked sad, but kept his face expressionless as he moved to get in the passenger seat. Dr. Rodriguez opened the back door and Eliana slid across before I climbed in after her. "Buckle up," Dr. Rodriguez said as he closed the door and got in the driver's seat.

I had trouble getting buckled due to the chains tangling with the seatbelt. Eliana noticed my struggling and leaned over to unravel the chains from the seatbelt and clicking it into place before doing her own.

I smiled over at her as Dr. Rodriguez pulled the car out of the garage. A guard, not the same as last time, met us at the gate. "Where you heading, Sergeant?"

"To take Christian and Victor to the camp for the next few weeks," Dr. Rodriguez answered.

He laughed. "Well, I wish them all the luck. Have a good day, Sir."

"Thanks. You too."

The gate opened and we pulled through. We passed the other gate where curious tourists were gathered. "I bet all of those alien enthusiasts would be shocked to find out there aren't aliens, but angels," Eliana said as we drove by.

Dr. Rodriguez looked back at her in the rearview mirror. "Who says we don't have aliens? There's more to Area 51 than what you have seen."

Her eyes widened. "You mean, aliens are also here?"

"I don't know," he said with a shrug. "I'm in charge of the angels. I don't have access to some of the buildings here, so aliens could very well be here."

"But I thought you were in charge of the whole base?"

"I am in charge of half of it. Dr. Patterson is in charge of the other half and is much more secretive than me."

"Isn't Dr. Patterson the man who shocked me a few days ago?" I asked.

He nodded. "He had a theory for his own research and wanted to do that test on one of my own subjects."

"But you have no idea what is going on with his research?" I raised my eyebrow in question.

"Nope," he said as we pulled onto the gravel road that led to the camp. He parked where he did last time and got out of the car before opening my door. He pulled on my chains after I unbuckled my seatbelt and I got out as Eliana and Victor opened their own doors.

We met them at the front of the SUV and started walking towards Sergeant Kirkwood's cabin. A few recruits standing by catcalled and looked Eliana up and down as we walked by. She was obviously uncomfortable, and I grabbed her hand and squeezed.

"They're just hormonal men who haven't had sex in a while, don't let it get to you," I whispered in her ear.

She giggled and squeezed my hand back. "Don't let go," she told me quietly.

"Never," I replied. However, Dr. Rodriguez yanked on the chains without looking back, making me lose my footing. I would have fallen if it wasn't for Eliana, who caught me by my arm.

She glared at the back of his head as we continued walking. Derek rounded the corner as we approached the cabin and smiled. He ignored Dr. Rodriguez as he looked at me and said, "Hey, Christian! Who's your friend?"

I smiled at how he showed his dislike for Dr. Rodriguez as I replied, "Hey, Derek. This is Eliana."

"His girlfriend," Eliana pointed out as she reached her free hand towards him.

"Ah. You're lucky to have him," he said as they shook hands. "I'm Derek."

"Are the others ready?" Dr. Rodriguez butted in.

Derek turned to him. "Yes, they are waiting inside. I had to run an errand before coming, so I'm just arriving."

We all walked in together, and Derek closed the door when we were all inside. He walked over to stand along the wall to the right next to Ben and Robbie. "Alright," Sergeant Kirkwood said from where he was standing in front of us. "The boys have read over the documents and have a few questions."

Dr. Rodriguez nodded. "I would be worried if they didn't. Ask away."

Ben stepped forward as he held the binder of papers in his hands. "So, on page 120, there is mention of him being able to wield a sword. Is that right?"

Dr. Rodriguez nodded. "Yes. He has his own sword and has been trained by me personally."

"Do you put the drug into his system while he is using it?"

"Yes. I tell him he may act normal, but not to kill me as we spar. He sparred with Victor without them, but I wouldn't recommend it."

"Did you bring his sword?" Robbie asked.

"It's in the car with his and Victor's belong-ings."

"Another question," Derek said, "what would you like us to focus on?"

"Aiming with his abilities, flying in different patterns, learning drills and codes, hand to hand combat, keep him training with a sword. After a few days, when he gets settled, he can participate in morning training with everyone."

"How do we do that with the chains?" Ben asked. "It will make everyone wonder."

"Once he realizes there is no chance of escap-ing here, you can disconnect the chains and leave the cuffs on so he can't use his abilities. Victor will also be with you and can guide you through everything," he explained as he gestured to Victor, who was standing next to him.

"One more thing," Robbie added. "On page 207, you say-"

Dr. Rodriguez interrupts him quickly, "I'm going to stop you from saying what I think you will ask. Page 207 has a footnote on it, correct?"

Robbie looked down at the page. "No, Sir, it doesn't."

"What?" he asked as he looked at the page. "Ugh. It didn't print. Well, that information is classi-fied to only a select few individuals. Not even Victor knows of it."

"Oh. Well, can I ask you about it later?" Rob-bie asked.

Dr. Rodriguez nodded and turned to look back at me. "Should we go get their things and check out your new cabin?" he asked them.

They all agreed, and we walked outside and to the car. Dr. Rodriguez unlocked and opened the trunk as we neared. There were two bags, one Victor's and one mine, and my sword and strap for my back.

Dr. Rodriguez handed me the strap and told me to put it on. I put it over my head and had to pull the chains through it to get it on properly.

He handed me my sword next, and I slid it into the sheath on my back. It surprised both me and Victor when he handed Victor a sword and strap too.

"What's this for?" Victor asked as he held the sword.

"I figured you would be the one to train Christian in sword fighting, so you need your own sword to do that."

Victor nodded as he attached the sword to the strap after putting it over his head. We grabbed our bags and followed them to the cabin we would be staying in. It was on the far end of the camp, away from most of the activity going on around the place, which made sense.

Robbie opened the door and smiled. "Welcome to your home for the next few weeks. You two are sharing that bunk," he told us as he gestured to the bunk bed to the right.

"I'll take the bottom, you take the top," Victor said sternly. I forgot about his plan to not be nice to me in order to not raise suspicions.

I nodded and threw the bag onto the top bunk as he did the same with his on the bottom. We turned to look at each other and if I didn't know any better, I'd say he hated my very existence. His eyes were dark and cold as he glared at me before turning to the others.

"Could you maybe show us how far along he is at sword fighting?" Sergeant Kirkwood asked Dr. Rodriguez.

Dr. Rodriguez nodded. "Shall we go to the building?"

Everyone nodded and we went to the building that I was shown off in last time. Once everyone was inside and the door was shut, Dr. Rodriguez handed a syringe to Victor. "I'll have you do it since you will be doing it for the next few weeks."

Victor nodded as he walked over to me, his eyes cold as ice. He injected the drug into my neck as he pulled my head to the side by my hair. Since his back was facing the others, he apologized with his eyes.

I understood. I really did. He was doing this to protect me; to ensure I had a chance of making it out of here alive.

He stepped back and waited for the drugs to take effect. Once they were, he looked over at his father and asked, "You want to spar with him?"

Dr. Rodriguez shook his head. "You can do it."

Victor pulled his sword out of the sheath across his back as he made his way over to me. He told me to take my sword out, but before I was able to, a loud bang was heard outside.

Everyone froze when the door opened and five men came in, all pointing guns at us.

CHAPTER THIRTY-SEVEN

None of us had guns. The only weapons were the swords Victor and I held, and they were no match against the five guns pointed at our heads. The cuffs were still around my wrists, so I couldn't use my abilities.

"You five, against the wall," one ordered everyone except Victor and I. They all held their hands up as they made their way over to the wall to the left.

"You two, sheath your weapons," another told us as he pointed his gun at us.

We sheathed our swords to our backs before holding our hands up in surrender. "Who are you guys?" Victor asked. "What do you want?"

The one holding me at gunpoint jerked his chin towards me. "Give us him."

I glanced over at Victor to see if this was his idea of 'getting me out'. He noticed and shook his head. My heart sunk.

"What?! Why?!" Derek asked from where he stood by the wall, clearly outraged.

"Just do what we say, and nobody gets hurt."

"No way will we hand over one of our own," Ben yelled over.

The one in front of me sighed. "Then you give us no choice." He reached into his pocket and pulled out what I thought was a bomb.

"Wait!" I yelled before he blew us all up. "I'll go with you. Just leave them out of it."

He smiled and motioned for me to go over to him with his finger. I did as he instructed, and he grabbed the chains around my wrists once I was in reach. He checked to make sure they were attached and once satisfied, he jerked me, so my face was inches from his. "No tricks."

I nodded and looked him in the eye. "No tricks."

He seemed satisfied and started pulling me behind him. I locked eyes with Eliana, and she looked so scared. *I love you*, I sent to her before being pulled out of the building.

I stopped in my tracks, shocked when I saw at least thirty men with guns outside and the entire camp on their knees along the buildings. They all watched as we walked by and to one of the cars. The man opened the back door and threw me inside.

I scrambled back when he threw the bomb looking thing inside with me and closed the door. Nobody else got inside and I panicked before it started to spin. A white mist started filling the car and I tried to pull the handle on the door.

It wouldn't budge.

I freaked out and started pounding on the window, but it was no use. The mist started to work its way into my lungs and I started crying as I felt hopelessness creeping through me. My fighting lessened as I collapsed across the seat and felt myself start to become paralyzed. My eyes closed soon after, but kept leaking tears as I laid there.

They opened the doors a few minutes later, laughing. "He put up a better fight than most. But even he couldn't fight the smoke bomb's effects."

One grabbed my face and shook it. "Not so tough now, are ya?" the man asked.

"Alright, boys! Let's go!" one ordered, and they put me in the middle seat, with two others on either side, before they started driving away.

* * * * *

I DRIFTED BETWEEN CONCIOUSNESS and unconsciousness for hours. The two guys on either side of me kept pinching my cheeks, pulling my hair, and I think they even took selfies with me at one point, but couldn't be sure.

They carried my limp and paralyzed body somewhere and handcuffed me to a pole a few minutes later. I knew it had to be a boat of some kind because the ground rocked back and forth. I felt like I was left like that for days. They came in once in a while, when I started to gain consciousness, and would feed me something before pressing a cloth to my face to make me pass out again.

"Almost there, big guy," a man told me as he fed me one time. I didn't know what it was that they fed me and didn't think I wanted to. All I knew was that it was food and was the only thing giving me the strength to even get close to consciousness.

Almost where? I wanted to ask. *Where are you taking me?* Of course, there was no answer as he shoved a cloth into my face and made me black out once more.

CHAPTER THIRTY-EIGHT

I was locked in a small cage as well as chained up when I was able to fully wake up. Two men with guns stood guard in front of me and whenever I asked them where I was, they would just bang on the cage and tell me to shut up.

I was tired, hungry, and my muscles ached from being in a confined space. After a few hours, a man walked in and the guards saluted as he approached my cage. He told them to leave as he bent down in front of me and looked me in the eyes. "What are you?" he whispered in a strong Russian accent.

I only glared at him, which made him laugh. "My spies tell me you have…abilities. That they aren't sure if you are human or not. So, what are you?" he repeated.

When I didn't respond, he kicked the cage and yelled, "WHAT ARE YOU?!"

"I don't know," I answered quietly. "I thought I was a normal human being until my 18th birthday."

"What happened?" he asked, starting to calm down now that I was talking.

"I don't know! Weird things started happening around me. Objects floated when I was near, I healed faster than ever seen before, and I could hear things that I couldn't before."

"Did they ever tell you what they think you are?" he asked as he bent down in front of me again.

"An angel. They think I'm an angel, or at least part of one. But I think they only think that because of the wings."

"Wings?" he asked with a raised eyebrow. "What wings?"

"Let me guess, your spies didn't tell you I have wings?" I asked with a raised eyebrow of my own. I sighed when he looked surprised. "I have wings and they resemble an angel's, so that's why they think I am one."

He stood up in one swift movement and made me jump when he yelled, "Demyan! *Idi syuda seychas zhe!*"

I had no idea what that meant, but a moment later, a boy around my age came in. He didn't seem fazed when his eyes focused on me, in a cage. He looked up at the man and asked, "*Da*, papa?"

He motioned for him to look at me. "This boy is what my spies have been telling me about. He is the secret American weapon that we now have our hands on."

"What does this have to do with me, papa?" he asked him in his thick accent.

"He needs to be taken care of. Such as let out to go to the bathroom, be fed and watered, and given showers when he needs them. Can you take care of that for me?"

The boy nodded. "Yes, papa."

"I will guide you on what to do these next few days, but after that, I am trusting you."

"I understand."

"Let's let him go to the bathroom now," he said before turning to me. He kicked the cage, making me jump again, before saying, "No running away, little angel. You understand?"

I nodded out of fear and he unlocked the cage. I crawled out and pushed myself off the ground to stand. However, he came up to me and kneed me in the stomach, making me drop down again. "No standing!" he yelled.

I glared up at him as I held the area where he hit. He used so much force, I didn't think I would be getting up anytime soon anyway. He picked up the chain that was still connected to my wrist and pulled. I was forced to follow him, like an animal, on my hands and knees.

He led me to the small bathroom to the left of where my cage was and told me I had five minutes to do my business before slamming the door shut. I sighed and rubbed my hands over my face before going to the bathroom.

Once I finished, I splashed some water on my face in the small single sink. I looked at myself in the dirty mirror and saw my fearful eyes. I was so scared. I didn't know what they wanted with me or how tortured I would be. All I knew was that I would be in that small cage almost 24/7 with little food and water.

He banged on the door, startling me. "You better be on your knees once I open this door, or we will have problems!" he yelled from the other side.

I rolled my eyes, but did as he said. I got down on my knees and hung my head as I looked at the dirty cement floor. I was so embarrassed by how he was treating me and how I basically did whatever was asked of me out of fear.

He opened the door and seemed satisfied with how I was obeying him. "See that, son?" he asked the boy. "The Americans used drugs to get him to listen. We use fear and pain to control him." He paused a moment before saying, "Let's get him back in the cage."

He pulled the chain, and I had no choice but to follow, on my hands and knees. I paused at the opening of the cage, not wanting to go into the confined space. He grabbed ahold of my hair and pulled my head up, making me cry out. "Get in," he hissed. "NOW!"

He let go of my hair and kicked me in the stomach before I got to move. I cried out and curled in a ball. Tears streamed down my cheeks as I held where he kicked. I could barely breathe and had to force my lungs to suck in air.

"On second thought," he said as he bent down in front of me. "Why don't you let me see those wings you were telling me about?"

I glared at him as he stood and turned to his son. "He told me he has wings. Can you believe that?"

"No."

"Me neither. Which is why I want to see them myself." He looked down at where I was still glaring at him. "If you don't do it, there are many worse things I can do than kick you."

I knew he wasn't lying because his eyes gave away that he was thinking about all the ways he could torture me. I slowly pushed myself up to my knees, grimacing at every movement, and willed my wings to come out.

They both gasped and widened their eyes. "Wow," the boy said.

They walked over and touched them. They both commented on how soft they felt and continued to stroke the white feathers. The man suddenly pulled a feather off, making me jump and my eyes water.

He didn't seem to mind or care as he studied the feather between his thumb and index finger. "Beautiful," he said. "Tell me, did it hurt when they came in?"

I didn't know why he was asking, but answered, "Yeah."

"If you could go back and change what happened. Having no abilities, wings, nothing. Would you?" he asked me.

"Yes. It has ruined my life."

"How so?" he asked curiously.

"Well, for starters, I wouldn't be here."

He chuckled. "That is true."

Christian, Alis' voice sighed in my head. *It's day 30 since you've been kidnapped and not hearing a response. Just please reply if you hear me.*

30 days?! I yelled back to her.

"Get in your cage," he ordered me.

I did as he said after retracting my wings and he slammed it closed behind me. Once it was locked, he told his son to bring me food before they both left, leaving me alone.

Alis? Can you hear me?

There was a pause before she answered, *Yes, I can hear you. What happened?*

Well, apparently, they kept me unconscious for 30 days. They are keeping me locked inside a small cage…I think I'm in Russia. Everyone here has Russian accents.

Are you okay? Are they hurting you? She asked worriedly.

Not too bad…yet. They just let me out to go to the bathroom and now I'm alone again…in a freaking dog cage.

There was a pause before she said, *Eliana wants to try to talk to you.*

I focused on imagining Eliana, her long brown hair and bright blue eyes. I then sent, *Can you hear me, angel?*

It took her a while, but I patiently waited until she said, *Christian?*

Even her thoughts sounded like she was crying. *Yes, baby. I'm here,* I answered.

Are you okay?

I'm okay now that I'm talking to you, I told her honestly. *How's Dr. Rodriguez handling this?* I asked both of them.

He's extremely mad and upset, but he doesn't seem as concerned about it as we thought. It's almost like he's convinced he will get you back.

How's Victor? I asked.

He's been up to something as well, Alis replied. *We don't know what, but he's been talking to someone a lot. Always on the phone, sneaking away, and stuff like that.*

The door opened again, and the man's son walked inside. I told them to hang on as he approached the cage, eyeing me wearily. He had a plate of food in his hands and my stomach growled in response.

He slid the plate under the bars of the cage before backing away, as if he was scared of me. He watched as I moved to pick up the plate and positioned myself to eat without the fear of choking. There were two chicken legs, mashed potatoes, and green beans on the plate, and I devoured it like a starved animal.

Once I finished, I pushed the plate back under the bars and it slid over to where he was still standing. He looked at me with wide eyes before bending down to pick it up. "Are you thirsty?" he asked me.

I nodded and he pulled a bottle of water out of his backpack before walking over. He seemed to think about how he would get it to me considering it wouldn't fit underneath the bars.

"If you think I'll try to escape, you're wrong. I can't feel my legs and don't have enough energy yet," I told him honestly.

He hesitated another moment before opening the cage door and handing the water bottle to me with a shaky hand. I took it and took a large gulp as he quickly closed and locked the cage.

Christian, you okay? Alis asked.

Yeah. Someone's here with me. Waiting until he leaves.

I watched him as he backed up and kept watching me. We just stared at each other until he finally turned on his heel and walked out the door. I sighed in relief and tried to get in a more comfortable position, but there is no comfortable position when you are in a cage.

Okay. I'm alone again, I told both of them.

Who was with you? Alis asked.

The boy who's supposed to take care of me. He brought me dinner. It's funny, I think he's scared of me, even though I should be the one scared of him.

I took another gulp of water as I waited for a response. My eyelids started to get heavy and I realized that the water had a weird flavor to it. I cursed. The water was drugged.

The water I just drank is drugged. Going to fall asleep soon, I sent them.

Okay, they both replied. *Keep us updated,* Alis told me before I slumped over and blacked out.

CHAPTER THIRTY-NINE

I woke up lying on a cold tile floor. I opened my eyes and looked around. I was in a different building that had a cage, almost like one you would see in an aviary or the bird section in a zoo, that took up half of it. A cage I was inside.

I looked around and noticed a room that was connected to it behind me. A hanging hammock bed was above me and required me to fly up to it. I stood up and looked around some more. There was a small cubby in the corner that appeared to have blankets, clothes, and a mini fridge.

I walked over to it and opened the fridge. Bottles of water were inside as well as cups of yogurt and fruits. I closed it and opened the door connected to the cage. It was a bathroom, with a shower, toilet, and sink inside.

I looked over my shoulder before grabbing some clothes out of the cubby and walking into the bathroom. Who knew if they cleaned me these past 30 days? I felt disgusting and got undressed before getting into the shower.

I let the water cascade over my sore muscles for a few minutes before shampooing my hair and rinsing my body.

I turned off the water and grabbed the towel hanging outside the shower. I dried myself and put the sweatpants on before looking at my reflection in the mirror above the sink.

Having not shaved in over 30 days, I had grown a small beard. I took the razor that was laying on the sink and shaved the best I could without shaving cream.

Once I felt refreshed and clean, I put the white t-shirt on and walked out of the bathroom. I looked up at the hammock hanging above me and decided to check it out.

I summoned my wings and flew up to it. I laid on it on my stomach and it rocked at the sudden movement. I let my wings drape over my back and closed my eyes before trying to talk to Alis. *Alis? You there?*

Yeah. I'm here, she answered.

I'm afraid to know how long I have been asleep, I admitted.

Only a day, she answered. *Victor wants to try to talk to you.*

Alright, I replied. I focused on trying to imagine Victor, his brown skin, black hair, and green eyes. *Victor? You there?*

I waited a while before I got his response, *Can you hear me, Christian?*

Yep.

This is cool. I wanted to tell you that we know where you are and are sending some troops to get you.

How do you know where I am? I asked curiously.

I sensed some hesitation before he responded, *Remember when dad said there was some classified information that even I didn't know about? Well, turns out that dad put a tracker in you during the last time he took samples. I guess it's a good thing we know this now and not when we got you out of there.*

There was a tracker inside of me? What the fuck? He seriously put a tracker in me like I was a fucking dog?

Where am I? I asked him. *Am I really in Russia?*

Yes. You are at a Russian military base on the east coast of Russia.

"You okay up there?" a voice asked from below me, still outside of the cage.

It scared me and I flipped off the hammock and almost hit the floor if it wasn't for my wings splaying out and softening the landing. The voice laughed, hard, and I looked back and saw the boy standing there.

"Sorry. I didn't mean to scare you that bad," he told me with a small laugh.

I pushed myself off the floor and retracted my wings. "It's cool," I told him with a shrug.

"This is a much better cage than what you were in," he admitted as he looked around.

I shrugged again. "It's alright. It's a cage, keeping me locked in here."

Christian? You there? Victor asked.

Not alone. Talk later, I answered.

"True," he admitted.

I crossed my arms over my chest before asking, "What's your name?"

He seemed shocked that I asked him a question. "What?"

"I figured that since you and I will be seeing each other for a while, I should know your name."

"Demyan," he said.

"I'm Christian," I told him.

"Why are you talking to me?" he asked, eying me wearily.

"I can't stay quiet forever. I need someone to talk to and you seem like someone who'd be willing to keep me company."

"Why me?"

"I don't really want to talk to your dad."

"I see," he said with a smile. "Well, it's good to know your name, Christian."

"Yours too, Demyan. What does your dad plan to do with me?" I asked him.

"I don't know. He doesn't tell me his plans. I only know that I'm supposed to take care of you."

All of a sudden, I felt a warm liquid fall out of my nose. I reached up to wipe it and found blood on my thumb. My nose was bleeding? I never had a nosebleed before, not unless I was hurt.

"You're bleeding," he said when he saw it.

"Yeah…" I said as I wiped it again and held my head back.

"Here, let me go get something," he told me before rushing out.

I continued holding it, unsure of what to do because I've never been in this situation before. He came back again with a box of tissues and tried to hand them to me. However, he couldn't because of the bars of the cage.

"Come in here. I promise I won't hurt you," I told him.

He hesitated only a minute before opening the door and coming over to me. He helped me sit and handed me some tissues to hold to my nose.

"Has this happened before?" he asked worriedly.

"No. I've never had a bloody nose before."

"Huh," he said as he helped me hold tissues up to my nose. "Maybe it's something bad…"

"I hope not," I told him.

"When's the last time you've used your abilities?"

"Before I was brought here," I answered, not wanting to give away that I knew how long it had been since I was taken from the camp.

"Did you ever go for a long period of time without using them?"

"I went two weeks and when I was able to use them, I lost control. Do you think this has to do with not using them?"

"It could be. I'm not a scientist, but I have a feeling that this is how your body tells you that you need to use them. You have to use them soon."

"But how? Your father would never let me use my abilities."

"I'll come up with something. I promise," he told me as he put a hand on my arm. He then checked my nose and declared that it had stopped bleeding as he helped me wipe the blood off my face and hands.

"Thanks," I told him.

"Demyan!" his father's voiced boomed from the doorway. We both turned to look and saw him striding over. "What the hell are you thinking?! Get out of there!"

"He was bleeding, dad. You told me he was my responsibility, so I'm taking care of him."

"I don't care!" his father yelled. "He could have escaped or hurt you!"

"I knew he wouldn't though!" Demyan said as he got up and walked out, leaving me sitting with bloody tissues and the box around me.

His dad quickly locked the cage and got up into Demyan's face. "Never go in there again. Do you understand me?"

Demyan nodded. "Yes, papa. I understand."

"Why is he bleeding?"

"That's what we were trying to figure out. I think it's because he needs to use his abilities. It's been way too long since he's used them."

"It's a trick, son," his father told him. "He wants you to think that so we will give him access to his abilities."

"I don't think so..." Demyan admitted.

"We will talk about this later," he told him before dragging him out of the building.

I sighed and leaned against the bars of the cage behind me. *You are going to have to tell your troops to hurry,* I told Victor. *Something is wrong with me.*

How so? he asked

My nose randomly started bleeding and my head is pounding, I told him as I held my head in my hands in agony.

It's probably due to you not using your abilities, he told me. *The troops should be there in a few days. Can you handle that?*

I'll try.

Alright, I'll let you go. Get some rest, we'll talk to you later.

I looked up at the hammock hanging above me and wondered if I actually wanted to use my energy to get up there. I groaned as I pushed myself off the floor, summoned my wings, and made it up in one flap.

I laid on my stomach and closed my eyes as my headache kept getting worse by the minute. It hurt like hell. The pain was so bad that I didn't know what to do with myself. I got up and landed on the ground, retracting my wings as I hurried over to the bathroom.

I barely had time to bend over the toilet before vomiting the little contents in my stomach. I sat on the floor and held my head in my hands, praying for the whole ordeal to end.

After a few minutes of dry heaving over the toilet, Demyan's voice sounded from outside the cage. "Christian?"

I pushed myself up from the floor and had to brace myself on the walls to keep myself from falling as I walked out. I leaned against the wall as I looked at him.

"You look like…shit," he said when he saw me.

"Thanks for pointing that out," I told him. "I feel like it too."

"I wish I could help, but dad thinks it's a trick to let you use your abilities."

"I know. I understand," I replied softly. I suddenly felt sick once again and ran to the bathroom to throw up. Since I didn't have anything left in my stomach, it was red bile. Blood.

Oh God. Something was definitely wrong with me. Vomiting blood wasn't a good sign, was it? *Victor?!* I practically yelled in my head.

Yeah? What's up?

I'm not sure if I am going to be able to wait a few days…

What?! Why?! he asked in a panicked tone.

I just threw up….blood. I'm so weak, I can barely stand. I don't know how long I have, I told him honestly.

Shit, he swore. *I'll try to figure something out. Keep me updated.*

"You okay in there?" Demyan asked.

"No," I answered as I pushed myself up. I walked out of the bathroom, holding onto the wall the entire time, and met his worrisome gaze. "Look, I need you to get your dad and bring him here. Something is really wrong with me and if he doesn't do anything, I don't know how much time I have left."

"Are you dying?" he quietly asked after a moment.

"I think so," I told him honestly.

It then seemed to register with him how bad the situation was. In a matter of a few minutes, I had gone from a simple nose bleed to vomiting blood, which wasn't a good sign. He rushed out of the building without another word, and I slumped against the wall. I leaned my left shoulder against it as I waited for him to return, hopefully with his dad.

A man walked inside the building with Demyan, not his father. "My father isn't here right now, so my older brother is the next option," Demyan explained with a shrug. "In fact, I think he's better, considering he's a doctor."

"Doctor in training," his brother growled as he looked down at me. "You look like hell," he said as he opened the door to the cage.

"Leo," Demyan hissed. "You're not allowed in there without papa's permission."

"How else am I supposed to check him out, Demyan?" Leo retorted.

Demyan just sighed in response as he paced outside the cage as Leo walked over to me. "Go outside and stand watch," he ordered Demyan, who nodded and walked out of the building.

He kneeled in front of me and looked me over. "Well, you certainly aren't lying when you say something is wrong. You look like death."

I only looked up at him, completely at his mercy. If he wanted to torture or kill me, there wasn't anything I could do to prevent it. He knew that too. He knew he could do anything and yet somehow, I knew he wouldn't.

"What hurts?" he asked.

"Everything," I told him. "My head is pounding, my muscles ache, I had a bloody nose earlier, and I am now throwing up blood."

He cursed under his breath and told me what I already knew, "Sounds like your body is shutting down. However, something has to be causing it. I have a feeling it isn't cancer, so what could it be?" he wondered to himself. He noticed the cuff on my right wrist and nodded to it. "What's that for?"

"It blocks my abilities," I answered with a cough. "I think that's the reason my body is shutting down. I haven't used my abilities in…a while and it's building up inside me with no way out."

"What happens if I take that off?" he asked.

"I don't know. The last time I went a long period of time without using my abilities, I almost took down the building. I lost control as the power took over my entire body."

"How long was that period of time?"

"Two weeks," I answered.

"Shit. It's been over month since you've last used them."

I widened my eyes, feigning surprise, and shrieked, "A month?!"

He nodded. "I heard you have wings. Can I see them?"

I nodded and summoned my wings. He gasped and looked at me with wide eyes. I expected his response, everyone had that response, but he gasped for a different reason. I could see it in his eyes. However, he didn't say anything. He blinked and cleared his throat. "They're magnificent. May I…touch them?"

I nodded again and he ran his hands over my right wing. He was fascinated and seemed speechless for a few moments until my nose started bleeding again. I reached up and held it as he moved to grab the tissue box a few feet away.

He helped me hold my head back at the right angle and held tissues up to it. I started crying as I told him, "I've been saying that I would rather die than turn into what they expect me to be, but now that I may be dying, I don't want to. At least, not here. I want to be with my friends."

"I'm so sorry," he whispered with tears in his eyes. "I wish I could help; I really do. But convincing my father to take that cuff off is like convincing a mountain to move itself. If you want, I could be your friend for the next few hours."

"Few hours?! How much time do you think I have?"

"At the rate you're going? Not long. A day. Two tops."

"Really?" I said with a sob.

"Want me to stay with you?" he asked as he stroked my wing gently.

"Can I be alone for a while? Come back to check on me?"

He nodded in understanding and got up before walking out of the cage. He locked the door and opened the door to walk out of the building. I saw Demyan look up and Leo shake his head, telling him nothing could be done, before it shut.

I broke down into sobs a second later. I moved to lay on my stomach and buried my face into my arms as I cried. *Victor?* I called.

Yes?

Please tell me the troops will be here sooner than you said.

They'll be there tomorrow morning at the earliest, he answered.

How many hours exactly?

About 12. How are you holding up?

A doctor came in to check on me. He says I won't make it much longer. If I don't make it, I want you to be the one who tells Connor and his family.

You'll make it. I'm in the plane with the troop. We'll be there soon.

I wanted to tell him that I was pretty sure I wouldn't make the night, but decided against it as I fell asleep.

CHAPTER FORTY

I woke up every few hours to Demyan and Leo checking on me, but wasn't able to acknowledge their presence. "He's not going to make it much longer," Leo whispered one time. "He's going to die here."

I felt his hand on my shoulder and it got warm as I felt a little bit of energy return in me. I had no idea how he did it, but I felt that if he hadn't done it, I would've died a long time ago.

He did that every time he came in and the energy would slowly leave my body shortly after he left.

In between consciousness, I sent Alis, Eliana, and even Angelica a goodbye and told them I loved them each deeply. I went unconscious before I got their replies.

* * * * *

I FELT DEATH CREEPING CLOSER, waiting for me with an outstretched hand. It was black and cold as it settled over me. There was no end and no beginning. "Christian!" it called to me. "Christian!"

"CHRISTIAN!" Victor screamed as he shook my shoulders, snapping me out of it.

I opened my eyes and saw his face in front of mine with my blurry eyes. "Christian," he sighed when he saw me open them.

"He doesn't look good," Robbie said from behind him.

"He's dying, isn't he?" Ben asked.

"Yeah. It's been way too long since he's used his abilities."

"We have to get out of here," Derek said. "How do we pick him up with his wings still out?"

I closed my eyes and willed my wings to slide into my back before anyone could answer. "Like that," Victor said with a smirk. "Good job, Christian."

"Could we take the cuff off now?" Ben asked.

"No. If we did that, it would be equivalent to setting off a bomb. Nobody near would survive. I have the key on me for when we are able."

Victor picked me up with the help of Derek and they made their way out of the building. Gun shots and shouts were everywhere as Russians fought Americans. All to get me back.

Men pointed at us and we were soon surrounded by Russian soldiers. "*Vzyat ego!*" one shouted as he pointed to me. They all swarmed us, and Robbie and Ben tried to fight them off, but there were too many.

"Take my cuff off," I told Victor. "I'll hold it on until you guys get out of the area."

"We're not leaving you," he replied.

"I'll be fine," I tried to reassure him.

"You sure?" he asked. I nodded and he pulled out the key to the cuff. He unlocked it and I held it on. "Let's go, guys!" he said and everyone on our side seemed to hear and started retreating, pushing and fighting their way out of the area.

He looked back at me one more time before the Russians grabbed me and started dragging me back towards the building. I didn't have it in me to fight and knew that once I took the cuff off, my abilities would be unleashed.

I waited a few more seconds before dropping it from my wrist. They dropped me when they felt my power surrounding them and looked scared.

I screamed as I bent to the floor and braced my arms over my head as my power took control. The building shook and the ground quaked underneath me.

Shouts were all around me, but nobody came near as the power pulsated from me. I continued screaming and the shouts started to stop. I glanced up and saw people were falling to the floor around me.

The walls to the building started to crack and I knew the building was about to go down. The lights flickered before the ceiling collapsed. I threw a shield around myself and closed my eyes as it came down on top of me.

Luckily, my shield held, and I wasn't hurt, or killed. I felt my power start to dwindle and slow down. The last thing I remember is looking up and seeing not just the building I was in, but all the ones around me, were destroyed and collapsed before blacking out.

* * * * *

I HEARD PEOPLE CALLING OUT commands as I was wheeled on a stretcher. "I need a medic stat!" Victor called out. He must have put another cuff around my wrist because I couldn't feel my abilities anymore.

"He took down those buildings like it was nothing!" Robbie exclaimed.

"He didn't do it. The power inside of him did," Victor replied. A medic came over and asked what was wrong. "This is Christian, the one we came here for. He was in the explosion and needs to be checked out."

"Would you boys step out for a moment while I check him out?" he asked. They agreed and left me alone with him. He looked my body over and touched a sore spot on my head before calling them back inside.

"He's perfectly fine. All he has is a small cut on his head. He's lucky, it could have ended a lot worse for him."

"Thank you," Victor told him with a sigh of relief. "Let's get him to the plane."

They put my arms over their shoulders and carried me down a hallway and into what I assumed was an elevator. I heard the doors close, and some-one press a button that dinged before we went up.

When the doors opened, I felt the cool fresh air hit my face and heard the waves of the ocean. We were on a boat, I figured out as I smelled the salty air and felt us slowly rock as they walked forward.

I cracked my eyes open and saw a military plane on the ship. I noticed a few men in uniforms waiting outside the door. They nodded in greeting before leading us inside. About 30 heads turned to look at us as we boarded. The seats were along the sides of the plane, facing each other, and Victor and Derek helped me sit in an open one.

They buckled my seatbelt and sat on either side of me. Robbie and Ben sat next to Derek. They noticed that I was awake, and Derek asked, "How are you, buddy?"

I gave them a small smile and a thumbs up, which made them laugh. "How was your near-death experience?" Ben asked me with a smirk.

"Fantastic," I muttered sarcastically. "When can I do it again?"

They laughed again. "How close were you?" a man asked me from next to Victor and all heads turned to look at him. "To death, I mean."

"A few hours later, I would have been dead. Maybe even minutes away from it."

"What do you remember?" another asked.

"It was black and cold. I saw an arm reaching out for me and it called my name," I answered. "It was as if it was waiting for me. Then, Victor was there and pulled me back to my body," I said as I looked at Victor.

"I knew you were close, but I didn't know you were *that* close," Victor told me.

A moment of silence went by, the only sound being the plane's engine as we flew. I broke it by asking Victor, "What does your dad have to say about all of this?"

"He is eager to have you back and plans to start where we left off," he answered. "He wants you to go to war in four weeks, so we really have to pick up our pace."

"Four weeks?!" I whisper-yelled.

He nodded. *I plan on getting you out before then though,* he told me in my head. *I have to figure out how to get that tracker out.*

Where is it? I asked him.

In your right wrist. It's so small that you probably didn't even notice any pain when he put it there.

I rubbed my right wrist and, now that I knew about it, could feel a small bump on the inside. I would have never noticed it if I didn't know about it.

"I barely notice it," I breathed so only he could hear me.

He smiled softly before clearing his throat. "You may want to contact your girlfriend. She's been worried sick since she found out how severe the situation was. When she got your goodbye, she called me, sobbing and crying hysterically."

I nodded and closed my eyes as I leaned back in my seat. *Eliana? You there?* I called to her.

Christian? she gasped in my head. *Oh my God! I was so worried!*

I'm on my way home, I told her as I smiled to myself. *I missed you so much, angel.*

I missed you too. I love you.

I love you too. I'll see you soon, okay?

Okay. Rest up.

I took her advice and let the sleep take over my body.

CHAPTER FORTY-ONE

Victor nudged me awake and told me it was time to get off the plane. I realized that my head was resting on his shoulder and that I was drooling on his shirt. *Gross*, I thought to myself before sitting up and stretching. I wiped the drool from my cheek as I murmured, "Sorry. I must have been really tired because I almost never drool."

He chuckled and batted his hand. "It's cool. I've dealt with worse things than a little bit of drool."

We stood up from our seats as everyone started to gather their things and slowly made their way out of the plane. "I found this in the rubble when we came back to get you," Victor told me as he handed me my sword.

I took it and smiled. Even though I didn't want to become a weapon and the man I hated gave it to me, I loved the sword. "Thanks. I thought I would never get it back."

I strapped it onto my back, and we made our way off the plane. It was sunny and warm outside, the feeling of summer creeping closer. Victor handed me sunglasses when I squinted, not used to seeing the sun for a while.

I put them on as he walked over to the parked white convertible Jeep Wrangler on the side of the runway. I followed him and saw Dr. Rodriguez leaning against the driver's side door. He pushed himself up as we neared and before he could say anything, Victor whispered something in his ear.

His eyes snapped up at me at whatever Victor informed him and he looked surprised. He shook his head, as if to clear it, and went to open the back door for me to get in.

"Before we go," I started, "is there a bathroom here?"

He nodded and pointed to the building behind him. "In that building. You can't miss it."

I walked inside the building and followed the signs to the restroom as I pulled the sunglasses off my face and onto my head. The men walking in and out looked at me as if I were a celebrity. Which I suppose I was, considering they all went to Russia for me. They whispered amongst each other and pointed me out as I walked by.

Once I made it to the bathroom, I took care of my business before washing my hands and walking out. The people still watched as I walked out of the building, pulling the sunglasses over my eyes, and over to where Dr. Rodriguez and Victor waited.

Dr. Rodriguez opened the door for me. Victor stopped me before I got inside. "I'll sit in the back. You sit up front."

I didn't protest and went to the other side and got in the passenger seat as he got in the back. Dr.

Rodriguez got in the driver's seat and started the engine before pressing the gas pedal and exiting the base.

"So, I heard you had quite the experience in Russia," Dr. Rodriguez said once we were on the road.

"I guess you could call it that," I said.

"You almost died," he pointed out. "Were you scared?"

I hesitated before replying, "I wasn't exactly scared of the dying part. More of dying alone and how my friends would handle receiving the news."

"Well, I heard you were very close to death. So close that it was calling to you."

I nodded. "Yeah."

He drove for about 20 minutes before the surroundings became familiar. A few minutes after that, he turned onto the gravel path of the training camp.

Most of the men who came to Russia were at the base already and were starting to settle back in. Some were training with guns and some were sparring, while others were unpacking their bags.

We got out of the Jeep and Victor grabbed his bag before we made our way to our cabin. We opened the door and saw Sergeant Kirkwood standing in the middle of the cabin. He smiled at me and to my surprise, hugged me. "It's good to have you back, Christian," he told me as he slapped my back.

"Thanks," I said awkwardly. "Umm. It's good to be back…I think."

He laughed and let go of me. "So, my men have been talking non-stop about you since they've gotten back. Say you took down not one, but four buildings like it was nothing."

"Four?!" I asked as I turned to Victor.

He nodded. "Four well-made buildings are nothing but rubble now."

"Holy shit!" I exclaimed.

Robbie, Ben, and Derek all walked in and put their bags on their bunks as Dr. Rodriguez announced he should leave. "I'll check in at the end of every week." He turned to look at the guys. "I hope to see progress when I come back."

"Yes, Sir," they all replied.

"I'll see you later, son," he told Victor before walking out with Sergeant Kirkwood, leaving us alone.

I'm going to keep the mean act going just to make sure nobody suspects anything, Victor warned.

I only blinked in response.

"So, where do you guys want to start?" Ben asked.

"I think we should start with a nap," Robbie yawned.

"I think Christian got plenty of sleep," Victor said. "It's time to get to work."

"He deserves at least one day to rest, though," Ben whined.

"No, he doesn't. Dad wants him ready in a few weeks, so we don't have a day to spare. We can work on flying tonight and he will attend the morning training tomorrow."

They all reluctantly agreed, and Robbie asked, "Since everyone at the base knows about Christian, could we maybe do it outside?"

"How about we wait a few days? Just to make sure we are safe," Victor suggested.

They agreed to that as well and we walked to the building where I would be training most of the time. The last building I was in before I was taken. I stopped before we walked through the doors and took some deep breaths as I had flashbacks of the event.

The guns to my friend's heads. The gun to my head. Being led out and to the car. Being locked inside the car and gassed unconscious. Waking up in the cage. It all came back to me and it felt as if I was reliving every moment in my head.

I was brought back to the present when Derek touched my arm. "You okay?" he asked with his brow crinkled in concern.

I swallowed and nodded as I followed them inside the building. He closed the door behind him, and we all stood in a circle in the middle of the room. "Sunglasses," Victor demanded as he extended his hand to me.

I took the sunglasses off and handed them to him. He put them on top of his own head before Robbie asked, "Could we maybe see you sword fight now? I'm still interested in seeing how good he actually is."

Victor chuckled. "He's very good. But sure," he answered with a shrug. He went over to pick up his sword, which was leaning against the wall next to the door. I already had my sword sheathed to my back and he told me to take it out.

"You're not going to drug him?" Ben asked with a raised eyebrow.

"No. I sparred with him without the drugs once, so it doesn't bother me. He knows if he injures or kills me, there will be major consequences."

He nodded in my direction. "You ready?"

I nodded as I twirled the sword in my hand.

"You may want to step back," Victor warned the others. Once they were a safe distance away, he turned back to me and we got in our fighting stances with our swords crossed.

"Begin," Victor said before we were engaged in combat. He spun and swung his sword out to my side, but I blocked his move with my sword. He pulled back and I swiped at his side. He anticipated my move and blocked me easily,

I ducked when he aimed for my head and swiped at his side as I did so. He jumped back a second too late and I nicked his side. Not enough to hurt him, just a scratch. He lashed out without thinking, bringing his sword to my chest. I used it to my advantage and quickly stepped to the side, making him hit nothing and stumble forward. I quickly turned and swiped my leg out, making him fall.

I put my sword to his chest and smirked as he looked up at me. "I win," I told him as I pulled my sword back.

He stood up and smiled. "Good job."

I sheathed my sword to my back as the others came over. "That was awesome!" Robbie exclaimed with a wide grin.

"It was really cool to watch," Ben admitted with a smirk.

"You were amazing," Derek told me. "How did you know you wouldn't accidentally kill each other?" he asked us curiously.

We glanced at each other. "We would stop before we got to that point," Victor answered. "Let's go over some flying for a while."

"Okay," Ben agreed.

Victor told me to summon my wings and I handed him my sword and sheath before willing them to come out, still wearing the shirt they gave me in Russia days ago. I was sort of surprised that he didn't drug me yet, but wasn't going to complain. I flapped my wings, not to lift off the ground, but to stretch them out.

"I bet you're dying to fly again," Derek declared as he stepped forward. "Being trapped in that cage they put you in probably wasn't big enough to do much, was it?"

I shook my head. "No, it wasn't." And he was right, my wings ached to fly around, just not inside…

"We'll be outside soon," Victor told me as if he could read my thoughts.

I nodded in understanding.

Victor cleared his throat before instructing me to fly around the room a few times to warm up. I flapped my wings and lifted off the ground. I flew around five times before he told me to land while he did something. He went over and pressed a button on the wall next to the door, one I didn't see until then.

I heard some noises coming from above and looked up. Six hoops, one on the short sides and two on the long sies of the room, lowered from the ceiling. They were big enough for my body to fit through, but my wings…they wouldn't fit through them.

"These hoops were put here a few weeks ago and they are for you to train," Victor explained. "If you had to fly between two very close buildings, you would need practice. To fly through them would require you to be fast and tuck your wings in to fit through them."

He told me to try, and I flapped my wings to lift off the ground again. I picked my speed up by going around, next to the hoops, a few times. Once I felt fast enough, I lined myself up with one of the hoops on the shorter sides and tucked my wings in tight to my body before going through. However, I started to fall faster than I thought I would and couldn't flap my wings in time. So, I landed on the floor with a thud.

Ouch. That's going to leave a mark, I thought to myself as I rolled onto my back with a grunt. "You alright?" Robbie called over with a cocky grin.

I turned my head to glare at him as I pushed myself off the floor. He just laughed in response. The others were smart enough to hold in their laughs, but I could still see their smiles.

"Try again," Victor told me once I stood.

I nodded and tried again….and again…..and again until finally, I got it right. It had to have taken me at least 20 tries to actually get it and flap my wings in time to keep me from falling to the ground. I then moved up to two back-to-back hoops, then three, and eventually, I got to all six.

By that time, it was late, and I was tired and sore. "Let's go to bed," Derek said when he saw me yawn after I landed in front of them.

The others agreed and we walked out of the building together. The rest of the base was already quiet, mostly everyone went to bed, save for the night shifters, and we climbed into our bunks after quick showers to do the same. My head barely touched the pillow before I fell asleep.

CHAPTER FORTY-TWO

Victor woke everyone up the next morning, declaring we should get ready for the morning training session. "Do we have to, man?" Robbie groaned from the top bunk across from ours.

We all chuckled, still half asleep, but got out of bed and ready for the day. Victor gave me a uniform, black t-shirt, camo pants, and black combat boots, and told me there were already slits in the back of the shirt, so I wouldn't have to change later.

Once we were all ready, we walked out of the cabin and to the field in the middle of the base. Men were already starting to gather as they waited for Sergeant Kirkwood.

Our group got some wide-eyed looks and points as we approached. "Hey, guys!" a man said as we stopped walking.

"Hey, Tony," Ben said with a smile and wave.

Tony looked at me and said, "You're the talk of the camp. I feel like I'm talking to a celebrity right now. I'm Tony, by the way."

I nodded in greeting. "Christian."

"You have to tell me; how does it feel to have so much power in your veins?"

I chuckled. "Definitely different. I mean, I thought I was human until a few months ago, so maybe I was always different and didn't know until the power showed itself."

"I can see that. I have synesthesia, where you see colors with music, and didn't know not everyone experiences it until I learned about it in college. So, you could have felt the power in you, and you didn't know any different."

I nodded before Sergeant Kirkwood came over and called out, "Alright, everyone. Ten laps around the track!"

"Yes, Sir!" everyone yelled before starting to go.

Before my group could go, he called us over by saying, "Christian's group, come over here for a second."

We jogged over and stopped in front of him. "You training outside today?" he asked. "I want to know so I can just warn everyone to stay out of the way."

"We plan on it, Sir," Victor said. "We might do some things inside first, but should be out here after lunch time."

Sergeant Kirkwood nodded and dismissed us by telling us to do our laps.

"Yes, Sir," we all said before jogging around the field. The rest of the men training were ahead of us by a lap, so we picked up our pace a little more. "I hate running," Robbie groaned on our fifth lap, making us laugh.

"At least you can make it around now," Derek said with a chuckle. "When we started training here, you could barely go around once."

"Really?!" I asked as I looked over at them with a smile. "Did you ever do football or anything in high school?"

Robbie shook his head. "And that was a big mistake."

I shook my head as I laughed.

"What about you, Christian?" Derek asked. "Any football?"

"He was our schools' quarterback," Victor answered for me. "Probably got some scholarships, that's how good he was."

They looked at me with wide eyes and I shrugged. "Not that it matters now."

"It's still cool!" Derek exclaimed.

We finished our laps a few minutes later and were out of breath by the time Sergeant Kirkwood called everyone to gather around him. "Today, you guys may see things that surprise or intrigue you," he started. "Christian and his group may be practicing outside today. That does not mean you can interrupt them by asking questions or get in the way to get a better view. If they report you to me, you will get kicked out of this camp immediately, is that clear?"

"Sir, yes, Sir," they all yelled.

"Good," he said with a satisfied smile. "Train hard today, boys!"

Everyone started dispersing and going to do whatever they had to do for the day. Our group went inside the building and warmed me up by making me fly through the hoops until they were one hundred percent sure that I had the hang of it.

By that time, it was lunch time, and someone knocked on the door to deliver our lunch. We sat on the floor as we ate, talked, and laughed about anything and everything.

When we finished eating, we held onto our water bottles and walked outside. After throwing our trash away in the trash can, we walked to the field and track we were at earlier. Victor wanted me to try flying outside, since I never had before then. It was windy, which would affect my flying and he wanted me to get used to it.

He told me he wouldn't drug me unless he had to because the cuff was blocking my abilities. We both noticed the crowd gathering to watch from a safe distance and knew the others did too.

He took a deep breath and whispered to me, "Try to ignore them."

I nodded and summoned my wings when he told me to. He instructed me to fly up a few feet to get a feel for the wind. I flapped my wings twice, which took me about ten feet into the air, and felt the wind through my hair. It felt so good to finally fly outside, with fresh air and unlimited room.

However, that was short lived when a sudden gust of wind came and blew me backwards. Like how birds glide in the wind with their wings spread wide, it took me back like I was a kite. I tried to get control of myself, but it was like learning to fly all over again.

I stopped… when I ran into a tree a few yards back. I landed on the ground with a grunt and laid there for a moment. The guys jogged over and laughed. "Are you okay?" Derek asked with a chuckle.

"Yeah. That's harder than I thought it would be," I admitted as I sat up, rubbing my head as it throbbed.

"We should have waited for a less windy day," Victor noted to nobody in particular.

"No, it's fine. I have to get used to it someday. Might as well get used to it now."

"Should we try again?" Ben asked.

We agreed and after helping me up, we walked over to where we started and tried again. I was expecting the wind this time, so it wasn't as much of a surprise.

I still wobbled for the next few tries, but eventually got the hang of it. I was able to keep control by flapping my wings more when the wind picked up. Victor then told me to try to take a few laps around the field and I did, enjoying the wind rushing through my hair and the sun shining down on me. I closed my eyes and took a few deep breaths to savor the feeling.

Everything looked small from how high I was. I had to be at least fifty feet above the ground and people watching from below looked like action figures.

I kept my eye on Victor, waiting for him to signal me to come down. He must have known I was content at the moment because he gave me a few minutes before beckoning me down. I landed in front of him and the rest of my team gracefully, noting their grins.

"Having fun up there?" Derek asked.

I nodded. "You have no idea."

"You have a visitor," Victor told me with a smile. He looked over his shoulder and called whoever it was out.

Eliana stepped out from behind the building and as soon as her eyes met mine, she started sprinting towards me. She ran right into my arms and wrapped her arms around my neck as she cried into my shoulder. I wrapped my arms around her waist and picked her up as I spun her around.

"I missed you," she whispered in my ear. "So much."

"I missed you too, angel," I whispered back.

"Is that his girlfriend?" I heard someone ask nearby, thanks to my super-hearing.

"Yeah," Victor and Derek whispered back.

Eliana pulled back enough to plant her lips on mine and the world around us seemed to disappear. It was just me and her. I kissed her back just as passionately as she did, happy to finally have my angel in my arms.

CHAPTER FORTY-THREE

Eliana stayed the rest of the day and left after dinner with promises of seeing me soon. The team and I walked back to the cabin and the guys told me how much they liked Eliana.

I smiled in response as Derek opened the door and we all walked inside. We sat on the couches in the middle of our cabin before Robbie asked, "What's the plan for the next few weeks?"

Victor answered, "Well, I was thinking we could dedicate each week to something different. Since dad gave us a timeline of four weeks, I figured that would be best. This week is obviously focused on flying, next week we can do some training with your abilities, the third week can be on sword fighting and hand-to-hand combat, and the last week we could work on things that need improving and putting everything together. How does that sound to you guys?"

We all nodded and agreed to Victor's plan. "Well, I'm going to get ready to go to bed," I said with a yawn. I stood up and grabbed sweatpants and a t-shirt before going to the bathroom. I brushed my teeth and got dressed before walking out.

The guys were all still sitting on the couches and looked over at me. "Go get some sleep," Derek told me softly. "We'll be quiet."

I nodded and climbed up to my bunk. I closed my eyes and tried to relax, but with my advanced hearing, I could still hear them whispering. I shoved the pillow over my head to muffle the sounds and fell asleep when they quieted even more.

* * * * *

I WOKE UP IN THE MIDDLE OF THE NIGHT to Victor yelling my name and shaking my arm. I realized that I must have had a nightmare because I was sweating and breathing heavily. "You okay?" Victor asked with his brow creased in worry.

I looked around the cabin and saw that I woke everyone up. I swallowed as I nodded. "Sorry, I didn't mean to wake you guys."

"It's alright, man," Robbie said with sleep written all over his face. "You've been through a lot these past few months. It's understandable if you have nightmares for a while."

"You want to talk about it?" Victor asked as he looked back at me.

I shook my head. "I don't even remember what it was about," I told him honestly.

"Okay. Well, if you ever want to talk about anything, we're here for you, man," Derek said.

I nodded in thanks.

"Let's try to get a few more hours of sleep," Victor said. "We can skip tomorrow's morning warm up."

We agreed and Victor slid into his bunk below mine and we went to sleep soon after everyone turned off their bunk lights.

* * * * *

WE WOKE UP TO SOMEONE KNOCKING on our cabin door. Victor got up to open it and Sergeant Kirkwood stepped inside. "I was checking in on you boys. You weren't at the morning practice."

"Yeah. We decided to sleep in because Christian had a rough night," Victor answered.

"Okay. Just making sure you were alright," he said before going out of the cabin and closing the door behind him.

"Get up and ready," Victor told us. "Time to start training."

We all got up and got ready for the day. I put on the usual training outfit before going to the bathroom to brush my teeth. Once everyone was ready, we all walked outside and went to the track field to practice my flying for the majority of the day.

I flew backwards, slow, fast, hovered, spun, did loops, figure eights, and many other things they told me to do for the entire day. We did that every day that week, each session getting more and more intense and crazy. We practiced outside when it was sunny, rainy, and windy, claiming it would be good for me to know how to fly in any weather condition. Every night, when my muscles ached, I would wake from a nightmare that I couldn't remember. I had a gut feeling that there was more to the nightmare than I knew, and the feeling kept growing.

After a week of training, Dr. Rodriguez came to the camp to evaluate my progress. Victor warned me the night before that his dad wasn't aware that we weren't using the drug and to expect it to be used when he was there.

"What have you worked on so far?" he asked us as we stood in the building with him.

"Flying," Victor answered. "We've worked on flying all week. He's getting very good."

"I need him to be perfect," Dr. Rodriguez growled.

"And we're getting there," Ben answered. "He really is making excellent progress."

"Show me what you've worked on."

Victor came over and stuck the needle into my neck as he gave me an apologetic look. He backed away and stood with the others while they waited for the drugs to take control.

Once I was fully stiff and was waiting for a command, Victor stepped in forward and said, "You may act normal. Just do what we say and don't do anything reckless."

I blinked and shook my arms out to loosen them from being stiff. I wasn't used to the drugs anymore, so it took some time to get used to. "Fly around the room until you're fast enough to go through the hoops."

I nodded and released my wings before shooting up and flying around the building. I flew around four times before having enough speed to fly through the hoops, tucking in my wings for a second each time.

After making it through all six in seconds, I landed in front of the group. Dr. Rodriguez looked impressed, but didn't say anything. Victor nodded in approval before telling his father, "We go outside for almost everything else."

Dr. Rodriguez nodded and we walked out to the field where, for the rest of the day, I was told to do certain things that I had been doing that entire week.

By the end, I was so tired that all I could think about was curling up in bed and sleeping for the rest of the day and night. However, I had to wait until Dr. Rodriguez left.

"You boys did good," he complimented my team. It bothered me how he gave them credit for all the work I did.

"Thanks, but that's all on Christian," Derek told him as he winked at me. "He has been the one doing all the hard work and putting up with us."

I smiled over at him and nodded in gratitude.

"Well, I'm very happy with your guy's work. If you don't mind, I'd like a few moments alone with Christian."

They hesitated before nodding and walking away. Once they were out of sight, he went to stand to my right. "You did well today," he said.

I nodded as I looked over at him. "Thanks," I mumbled.

"Are the drugs still in your system?" he asked.

"Yeah," I answered through clenched teeth. I hated that even though I could act normal, I still felt the effects of the drug.

"Well, I'm ordering you not to tell the team this, but I think I'll ship you to war earlier than expected. Probably in two weeks instead of three."

My heart sank, but I remained silent. Two weeks?! And why did he order me not to tell the team? Did he not want them to intervene?

"Keep up the good work and I will see you next week," he told me before slapping me on the back and walking away. I stood there for a moment longer and then turned and walked back to the cabin.

I opened the door and their heads turned to look at me as I closed it behind me. "What did he talk to you about?" Victor asked worriedly.

I shrugged. "Just wanted to compliment me on my progress." I wished I wasn't under orders to not tell them that I was being shipped to war earlier than they thought.

"Oh," was all he said, like he expected more.

"I'm exhausted," I sighed. "I'm going to get a shower and then go to bed."

I walked into the bathroom and got a quick shower before getting dressed, brushing my teeth, and walking out. I was so tired that I could have fallen over. I told the guys goodnight before climbing into bed and instantly falling asleep.

CHAPTER FORTY-FOUR

I heard the guys whispering in the morning, but I couldn't wake up yet. "He was really tired last night," Derek said. "Let's let him sleep for a while longer."

"He didn't even have a nightmare last night," Ben added. "That shows how exhausted he must have been."

"Yeah," Victor agreed. He hasn't even been trying to keep his act of hating me up because we all have gotten so close. "At least they let him have one night of peace." He paused. "I wish he would tell us what dad told him. I know there was more than compliments. It was written all over his face when he walked in."

"I know. I saw it too," Ben whispered back. "Hopefully, he has a good reason not to tell us."

I shifted so I was laying on my left side, with my back to them, in hopes to get a few more minutes of sleep. They noticed the movement and quietly chuckled amongst each other before Robbie said, "Is it bad that I don't want him to go to war? Like, I know he's not an animal, but I'm getting too attached to him."

"Aren't we all?" Victor replied.

"I've been trying not to get too attached, which is why I don't talk to him much," Ben started. "But I'll admit, I will miss him."

"Let's worry about this later," Derek interrupted. "That's not for a few more weeks. Let's focus on now."

"Time to wake him?" Robbie asked.

"Yeah. We should probably start training," Victor answered.

"Christian," Derek said as he gently shook my shoulder. "Time to get up."

I groaned and pulled the blanket over my head. "Five more minutes."

They all laughed. "That's it. I officially declare that we keep him," Robbie stated with a chuckle.

"Sorry, big guy," Derek said, "but it's time to get up."

I turned my head and looked back at him. "Did you just call me 'big guy'?"

He laughed. "Maybe."

I smiled before chucking my pillow at his head. He laughed and threw it back at me. My smile fell when I remembered that Connor and I always did the same thing to each other. I missed him so much. He was practically my brother and I knew he must have been wondering where I was and if I was okay.

"What's wrong?" Victor asked.

"Just missing when things were normal," I answered honestly. "I wish I could see Connor one more time."

"Who's Connor?" Derek asked as he looked between Victor and I.

"Connor is Christian's best friend," Victor answered for me. "If you ask me, they are like brothers. Almost inseparable."

"Ah," he replied. "Sorry, man. Wish I could help."

I shook my head. "It's cool." I got out of bed and grabbed some clothes without saying anything else to them. I walked past them without meeting their worried stares and into the bathroom.

I got dressed slowly, not wanting to face them yet. I felt something I've never really felt before. I felt…homesick. I wasn't used to feeling this way since I've never really had a place to call my home. I guess, in a way, the Peters' house was my home. It was the one place I felt safe and surrounded by people who cared about me. I missed each and every one of them deeply.

A knock sounded on the door, startling me from my thoughts. "You alright in there, man?" Robbie asked.

"Yeah. Be out in a minute," I called. My voice was hoarse, and I realized I had been crying without knowing it. I looked in the mirror and saw my cheeks were red and puffy. I splashed some water on my face to bring the color back into it.

Once I got myself in check, I opened the door. All heads turned to me and I forced myself to smile, but they knew me too well. "Dude, you sure you're okay?" Ben asked.

"I will be," I answered with a sigh. "I just need a distraction."

"Well, let's go train with your abilities," Victor said.

I nodded in agreement and we walked outside. We walked to the field and Victor told me he had to use the drug. He told me that if his dad somehow found out he wasn't giving it to me, bad things would happen.

I allowed him to press the needle into my neck and he stepped back as they took effect. They waited a few minutes before Victor came up to me and took the cuff off my wrist. "Okay," he said as he took a deep breath. "You may act completely normal except you have to listen to us and not hurt or kill anyone. Don't try escaping either, even though I know you won't."

I blinked and shook my arms to get rid of the stiffness from the drug. "I hate this drug," I mumbled.

"I know," he told me with a grim expression. "You and me both."

"What should we do first?" Ben asked.

"I think we should work with simple things and go from there," Victor answered before turning to me. "How fast do you think you can run with your abilities?"

I shrugged. "I don't know."

"Try running around the track as fast as you can," he said as they moved out of the way.

I got ready to run at one of the starting places before taking off and calling my abilities as I did so. I was very surprised by how fast I actually went. The entire world seemed to slow down, and I noticed everything. From the bugs flying to the people watching around me. I saw every flap of the wings of a fly, a man moving extremely slow, and even a bird seemed to stop moving overhead.

I got back to the place I started before the guys could even blink. I stopped and was breathing heavily. Even though it was quick, I still ran a full lap. "Ready?" Victor asked once time resumed to normal. He noticed me breathing heavily. "Wait. Did you…?"

I let out a breathy laugh as I nodded. "Yeah."

"Wow." Robbie looked at me with wide eyes. "You might be faster than The Flash."

I laughed as Derek suggested, "We should set up a camera and record to slow it down."

"I think we have some," Victor replied. "I'll be right back." He walked away and came back a minute later with a camera in his hand.

"Do it again," he said as he pointed the camera so it could film the whole field.

I nodded and started running again. Again, I reached the point I started at within a blink of an eye and nodded to let them know that I did a full lap.

He brought the camera over and angled it so we could all see. "I slowed it down the best I could," he explained. We watched the video and I moved so fast that all we could see was a bright blue streak go around the track.

"Holy crap!" Robbie exclaimed. "You seriously are The Flash in real life."

All of us laughed and we watched the video one more time before Victor declared we should get to work. For the rest of the day, they had me make balls of electricity, fireballs, use telekinesis, run some more, read their minds, and so many other things that by the end of the day, I was exhausted.

"Let's go get you to bed," Derek told me as we walked back to the cabin. "You look drained."

"I am," I told him. I could barely keep my eyes open as we walked. I didn't even bother to get dressed before collapsing in bed without a word. I was out before any of them could say anything.

CHAPTER FORTY-FIVE

The rest of the week went by in a blur. We would practice things I didn't even think I could do until we tried them. Each night, I passed out, so exhausted that even the nightmares couldn't wake me. I knew the guys made me tired so I wouldn't have nightmares at night, and I wasn't complaining.

The night before Dr. Rodriguez's second evaluation, we all lounged on the couches in our cabin. I smiled as I watched my new friends interact around me. Robbie was obviously the clown of our group, the one who seemed to know how to make a down moment better. Ben was quiet and observant, only speaking occasionally. Derek was the caretaker; he took care of us if we needed anything. I got hurt a few times, nothing serious, but Derek would always be at my side first, making sure I was okay. And then there was Victor, the leader. He made sure we all stuck to schedule and yet had time to enjoy ourselves as well.

"I thought we deserve a treat, so I decided to invite a guest, who also brings food," Victor explained. "They should be here soon."

"Who?" I asked with a raised eyebrow.

"It's a surprise," he answered with a cocky smirk.

A few minutes later, a soft knock sounded on the door. Victor got up to answer it and I propped my legs up on the space he was sitting as he opened it.

"Pizza delivery!" her voice sounded. My ears perked up in recognition because it was Eliana.

"Come on in," Victor told her before opening the door to let her in. She came inside with two boxes of pizza in her hands and a plastic grocery bag hanging from her right arm. "Here, let me help," Victor said as he took the pizza from her.

"Thanks." She looked over at me and smiled as they came over to put the food and drinks on the coffee table. Victor pushed my legs off his spot with a laugh before sitting next to me.

Eliana fit between us and snuggled into my side. I wrapped my arm around her and kissed her head. "I missed you," I whispered in her ear as the guys started talking again.

"I missed you too," she said as she tilted her head to look up at me. She leaned in and placed her lips on mine for a second, but didn't do it too long due to not being alone.

"Who wants pizza?" Robbie asked after a moment of awkward silence passed.

We all laughed, but agreed. We each got a slice of pizza and a can of soda from the bag and ate in silence. Once we finished eating, Eliana leaned into my side as she asked, "What have you guys been up to this past week?"

"Christian has been training with his abilities from morning to night," Derek answered. "I'm not sure how he has put up with us so far."

I rolled my eyes. "Because you are much more tolerable than Dr. Rodriguez. I'd hang with you any day if it means I don't have to deal with him. Plus, you guys are my team. My friends."

"Come out and say it already!" Robbie exclaimed. I gave him a puzzled expression and he rolled his eyes. "Admit it, you love us."

We all laughed. "I do," I said with a chuckle. "I love you guys as if you were family."

We talked for hours, acting like normal teenagers. Acting as if I didn't have powers and wasn't being turned into a weapon. We laughed, cried, and comforted each other until we were all yawning. I must have fallen asleep with my arm wrapped around Eliana because I half-awoke when she shifted in my arms.

"Did he fall asleep?" she whispered. "I can't see his face."

"Yeah," Derek answered. "He's out like a light."

"Like every day this week," Victor stated with a sigh. "I'm surprised he lasted this late."

"Why is he so tired?' she asked.

"Using his abilities wears him out," he answered. I felt him shift his position next to us. "Think of it this way. If you had to take all the energy from your body and channel it on one thing for an entire day, would you be exhausted?"

"Probably," she murmured. "Is that how he feels when he uses his abilities?"

"I don't know," he answered quietly. "That's just how I understand it."

"Can I ask you a question that has been bothering me for a while?" She paused and I imagined Victor nodding. "Do you know what happened to John? The boy who…" she couldn't finish, but Victor knew who she meant. The boy who raped her.

"What do you mean? What happened to him?" he asked, his voice laced with concern.

"That's the thing I don't know. He disappeared, not a trace of him, a few days after I told Christian. And I knew he told you, so I thought that maybe you would know."

"I don't. I cornered him and beat the shit out of him, but other than that, I didn't cause his disappearance."

"Who's this John guy and what did he do?" Ben interrupted.

"He went to our school and… wasn't a good guy," Victor answered.

"I want to know what he did so I can beat him myself," Derek growled.

"He…he raped me," Eliana said quietly as she started fidgeting with the cuff around my right wrist, that was resting on her shoulder.

"He what?!" they all shouted.

I stirred and moaned, "Keep it down. Some of us are trying to sleep."

They laughed quietly before Derek whispered, "I'll kill this guy if I ever see him."

"Jump in line," I mumbled, still half asleep.

"When did this happen?" Derek asked quietly.

"A few days before grandma brought me to the lab with her. I went to his place because we had a project to do, but when he tried to kiss me, I tried to leave. He ran after me and pushed me onto the couch…and you can determine the rest."

"Oh my God, Eliana," Robbie breathed. "I'm so sorry."

"I'm still terrified of being alone with most guys, but when I'm with Christian, I feel safe," she explained as she kissed my fingers.

"I understand," Robbie said.

"And now that I know he won't be around much longer, I am becoming more terrified." There was awkward silence before she yawned and snuggled in closer to me. "I'm going to fall asleep here."

They all chuckled, but a few minutes later, she fell asleep. I knew she did because her breathing slowed down, and I heard her heartbeat slow as well.

"I think we should go to bed too," Derek whispered.

"Yeah," Victor said before standing up from next to us. "Help me move them so they are laying down."

Someone helped him adjust us so we were laying on the couch, on our left sides, with Eliana's back pressed against my front and my arm around her middle to ensure she wouldn't fall.

Eliana sighed in contentment and snuggled back closer to me, making them laugh quietly. "It's going to kill her if something happens to him," Ben stated as someone draped a blanket over us.

"I know," Victor whispered back. "Let's go to bed."

I heard them climb into their bunks and someone turned the light off before I fell asleep once more.

* * * * *

ELIANA WOKE ME IN THE MIDDLE OF THE NIGHT, when she was having a nightmare. She was tossing and turning against me as soft whimpers came out of her mouth.

I woke her gently by kissing her neck and whispering, "You're okay, angel. It's a nightmare. You're safe with me. I love you."

She turned so her chest was against mine and cried into my chest. I kissed her head and reminded her that she was safe here, that no one could hurt her.

"It's like he lives in my head. He's there every time I close my eyes, always pulling my underwear down," she whispered.

I knew she meant John and told her, "Nobody should ever have to go through what you went through. I wish I could have been there to stop him myself. When I had that vision, it pained me so bad that I couldn't do anything to help you; to save you. It was agonizing to not be able to be your guardian angel in that moment."

"You have been the best guardian angel anyone could ask for," she whispered as she looked up at me. "And I love you for it."

She leaned up to kiss me and there was no gentleness to the kiss. She put all her determination into it, all her love and passion. I returned what she gave me, and she moaned in response.

She pulled back after a moment and I said, "I love you so much, angel. Now, go back to sleep."

She smiled and settled into my chest before falling back to sleep moments later. I stayed up, looking at the wooden beams on the ceiling, wishing things could have been different; that we could be a normal couple instead of me going to war against my will.

I fell asleep when I couldn't keep my eyes open any longer and my head hurt from wondering so much.

CHAPTER FORTY-SIX

"Good morning, boys," Dr. Rodriguez said loudly, startling all of us awake.

I shot up, nearly knocking Eliana off the couch. I caught her before she could fall and wrapped my arm around her middle. "What the hell, dad?!" Victor yelled from his bunk.

"Dude, you almost gave me a heart attack," Robbie grumbled as he rubbed the sleep from his eyes.

"Well, looks like you had an eventful night," Dr. Rodriguez stated as he surveyed the room, noting the pizza boxes and cans of soda on the coffee table. His eyes landed on Eliana and he smiled. "Well, hello, dear. Haven't seen you in a while."

"I've been busy," she told him with a shrug.

"Looks like you've been very busy," he said as he looked her up and down, pressed against me with a blanket wrapped around both of us.

I growled possessively, reminding him that if he laid a finger on her, I would destroy him. I pulled her closer to me and she knew better than to argue in front of him.

"I'll give you boys ten minutes to get ready and to get her off the camp's ground," he said before turning on his heel and walking out the door.

We all stared at the door for a moment until what he said sunk in. "I better go," Eliana said as she wiggled out of my embrace. "Don't want to get you into trouble."

"I can walk you out," I told her. "Just let me get changed really quick."

She reluctantly nodded and I quickly got up and changed in the bathroom. She was waiting by the door when I walked out, and I took her hand before opening the door to the cabin. "I'll be back in a minute," I told the team before we walked out. I checked to make sure Dr. Rodriguez wasn't in sight, and once I was sure, we started walking towards her car.

She got her keys out of her purse and unlocked it before turning to me. "I love you," she said before standing on her tiptoes to kiss me.

"Love you too," I told her as she stepped away and got into her car. I waved as she pulled out of the camp, and walked back to the cabin, where the guys were waiting.

"Ready to deal with dad all day?" Victor asked with a smirk.

"Hell no!" I exclaimed, making them all laugh. "I already can't wait until I can go back to bed."

"Me neither," Robbie said with a yawn.

"Let's just get this over with," Victor said with a sigh before leading us out of the cabin and to the field, where Dr. Rodriguez was waiting for us.

"What did you work on this week?" he asked.

"Abilities. Almost anything you can think of," Ben answered.

"Let's get started then," Dr. Rodriguez said with a grin.

Once I was under the drug's effect, I was at their mercy, or should I say, Dr. Rodriguez's mercy. He asked them what I have been practicing and commanded me to do them. Unlike the team, he didn't give me breaks or much time to gather my bearings.

"He must be ready to go to war, which means no breaks," he told Victor when he questioned whether I should get a break. "He may be used for hours, or even days, at a time. He must get used to it."

Victor backed down, but looked more and more worried as the day went on. I was so tired, hungry, and thirsty that I could have dropped to my knees and begged for a break. Of course, the drug wouldn't let me do that, but I felt that if I had to go any longer, I would pass out.

"Dad," Victor said around dinner time. "I think he deserves a break. He doesn't look too good."

The team agreed with him and Dr. Rodriguez looked from them to me. "How are the drugs holding up?"

I licked my dry lips with my sandpaper-like tongue before answering, "They're weakening."

"Please, dad. Give him a break. Unless you want to push back the date because he gets injured or sick, I suggest you stop."

"Fine," Dr. Rodriguez sighed, finally giving in. "I want him all day next week, though. From dawn to dusk. No breaks."

Victor nodded. "Okay."

After that, Dr. Rodriguez left the camp and Victor came over to me. He put the cuff on my wrist before we slowly made our way back to the cabin. I rushed to the mini-fridge and grabbed a bottle of water. I drank half of it without any breaths in between gulps.

"Thirsty much?" Robbie asked with a chuckle.

"Maybe a little," I answered sarcastically. "What's for dinner? I'm starving."

"I don't know," Victor answered. "I'll bring it back here."

I nodded and sat on the couch with a sigh as he left. I kicked off the combat boots and propped my feet onto the coffee table. The guys sat around me while we waited for Victor to show up with the food. I closed my eyes and rested my head against the back of the couch. I was so tired that all I could think about was crawling into bed. I didn't even want to eat due to being so tired.

"You okay, man?" Derek asked as he put his hand on my shoulder.

"I don't feel too good," I murmured as my stomach swirled.

"You going to be sick?" he asked. "'Cause you look like you're going to be sick."

I shook my head, but a few seconds later, I jumped up and went to the bathroom. I threw up in the toilet and flushed it before grabbing my toothbrush and brushing my teeth to get rid of the acid taste.

When I walked out, I walked straight to my bunk and climbed into bed. "Tell Victor that I'll eat later," I told the guys. "I'm going to bed."

I closed my eyes and fell asleep without hearing their responses.

* * * * *

VICTOR NUDGED ME AWAKE sometime later. "Christian," he sighed. "You have to eat something."

I moaned. "I'm not hungry anymore. I'm too tired to eat anyway."

"Just leave him be," Ben whispered. "He'll eat when he wants to eat. He threw up earlier, maybe that changed his appetite."

"I'm just worried that he doesn't have enough in his system to get his energy back to normal," Victor replied.

"Maybe we should take tomorrow off, just so he gets a day to regain his energy."

Victor sighed. "I guess that wouldn't hurt. I can't believe dad kept pushing him like that. It makes me so mad that he wouldn't even give him a drink break."

"Yeah. Let's let him sleep for now. Hopefully, he'll eat when he wants to."

"Okay," Victor agreed, and they walked over to Robbie and Derek, who I heard whispering on the couches.

Derek whispered, "He okay?"

"Honestly? I'm not sure," Victor answered. "Hopefully, he will eat soon."

"He will," Derek said confidently. "He was so tired that he could barely stand. Just let him sleep and then he will eat."

Someone came back over and reached up to my bunk to pull the blanket over my shoulders. They then walked back over to meet the others as Robbie asked, "Should we invite Eliana tomorrow? Maybe she can make him feel a little better."

"I'll give her a call," Victor replied before walking out of the cabin. I fell asleep sometime after that and didn't wake until morning.

CHAPTER FORTY-SEVEN

I was lounging on the couch, still feeling weak and tired, when Eliana arrived. The guys were out running some errands around the camp, so we were alone. She sat by my feet and said, "You look like crap."

I rolled my eyes, but smiled. "Thanks. I feel like it too."

"Really? I would have never guessed," she replied sarcastically. She got serious after a moment. "Seriously though. You don't look like yourself."

"I'm just tired," I told her with a shrug. She gave me a look that told me she didn't believe me, and I laughed. "Okay. I feel…drained. Drained of my energy and I can't seem to get it back quick enough. Like when you have the flu, ya know?"

"I guess that makes sense," she said thoughtfully. "I hope you feel better soon." She came up and laid on my chest, basically her whole body on mine, and looked up at me from under her full eyelashes.

"You look pretty today. Did I tell you that?" I asked. She did look pretty. No, she looked better than pretty. She was wearing a very cute black romper with sunflowers over it. Her long brown hair was straightened, and her makeup was subtle, only basic colors and eyeliner that made her blue eyes pop.

"Thank you," she told me with a blush.

"You're perfect," I whispered.

She rolled her eyes. "I am far from perfect."

"Then you're perfectly imperfect," I came back with a smile.

"Can you be anymore cuter?" she giggled.

"Oh? I'm the cute one in this relationship?" I asked with a chuckle. "I thought you were."

She laughed and it was the most magical sound I'd ever heard. It made me feel warm and happy inside, making me smile widely. "I love you," I told her.

"I love you more."

We laid there for a few minutes, content with just listening to each other's breathing, until the guys came back in. Robbie covered his eyes when he saw us and joked, "Are we interrupting something?"

Eliana and I both laughed as she rolled off me. "No. You're good," Eliana said with one more laugh. "We were just talking."

"Sure," he said with an eye roll. "They were 'talking'," he said to the others, using air quotes.

I chucked the pillow from the couch at his head with a laugh. "You are so weird."

"Thanks, but I already knew that," he replied as he threw it back. "You don't have to remind me."

"Just making sure you knew," I told him with a smirk. "Because it'd be very awkward if you didn't."

"You're lucky you scare me with those freaky powers of yours and the sword fighting."

I laughed and everyone smiled, seeming happy that I was starting to feel better. I stood up and walked over to Robbie. "I'm scary?! Really?" I told him with a laugh. "You do realize that I would never hurt anyone…at least, not on purpose."

"He's right, man," Victor said as he slapped Robbie on the back. "Christian would never hurt a fly."

"I don't know about that," I told them with a smirk. "Flies are annoying."

"So just don't annoy you, got it," Robbie whispered to himself, making everyone laugh.

For the rest of the day, we lounged on the couches and talked. We were all becoming close and it was hard to imagine myself not being there. I remembered what Dr. Rodriguez told me last week, that I was to be shipped to war at the end of this week.

"What's wrong?" Eliana asked when she noticed something my expression.

"I wish I could tell you," I told them as I looked down at my hands in my lap. "But I can't."

"Why not?" Ben asked.

"I was ordered not to tell anyone when I was obedient... by Dr. Rodriguez."

"Can you try telling us?" Victor questioned.

"Just…know that I will miss you guys when I…leave," was the closest hint my mind would allow me to say. I prayed they would somehow understand what I was trying to say, but they only looked more confused.

"We'll miss you too, man," Robbie said. He then changed the subject to something happier, but I looked over at Victor and saw him watching me with a thoughtful gaze. It appeared as if he was trying to put together what I couldn't say, and I just hoped he would do it in time.

* * * * *

ELIANA SPENT THE NIGHT AND we slept together on the couch. I woke up feeling like myself again and was ready to start the day. Eliana wanted to stay and watch for the day, so we all agreed. We got dressed and walked outside, enjoying the nice sunny weather.

Victor and I had our swords strapped to our backs and the men on the field gave us double looks before clearing the area. They knew that when we were outside, they were to stay away from us.

"Let's do some warmups to stretch our muscles," Victor instructed. We took our swords out of their sheaths and did various exercises with them. From holding them out with straight arms to thrusting them out, all while monitoring our breathing and working on our footwork.

He told me to put the sword down as he did the same. "I think we should work on hand-to-hand combat first. If you got captured by the enemy, the first thing they'd do is take your sword, so it'd be good to know how to fight without your sword and abilities."

I nodded in agreement and he walked over to me. "We will practice falling first. That way you know how to lessen the chance of you getting hurt and how to get back up."

For the next hour, we went over various ways I could fall and how to get back up, or still gain the upper hand from the ground. The number one rule when falling is to exhale on impact so your body absorbs the brunt of the fall.

By the end of the hour, my side, arms, legs, and even bottom hurt from falling on them so much. Victor gave me a break and we took drinks from our water bottles as the others came over. "Some of those falls looked like they hurt. You good?" Derek asked.

"I'm good. I'll be sore for a while, but nothing I can't handle."

"You still okay to move on?" Victor asked as he capped his water bottle.

I nodded. "If your dad wants me all day next time, then I might as well build up my endurance."

Eliana came over and surprised me when she gave me a hug. I wasn't complaining, but asked, "What's this for?" as I wrapped my arms around her.

"It never really sunk in that you're doing all these things to keep me safe. It hit me when I was watching you, I remember that he threatened me if you ever do something wrong. I just felt the urge to hug you because of that."

I rubbed her back. "I'm doing it, so we have a possibility to be together, to be normal."

She pulled back and stood on her tiptoes to give me a kiss on the cheek. "And I love you for that."

"Alright, Eliana. I'm going to steal him from you now," Victor said as he took hold of my arm and gently tugged me back to where we were training.

She pouted her lip and I laughed before blowing her a kiss. I turned my attention to Victor, and he took a deep breath before saying, "Now, I want to go over the basic fighting stance."

"Okay," I answered with a nod.

"The fighting stance is simple and yet complex at the same time. You want to hold your hands up in relaxed fists to protect your head and face. And you also want to keep your knees bent and feet slightly apart, but be ready for the attacker to make a move on you."

He demonstrated and told me to try to copy him. He fixed a few things, such as where to position my feet and to bend my knees. He corrected me on where to hold my hands so my face would get the best protection.

Once I had the stance down, he told me to punch with my right hand and to hold it. "You have to keep your thumb around your fingers and hit with the top of your knuckles to ensure you don't shatter your hand," he explained as he adjusted my fist. He guided me through the punch in slow motion.

For the rest of the day, we covered punching. I was surprised by how many mechanics actually went into punching. Victor was patient with me when I kept asking questions and making mistakes that he corrected over and over.

We sparred, with punches only, after I got the idea of how everything worked. He corrected me as we went, but after a while, we were going at a steady pace and I actually gained the upper hand on him a few times.

"I think you're ready to do some kicks tomorrow," he told me as we walked back to the cabin. The others left us alone a few hours ago and were waiting for us there. Eliana left the camp after lunch, claiming she had homework to do and that she would see us later.

The guys were lounging on the couches, looking bored to their minds as Ben stared at the ceiling, Robbie threw a ball up and caught it, and Derek appeared to be asleep. Victor and I laughed when they looked so excited to see us.

"You know you could have stayed, right?" Victor asked with a smile.

"But we felt so awkward just standing there watching you guys," Robbie answered. "And we were hot, so we came into the nice cool A.C."

We both chuckled to ourselves before I asked, "What if we were hot too?"

He shrugged. "You could have joined us."

"And risk losing another day?" Victor exclaimed as he walked over and sat on the couch with a sigh in relief. "Dad would literally kill me if we let that happen."

I agreed and added, "After he kills you, he'd probably kill me."

"He probably would," he confessed.

We ate dinner and talked for a little while before going to bed. I had a nightmare that I couldn't remember in the middle of the night and thankfully only woke Victor. He woke me up and made sure I was okay before crawling back into his bunk below me.

I fell asleep hours later because I kept thinking about how I most likely wouldn't be there next week, and nobody knew but me. I worried I would never see my friends again, and more importantly, Eliana. She was my soulmate. She had to be. Even before I knew her, I knew something was different. I loved her and would do anything to keep her safe, just like I would for Connor. I would do anything at all to keep them safe.

Absolutely anything.

CHAPTER FORTY-EIGHT

The next day, Victor and I went over kicking, as he said. He told me the most vulnerable parts to hit and how to kick them. He taught me that kicking the back of the knees would make them collapse to their knees and that kicking them where the sun don't shine was also an option, as long as they were male.

By the end of the day, I knew how to kick and punch well enough to at least protect myself. Victor seemed happy when I beat him at three sparring matches back-to-back and declared that I was 'good enough'.

The following day, we started using swords again and he taught me some moves that his dad didn't. He taught me how to roll out of the way if an attacker was making a blow that I wouldn't be able to duck or jump out of the way for. He demonstrated how to get myself out of a sword to throat situation if I was laying on the ground by kneeing the attacker in the stomach and taking the opportunity to get back up.

The next two days, he had a few others who knew how to sword fight join us and taught me how to fight off multiple attackers at once. The number one rule he gave me was to never turn my back to an opponent unless he was down for good.

"I think he's got the hang of it," one of the men said with a wince. I kneed him in the groin earlier and even though he said it was fine, I still felt bad for doing it. He just waved me off and told me that it was all about teaching me.

"He's beaten us four times now," another said. "He's got this down."

Victor nodded and looked me in the eyes. "You feel good about it?"

I nodded as I sheathed my sword to my back. "Yeah. I think so."

"Alright then," he replied with a smirk. "Thanks for your help guys! That will be all."

"Good luck, Christian," they told me before dispersing.

"What now?" I asked him once they were gone.

"We relax and get ready to face dad tomorrow. Eliana should be here in an hour."

I nodded. "Sounds good."

We walked back to the cabin and met the rest of the team. Since they weren't able to help train me, they had been doing their own things such as training with the others, doing errands for Sergeant Kirkwood, and watching us.

"Hey," Derek said when we walked inside. "How did the last hour go?"

"Christian beat the guys at two more sparring matches," Victor answered. "I think he's ready for tomorrow."

"How's Tony?" Ben asked.

"He's going to be sore for a while," Victor answered with a chuckle.

I assumed Tony was the one I kneed in the groin and said, "I still feel bad about that."

"Like he said, it's all about training you," Victor told me as he slapped me on the back. "Don't sweat it."

"Eliana should be here soon," Robbie told us. "With food."

We all laughed because he seemed more excited for the food than anything else. We walked over to sit in our usual spots on the couches. "I'm starving," I groaned. "Hopefully, she gets here soon."

"Same," Victor replied as he folded his arms behind his head and leaned back.

Eliana came in a few minutes later and we all jumped up excitedly. She smiled as she said, "You guys missed me that much?! I feel so loved."

Robbie took the pizza box out of her hands and said, "We are starving."

"So, you're excited for the food?" she questioned with a raised eyebrow.

"Yeah!" he exclaimed like it should have been obvious. "I mean, Christian probably missed you, but we are all starving."

I wrapped my arm around her shoulders and rubbed her arm. "I missed you," I told her as I kissed her head, "but let's eat."

Robbie already opened the box and was taking a slice out as we walked over. We each took a piece and moaned as the cheesy pizza met our taste buds. We sat back and ate as we talked about how my sword fighting has been going.

Eliana seemed very proud to say that her boyfriend knew how to wield a sword. I smiled when I heard her call me her boyfriend and kissed her. "I love you," I whispered.

"Love you too," she whispered back. "You okay? You haven't seemed like yourself lately."

I sighed. She knew me too well. I couldn't get it off my mind that tomorrow, I might be shipped to war, and they didn't know. I hoped that Dr. Rodriguez was telling me it just to get to my head, but had a feeling that it wasn't the case.

"I'm just not looking forward to leaving you guys," I answered after a moment of silence.

They told me they weren't looking forward to saying goodbye and Victor kept glancing over at me for the rest of the night. *What?* I asked him after he looked at me for the hundredth time.

He shook his head. *Trying to figure something out. I know something's wrong and want to fix it.*

I wish I could make it easier for you, I told him honestly. *But you know your dad…*

Yeah… I know, he told me before turning to join the conversation the others were having around us.

Eliana left a few hours later and I walked her to her car. She turned to me and said, "Good luck tomorrow."

"Thanks," I replied as I kicked the stones with the toe of my boot. "I love you."

"I love you too," she breathed, as if she knew something was wrong. "I'll see you soon, okay?"

I rubbed the back of my neck, but nodded. I pulled her to me by the belt loops of her jeans to give her one last kiss. I kissed her with every ounce of hope I had left. Hope to see her again. Hope to have a normal life together.

"I love you," I told her one more time before letting her go. I opened the car door for her, and she climbed inside. She started the car and I watched until I could no longer see the red brake lights anymore.

I slowly made my way back to the cabin and the guys were whispering about something, but stopped when I walked in. "I'm going to bed. Long day tomorrow."

They nodded and I got changed before climbing into my bunk and forcing myself to fall asleep.

CHAPTER FORTY-NINE

Dr. Rodriguez watched me do hand-to-hand combat with Victor and then, without a break for me, sword fight with him too. He then made me spar the guys from the last two days and seemed impressed.

"I want him for the rest of the day," he told the team after I beat them five times in a row. "Alone."

They glanced at each other, but agreed and left me alone with him and my stomach dropped. *This is it*, I thought. *This is how he's going to get rid of them to ship me away.*

"You've improved so much," he told me as he looked me over. "You look better too."

I knew I did. Being in the sun had made my pale skin tanner and sword fighting and training has made my muscles stronger and more defined, especially in my arms. With the sword strapped to my back, I looked like a soldier ready for battle.

"Come. Follow me," he told me before leading me to a building nearby that I hadn't been in. It occupied multiple vehicles for the military and when we stepped inside, The door slammed shut behind us. I turned back, but nobody was there.

It's just the wind, I tried to reassure myself. *Only the wind.*

"You mind helping me with something?" he asked as he opened the back of one of the box trucks.

I hesitated, but climbed in after him. Multiple boxes and crates were inside the truck and he told me to take my sword off my back. I unsheathed it and handed it to him. He put it in a box and closed it. I panicked because I then realized it was a trap.

He was shipping me to war today.

And he just took my weapon.

I looked back, thinking I might be able to run, but stopped when two men appeared behind me, blocking my exit. I turned back to Dr. Rodriguez and saw him opening the top of a bigger crate. "Get in," he ordered.

I stared at him in shock. "What?"

"Get in," he repeated.

He wasn't serious, was he? *He's literally shipping me to war?! In a fucking box?!* I thought. However, as I studied him through my glare, I realized that he was not kidding and was completely serious. *Maybe if I stall enough, Victor will come and stop him.*

He looked past my shoulder and nodded to the men behind me.

I looked back and saw the two men walking towards me. I panicked, unsure of how to get out of the situation considering I had the cuff on my wrist. The first man went to grab me and I ducked, but the second took the opportunity to grab me and stuck a needle into my neck. He held me to him as I collapsed, unable to stand. *Fucking sedative,* I thought as they lifted me up and placed me inside the crate.

It wasn't a strong dose because I knew I wouldn't pass out. He wanted me to be awake. He closed the lid and I heard him lock it. I looked up and saw a few small holes that were likely there so I could breathe.

I sat with my legs close to my chest, cramped inside the small space. I heard the truck start a few minutes later and it lurched forward making me hit the hard side of the crate with my shoulder. I winced, pain shooting through my body.

How long am I going to be in here? I thought to myself as we hit a bump, causing me to hit my head on the top. I reached up and tried to push the lid off, but it was secure.

A few moments later, the truck suddenly stopped. Not a subtle stop like you would feel when stopping at a stoplight or stop sign, but a full-on jerking stop.

I heard the back of the truck open and thought we arrived at the airbase. However, I then heard a voice, "Christian? You here?"

Connor?

"I'm here," I managed to get out.

"Where are you?" he whispered in a panicked tone.

"In the crate," I said, "just follow my voice."

I heard him rustle with the lock and curse. He sighed in frustration and said, "I'm going to break the lock. One second."

He walked away, but came back after a moment and hit the lock with something hard. It busted and he quickly threw the lid off. I squinted at the light that filtered inside and he helped me stand by putting his hands under my arms.

He was the only thing supporting me because my legs fell asleep from being cramped and because of the sedative. I told him to hand me the sword in the box next to mine and he looked at me with wide eyes.

"Since when do you know how to use a sword?"

"Since they turned me into their weapon," I answered as he bent down to pick it up.

"It's heavy," he told me as he weighed it in his hand.

"I know," I said through a clenched jaw as he handed it to me. I slipped it into the sheath still on my back before he helped me step out and we walked to the open door of the truck. He helped me get out by holding my arm as I slowly slid myself to the ground. He kept his grasp on my arm as he jumped out himself. He quickly closed the door to the truck before turning to the road behind us.

He walked off to the right, towards the trees and walked into them. He helped me walk towards a car parked on the other side of the trees, along a gravel road.

"How are you here?" I asked him as we got closer to it.

"Victor contacted me a few weeks ago and told me he needed help with something. We made a plan to get you out and went through with it. So, he stopped the truck and caused a distraction while I got you out. He'll meet us soon."

"What about Angelica and Alis?" I asked as he helped me into the passenger seat.

"Who?"

Shit! I thought. "We have to go back to the lab!" I told him.

"Why?" he asked, clearly confused.

He quickly closed the door and rushed to the driver's side. *Alis! Angelica! Can you hear me?* I screamed in my mind as he started the car.

We can. What's up? Alis said.

I told Connor where to go as he drove. *Get ready to leave.*

We stopped before we could be seen by anyone working outside and I got out of the car. "I'll be right back. I'm going to get two others like me."

I summoned my wings, but before I took off, Connor opened his door and stood with his arms resting over the window. "Please be careful."

I nodded. "I'll see you soon." I turned back towards the fence and flew over it. I landed in a shadowy spot by the main doors of the building. I made my wings recede into my back before walking inside.

Three guards turned at my entrance and pointed their guns at me. I pulled my sword out and

got into a fighting stance. They appeared to have orders not to kill me because they hesitated. That was
all I needed to gain the upper hand.

I swiped my sword at the nearest guard and
nicked his arm. He cried out in pain as he clutched it.
I spun around and gave him a back-kick to the head.
He fell, losing consciousness. I turned to the next
guard and swiped his leg with the sword. He fell, no
longer able to stand due to the wound. I brought the
handle of the sword to his head to knock him out.
The last guard pointed his gun at me, but I swiped at
his ankle and knocked him out the same way as the
second. I picked his gun up after I sheathed the
sword to my back.

I rushed towards the room that I was held in
for the last few months. I was happy to see the girls
already waiting for me. I held the gun up to the
guard's head and ordered him to open it.

He nodded, scared to death, and opened the
door to the room. They rushed out, and I hit the poor
guard's head with the gun to ensure he wouldn't do
anything.

"How did you get out?" Angelica asked.

"Unimportant. Right now, let's focus on getting the hell out of here," I told them as I grabbed
each of their hands. I dragged them down the hall
and out the door.

I stopped short when I saw a line of guards in
front of us. We couldn't fly because the roof was still
above us. *Any plans?* I asked the girls as we backed
up slowly.

Try another door? Angelica suggested.

Let's run, I said.

We all turned and ran back into the building. Angelica went first, I was second, and Alis took the back.

I heard a gunshot and stopped to make sure Alis was still following. However, I saw she was still outside, and was now on the ground. *Alis!!* I screamed to her as the men surrounded her.

Angelica turned and screamed her sister's name out loud when she saw. She tried running to her, but I pulled her back by the waist. "We can't, it's a death sentence!" I told her.

She sobbed and fought my grip, but I held onto her. *Go! Alis* screamed in our heads. *They shot me too close to my heart. I'll be dead in a few minutes. Don't worry about me! Save yourselves.* She then told me, *Take care of my sister, Christian. She will need you to protect her. And don't forget to be extraordinary because you are.*

I pulled Angelica behind me and she finally started running towards the other exit, the garage. We opened the door and ran out before I summoned my wings. Someone hit me in the head with the handle of their gun. I cursed and faced my attacker. "You're not going anywhere," the man snarled.

I blinked back the spots and focused on kicking his ass. I went to tackle him, but a gunshot sounded. It wasn't him who shot it. It was Dr. Rodriguez, who was behind the guard with a pissed expression.

I doubled over and grunted when I felt the pain in my right side. I placed my hands over it and felt the blood gushing out of my wound. I looked back at Angelica, who was curled in a ball on the ground and sobbing.

I knew I couldn't let them take her back inside; I had to get out of there. So, I mustered up every ounce of my energy and picked her up before taking to the sky. I went high enough so the clouds covered us until we neared Connor's car.

Once I landed, I saw Connor jump out of the car and rush over. "I thought there were two?" he asked.

I shook my head and let a few tears slip for Alis as I retracted my wings. He stopped when he noticed them. He ran his hand through his hair as he said, "Shit."

Angelica shook with sobs against me, and I placed her in the car's backseat. I turned to face Connor, who now took in my appearance. "Christian. You're bleeding," he told me as he looked at my stained shirt.

"We'll worry about it later," I told him as I walked around to get in the passenger side.

He climbed into the driver's seat and sped away from the base, that was now in full lockdown and men with guns were running everywhere. I pulled my shirt over my head and examined my side after turning the light on. The bullet was still inside and was blocking most of the blood from getting out, but I had to get it out soon; had to get it out before I started healing.

"Shit," Connor swore when he glanced over at me. "Were you shot?!"

I nodded as I opened his glove box. "Got any tweezers in here?"

"Mom should have some in there somewhere. Are you going to take it out now?" he said, horrified at the thought.

"I have to get it out before I heal," I told him as I dug around. "Just focus on driving."

I found a pair of tweezers and some hand sanitizer. I washed the tweezers and my hands. Before I went for the bullet, I focused on the cuff locked around my wrist. I wouldn't be able to heal with it on my wrist, so I realized I had to take it off before I took it out.

I used the tweezers and picked the lock of the cuff. After a few moments, it finally clicked and unlocked. I washed the tweezers again after the cuff fell to my lap. I looked down and took a deep breath before going for the bullet. I hissed as the tweezers were inside the wound and saw stars as I got hold of the bullet and pulled it out.

I dropped the bullet into the cup holder and wrapped my shirt around my middle. I sighed when I felt myself start to heal. "Mom's so going to kill us for getting blood in her car," Connor said with a laugh.

I looked over at him. "And I'm not done yet. You got your pocketknife on you?"

He nodded and reached into his pocket as he drove and pulled it out before tossing it to me. I opened it and breathed, "This is not going to be fun." I felt for the tracker in my wrist and once I knew where it was, I cut through the skin to get to it.

I hissed as blood seeped from it and Connor screeched, "What the hell are you doing?!"

"Getting the tracker out," I answered with a clenched jaw. I felt the little device that allowed Dr. Rodriguez to track me in my wrist and dug it out.

"That was in you?!" Connor asked.

I nodded and put the window down to throw it out. I grabbed paper towels out of the glove box and held it to my wrist before I looked back at Angelica and saw her sleeping across the back seat. I turned back around and let the tears flow. I couldn't believe Alis was dead, that she sacrificed herself like that. I thought about how I would never forget her laugh, smile, and encouraging words.

Connor looked over and noticed my tears. "Want to talk about it?"

I shook my head and rested it against the cool glass of the window. "Maybe later," I told him.

I started to feel tired and fell asleep soon after.

CHAPTER FIFTY

Connor slammed his door after he got out, startling me and Angelica awake. I looked down and saw my wound was almost fully healed on my stomach and my wrist had a slight scratch left over. I saw Connor going up the porch of the log cabin in front of us and knocking on the door.

Angelica started sobbing again, and I climbed into the back to comfort her after pulling my shirt over my head. I sat in the seat and placed her on my lap as I rocked her back and forth. "It's okay," I whispered to her as she cried into my chest.

"Is she really gone?" she whispered.

My own tears threatened to spill over again as I answered, "Yeah."

She shook harder as she sobbed, and her skin started getting hot to touch. Her abilities. Fire. Not good. I quickly opened the door and climbed out of the car with her in my arms. I placed her in the grass, and she started to smoke. Literally smoke.

"Angelica," I said. "Calm down. You're losing control."

She kept smoking, and it kept getting worse. So, I created a rain cloud above her, putting out the fire she was creating.

Linda rushed out of the cabin and exclaimed, "What in the world?"

I forced myself to smile as I looked over at her. "Hi, Mrs. Peters."

Angelica started to steam as my water hit her. "We have to go back for her! She can't be gone," she sobbed as she attempted to get up.

I bent down next to her and grabbed her wrists, pinning them above her head. I cursed and pulled back when she burned me. I put a coating of ice over my hands and tried again.

She fought my grasp, cursing and swearing at me. I straddled her small body as I held her wrists down. "Angelica!" I yelled at her. "We can't go back! She's gone and I'm sorry for that."

She screamed and her body erupted in flames, but didn't burn her clothes. I jumped off her and cursed. She got up and came over to me. She started throwing fireballs, which I put out with simple flicks of my hand.

She groaned in frustration and came over to start punching me, without the flames, thank God. I let her for a moment; she wasn't causing me any pain. But I soon grabbed her wrists, stopping her, and told her I was sorry before convincing her mind to go unconscious.

She slumped against me, and I sighed in relief. I quickly glanced over my shoulder when I heard a twig snap behind me. I relaxed when I saw Dan, holding his hands up to tell me he meant well. "What the hell did they do to you?" he whispered as he slowly approached me.

I glanced over at Connor and he shrugged before saying, "I didn't tell them much about why they took you. I don't even know the extent of everything."

I nodded in understanding before Linda said, "Why don't we go inside?"

We agreed, and I picked up Angelica as we walked inside. We walked into the living room and I sat down on one of the couches with Angelica on my lap. I didn't want to let go of her yet.

Connor sat next to me while Linda and Dan stood in front of us. "Christian," Linda said with a worried tone, "you're bleeding."

I looked down at my side, my shirt was covered in blood. "It's dried up now," I said with a shrug. I shifted Angelica so I could pull the shirt off my side enough to reveal the slight scratch that still had to heal.

"Christian is a badass," Connor told them with a smirk. "He got shot and still escaped. He took the bullet out himself while I drove. Even took a tracker out of his wrist."

I cringed and looked up at them. "I may have gotten blood in your car. Sorry about that."

Linda bent down in front of me. "You're safe, that's all that matters."

I noticed the tears in her eyes and nodded. Angelica started to stir in my arms, and I put her next to me, opposite of Connor. I put my head in my hands after resting my elbows on my knees and started crying. Linda hugged me to her and rubbed my back.

"What happened back there?" she asked me.

"She's dead," I cried over and over. I didn't care if she understood or not. "It's all my fault."

She rubbed my back. "Don't say that," she said as she rested her chin on my head. "I may not know what happened, but I know that whatever it was, it wasn't your fault."

"Why don't you explain what happened," Dan suggested.

I pulled back from Linda and they both sat in armchairs near across from us. I wiped my eyes and explained, "The government took me as an experiment. I came into abilities on my 18th birthday, after I came to your house. Victor found out, and they took me. When I got there and woke up from the drugs," I gave Connor a pointed look, "I met my 'cellmates', Angelica and Alis," I choked back a sob. I explained the experiments and going to train with the troop until Connor came while I was being shipped to war. I told them about being kidnapped by Russians and almost dying there. Then, I explained how Alis died. How I should have let her go before me, or went back for her, or have done something.

Once I finished, they all looked at me with wide eyes. "Jesus," Dan said as he ran his hand through his hair. "So, what happened earlier… those were your abilities?"

I nodded. "Yeah. I can do almost anything. While Angelica can manipulate fire. Alis saw the future." I paused. "She knew," I whispered to myself. "She told me to take care of Angelica if something ever happened to her. She knew she was going to die." I choked back a sob.

"Do you know what you are?" Linda asked. "How you got your abilities?"

Dakota trotted into the room from the kitchen behind us and her ears perked up when she saw me. She came over to me and rested her muzzle on my lap as she looked up at me with her bright blue eyes.

"They think we are angels," I explained as I stroked her soft head. Connor grinned because he knew why. "We have…wings. We come into them a week after we turn 18," I explained. My back ached at the memory and I cringed. "That was not a fun day."

"So, you have wings?" Dan asked.

I nodded. "Would you like to see?"

They both nodded, and I told them I should probably do it outside, not wanting to break anything. "They're that big?!" Linda exclaimed.

Connor put his hand on her shoulder. "Mom, they're huge."

I laughed and followed them through the kitchen and into the backyard. "There is no one around for 4 miles, so you should be okay," Connor explained.

I nodded and was grateful for the number of trees surrounding the area. I closed my eyes and willed my wings to come out. I heard everyone gasp and opened them a second later. I looked over at Linda and Dan, who were standing with their mouths hanging wide open.

I gave my wings a flap to stretch them out before Linda slowly approached me. "Can I…touch them?" she asked as she hovered her hand over them.

I nodded and shivered at the feeling of her hands as they slid over the membrane of my left wing. She giggled. "Does it feel good?"

"Yeah," I breathed as she ran her fingers over them.

Dan asked if he could feel them, and I nodded. He ran his fingers over the other wing as Linda continued to do the same. My legs almost gave out at the amazing feeling. "They're so soft," Dan breathed as he inspected the feathers. "Can you fly with them?"

"Damn right he can," Connor answered with a smirk. My wings tingled at the thought of flying outside, on their free will. Connor somehow knew and said, "Go ahead. You know you want to."

I looked back at Linda and Dan, and they stepped back to give me some space. I flapped my wings once and lifted a few feet off the ground. I flapped again and was about 10 feet off the ground. I flew around the yard, weaving through a few trees as I did so, before landing in front of them once more.

Dakota jumped up at me excitedly and I laughed before petting her. She then sat in front of me and leaned into my touch. I laughed before Angelica stepped out of the house and walked over to me. It shocked me when she gave me a hug. "I'm sorry I yelled and tried to hurt you. I was just really upset and lost control. I know there was nothing you could have done. You saved me, and someday we will get our revenge."

I rubbed her back and told her, "And I'm sorry I had to make you go unconscious. I regretted it the minute I did it."

She pulled back and looked at me with forgiving eyes. "You did it to protect you and me. In a way, I'm glad you did it."

I introduced her to the Peters, and they said their hellos. "Want to fly?" I asked Angelica with a tilt of my head. "I never got to fly with you yet. Never got to see those beautiful wings."

She blushed and nodded. She closed her eyes and her black wings emerged from her back and out of the slits in her shirt a moment later.

"Wow," Connor breathed.

I looked over at him and saw him looking at Angelica with awe written all over his face. He looked like he would bow in her presence if she asked him to. He noticed me staring at him and coughed before looking anywhere but over where we were standing.

"Race you to the trees and back!" Angelica yelled before taking off.

"Hey! That's cheating!" I yelled as I flew after her. She was fast, I'll give her that. She beat me by a landslide and grinned as she hovered in the air. I collided with her and wrapped my arms around her waist. She laughed as I tickled her and soon said, "Mercy!"

I stopped and she let another laugh escape before looking up at me and saying, "Thanks, Christian. I didn't realize how badly I needed to laugh."

I shrugged. "No problem."

We landed on the ground and turned to face Connor. Linda and Dan must have gone inside to do something. "Where's Ginny?" I asked him as we made our wings retreat.

"She should be here soon," he answered.

"Victor is here," Linda called from inside.

"Send him out here!" Connor called back.

A moment later, Victor came out of the back door and smiled when he saw me. "Glad to see you are alive," he told me. "However, you did take over my job of getting the girls," he said as his gaze slid to Angelica. His brows creased in confusion and worry. "Where's Alis?"

I shook my head solemnly, silently telling him she didn't make it out.

"Oh no," he said quietly. He looked over at Angelica. "I'm so sorry, Angelica. This must be very hard for you."

She started to tear up as she nodded in gratitude. I heard a car door slam and heard two female voices. "Ugh. I'm so hungry," Ginny said.

The other girl giggled. "Same."

I widened my eyes. I recognized that voice. It was Eliana's voice.

CHAPTER FIFTY-ONE

Even Victor looked surprised when they walked outside. They both stopped when they saw me standing there with my wings still out. "Christian?!" they both exclaimed.

"Eliana?!" Victor and I both responded.

Ginny and Connor looked confused. "Wait," Ginny said as she held her hand up, "you know each other?"

"Yeah, her grandma works at the base," I answered as I retracted my wings. "She's my girlfriend."

She blushed as they looked at her. "What?!" Ginny exclaimed before hugging her. "Why didn't you tell me this?"

"I had to keep it a secret to protect him," Eliana explained. "I love him and didn't want him to be in any more trouble than he was already in." She walked over and gave me a quick kiss. "I don't know how you are here, but am so happy to see you."

"Where are we exactly?" I asked Connor.

"A family friend gave us their log cabin after I asked them for it," he answered with a shrug. "I told the family to meet me up here last night. We are about a half an hour from school so we can still go to not raise suspicions that we brought you here."

"Sounds good," I replied before yawning.

"You should go to bed," Victor said. "You've had a long day."

I nodded and we walked inside. Linda and Dan were standing in the kitchen and turned to look at us. "We don't have as many rooms as we do in our house, so a few of you may have to share," Linda told us.

"Can Eliana stay with me?" Ginny asked.

Eliana looked up at me and I shrugged. "I can room with Connor." I looked over at him and smirked. "Like old times."

He smiled and nodded. "Victor and Angelica can have the other two rooms," he said. "If that's okay with you?"

They agreed and Linda showed us our rooms. Connor and I were the first door to the right of the hallway, Victor and Angelica were the rooms across from us, and Eliana and Ginny were next to our room. "Dan and I are at the end of the hall if anyone needs anything."

We thanked her and after Eliana gave me a kiss, we retreated to our rooms. Linda looked con-fused, but didn't question how Eliana and I knew each other when she saw how tired I was.

Connor and I closed the door, and I took in the blue walls and bookshelves taking up the walls. "Whose place is this?" I asked him.

"Brayden's," he answered.

"Is he…okay?" I asked because Brayden was one of the five boys I was forced to electrocute before erasing their memories.

"He's been off lately," he answered honestly. "Why do you ask?"

I sighed and sat on the bed before saying, "He and four others from school snuck into Area 51 and were caught. I was forced to help interrogate them and shock them until they passed out before erasing their memory of that day."

"Oh God," he breathed. "No wonder they had been acting strange."

"Yeah…" I looked over at the door next to the bed and asked, "Is that the bathroom?"

He nodded. "Go ahead. Take your time. There should be clothes in the closet in there."

I got up and decided to get a shower in the morning as I went to the bathroom. I found pajama pants in the closet and put them on after taking my uniform off. I didn't bother putting a shirt on and walked out.

Connor was laying on the bed, flipping through TV channels, and looked over after turning it off. His eyes went right to the brand on my stomach before traveling up to meet mine. "Did that hurt?"

I nodded. and whispered, "Like hell."

"I'm sorry, Christian," he said after a moment of silence passed. "I tried so hard to find you, but couldn't. I was mad at the world for taking you from me. You're my brother and I was supposed to have your back."

"It's cool. You're here now. That's all that matters."

I yawned and he got up. "Get some sleep. I'll be back in a few minutes."

He left the room and closed the door behind him after allowing Dakota to prance inside. She hopped onto the bed and I sighed before climbing into the soft and fluffy bed with her. The blankets were so much softer than the ones I was given the past few months and I fell asleep after turning the lamp off on the nightstand.

* * * * *

I WOKE UP FROM A NIGHTMARE to Connor shaking me awake. I opened my eyes as I took in a deep breath. Connor looked down at me in worry and concern. "You okay?"

I swallowed and nodded. "Sorry, I should have warned you about the nightmares."

"You've been having them for a while?" he questioned.

"Almost every night," I said quietly as I diverted my gaze from his. "I almost never remember them."

"Hopefully, they'll die down now that you're out of there," he told me.

"Yeah…hopefully."

"You okay to go back to sleep?"

I nodded and rolled on my side, so my back faced him. He settled back down beside me, and I let the tears flow. I wished I had answers as to why I had those nightmares all the time. I wished I could make them stop and go away. But I knew they would always be there; would always haunt me.

I fell asleep after my tears dried up and didn't have any more nightmares that night.

CHAPTER FIFTY-TWO

The next morning, I woke up by myself. I figured Connor went to school as well as everyone else who was supposed to. I walked out of the room and saw Linda sitting at the kitchen table with a coffee in front of her. She glanced over at me and gave me a soft smile. "Good morning."

"Morning," I replied with a yawn.

Her eyes traveled down to the brand, but she didn't seem surprised. "Connor told me about that this morning before they left." She stood up and gave me a hug. "I'm so sorry, honey."

"It's okay," I replied as I hugged her back. "You couldn't do anything."

"I love you like a son," she cried. "I should have done more to find you."

"I should have trusted you enough to come to you for help. I was just scared of what was happening to me and didn't know who to trust."

"Don't blame yourself," she told me as she pulled away from me. "You didn't have much time to process it yourself, let alone tell someone else. All that matters is that your here now."

"Thank you," I replied. "For risking everything to keep me safe."

"We love you, Christian. You're part of our family."

Victor walked out of his room in only his pajama pants as well and told us good morning before heading to the fridge. "Can I have one of these yogurts?" he asked.

She nodded. "Take whatever you'd like."

"Get me one too," I told him.

He tossed one across the room at me and I caught it easily. Linda got us spoons and we ate before going to get dressed. Victor gave me a duffle bag with some shirts that had slits in the back to accommodate my wings, so I wouldn't have to take it off whenever I used them. He left after claiming he had to throw his dad off our trail by being seen away from where we were.

Linda told me that Dan went to work, which meant Linda, Angelica, and I were the only ones left. Angelica was still asleep, and I went into the living room to sit on the couch.

A little while later, I was watching TV with Dakota curled up next to me, her head in my lap, when Linda's phone rang. She got up from the kitchen table and went to answer it. "Hello?" she said.

I tuned into my super-hearing to hear who it was, just to make sure it wasn't trouble. "Mrs. Peters?" Dr. Rodriguez's voice asked.

I jumped up from the couch and went into the kitchen, Dakota following me closely. She looked at me with a confused expression as she answered, "Yes?"

"Hello. I was wondering if I could speak to Christian," he said.

She gave me a panicked look before saying, "Christian Hoyt? I'm sorry, Sir, but we haven't seen him in months."

He laughed. "I know he's with you."

"What are you talking about?"

"I would give up this act, ma'am. We have someone who you care deeply about."

"Who-"

I took the phone out of her hand and held it up to my ear. "What have you done?" I ordered in a stern voice.

"You really thought I would have left you go that easily?" he asked with a malicious laugh. "The bullet I shot you with had a piece that holds the obedient drug and is in your body. I can press this button and it will enter your blood stream," he paused for a second.

I felt a slight burning in my side and cried out as I doubled over in pain. Linda rushed over to my side, but I waved her away as soon as I realized the serum was somehow taking control.

After a moment, I was standing up straight and unblinking. "What the hell?" Linda whispered as she waved her hand in front of me.

"Now, listen carefully," he told me through the phone. "I have your friend Connor here with me, and if you want him alive, you better follow orders."

Linda ripped the phone out of my hand. "What did you do to him? What do you mean you have my son?!"

"This is between Christian and I, ma'am," he said.

"No. No. No. This involves me too now. You see, you're messing with my sons! Even though Christian isn't mine biologically, he's still my son. And you just messed with the wrong mama," she said angrily.

He ignored her and said, "Put Christian back on." She hesitated before putting the phone in my hand and guiding it up to my ear. "Walk out of the house and meet me at your school in the next 20 minutes," he told me quietly so Linda couldn't hear. "You may act semi-normal until then, but don't talk to anyone."

He hung up and I blinked a few times to clear the haze over my mind. I went to grab my shoes out of the room, not bothering to look at Linda.

She stood behind me with worry radiating off her. "What did he do to you?"

I held back as long as possible, wanting her to follow me so she could take Connor and run if they had to. I couldn't hold back long, though, the obedience was yelling at me.

I walked out the door and Linda called for Angelica as she got her keys, but didn't wait for her. I summoned my wings and took off as she got in the car and started it.

I flew towards the school as she drove below. I knew I had to obey, but even if I didn't, I would still be getting there as fast as I could. I was angry as hell at him for dragging my best friend into this. I knew that people were pointing and shouting at me as I flew towards the school, but didn't care.

When it came in sight, I flew faster than I ever had before. I saw the trucks sitting outside the school and the small crowd that had gathered to see what was going on.

I did a three-point landing, my fist hitting the ground and creating a boom with force. My wings tucked proudly behind me as I lifted my head to look at Dr. Rodriguez.

He was leaning against the side of the wall with an amused expression on his face. He pushed off the wall and came over to me as I slowly stood up. He lightly slapped my face as he said, "Good boy."

Linda came barreling through the crowd angrily. The crowd watched with wide eyes and agape mouths as she strode over to us. "How dare you!" she yelled as she pointed an accusing finger at Dr. Rodriguez. "Where is my son?"

He sighed and turned away from me to look at her. "He's in the truck. We'll get there in a moment." He turned back to me and ordered, "Give me your hands."

I slowly put my wrists together and brought them near him, but was stopped when Linda pushed me back and stood between us. "You're not taking him!" she yelled. "He deserves a better life than what you are giving him!"

He chuckled. "He belongs to me. He's property of the government."

"He's a kid!" she screeched. "He doesn't belong to anyone."

He glanced at something behind me and nodded as he continued arguing with her. Someone came behind me and tried to grab my arms as Eliana rushed out of the building and joined the argument. I fought him and saw Connor come out of the truck, with a gun to his head.

And the person holding that gun was Angelica.

I widened my eyes in surprise that she would betray me like that. Connor looked at me with wide eyes, as if he was as shocked as me. Dr. Rodriguez suddenly grabbed Eliana and put a gun to her head too. "Surrender yourself now or your girlfriend and friend will die," he growled to me.

Eliana and Connor were the two people I would do anything for, and I realized that this was my worst nightmare. All the nightmares I had came rushing back to me and suddenly, I remembered what it was about. It was that exact scene: my two best friends held at gun point because of me.

I put my hands up in surrender and said, "Fine. You win. You can have me. I will be your obedient little weapon."

He smiled wickedly and nodded to the men behind me. They came over and went to snap the cuffs around my wrists. However, I spotted the guns strapped to their waistbands and changed my mind. At the last minute, I jabbed my elbow into one of the men's side and he doubled over, giving me a chance to snatch his gun out of its holster.

I brought the gun to my head. I knew it was the only way to prevent people from dying because of me. Even if I killed Dr. Rodriguez, they still wouldn't stop trying to create a weapon out of me.

"Let all of us go or I'll pull the trigger," I told him, dead serious.

"No!" Eliana cried. She knew I was serious. I told her I would kill myself before they made me their weapon.

Dr. Rodriguez only laughed, not knowing how serious I really was. "You'll never really be free. Even if I did let you go, which I'm not, the other bases would start looking for you."

He glanced over at the guard, trying not to make it obvious, but I saw it. The guard went to take the gun out of my hands, but he was too late. I already squeezed my eyes tightly shut and pulled the trigger. The gun fired and I felt the sharp pain as the bullet went through my head. I knew it was Linda who caught me before everything went black.

THE END FOR NOW…

ACKNOWLEDGMENT

Where to start? Thank you to all my friends and family for supporting my writing and encouraging me to continue writing when I felt like giving up. Mom, you always encouraged me the most. Even though you probably never knew it, by telling me that you've always loved my writing made me want to keep going. All the friends, mostly Hannah and Katie, who asked how my writing was going and kept pestering me by asking when I would finally publish, thank you.

Thank you to my cover designer, Callie, from Literary Designs for creating this amazing cover and working with me. Thank you to my beta readers for volunteering their time to read my final manuscript and giving me feedback on how to make the story even better.

Thank you to the NaNoWriMo community because without you, this book would have never even happened. I didn't start taking writing seriously until I found this wonderful community of writers all over the world and participated in my first NaNoWriMo in November of 2019.

I can't forget about the characters who have lived in my head for years now and forced me to write. Even though they were loud at times and gave me the silent treatment other times, their story came together. They never stuck to plan and made me gasp out loud at times when a plot twist would come up. Can't wait to work with them some more!

Thank you, the reader, for purchasing the book and making it this far. I hope the cliffhanger doesn't kill you, I promise I'm writing book 2 as fast as possible. If you could take the time, it would really help if you wrote an honest review on Amazon or Goodreads, not just for me, but for any authors. I love you all and hope you are just as eager as I am to see what happens next in this series.

ABOUT THE AUTHOR

A. R. Stein can usually be seen with her nose in a book, and that book is most likely going to be fantasy. Deep down, she has always known that she would write a novel, but didn't realize she had to use her creative thinking until she stopped using it to focus on her studies in Computer Science. After winning her first NaNoWriMo in 2019 with the rough draft of 'The Experiment', which later came to be Project Obedience, she realized she loved to write more than she originally thought. When she is not reading or writing, she can be found horseback riding, scrolling through social media, and coming up with new ideas for novels almost anywhere. No, seriously, she currently has over 10 novels in progress and gets a new idea at the most random times.

Stay in Touch!

Instagram: @author_a.r.stein
Facebook: Author A. R. Stein
TikTok: @author_a.r.stein
Facebook Spoiler Group: Project Series